SWOR[illegible] OF BABYLON

(MATT DRAKE #6)

BY

DAVID LEADBEATER

ISBN:9781500690526

All characters in this book are fictitious, and any resemblance to actual persons living or dead is purely coincidental.

Other books by David Leadbeater:

The Bones of Odin (Matt Drake #1)
The Blood King Conspiracy (Matt Drake #2)
The Gates of Hell (Matt Drake 3)
The Tomb of the Gods (Matt Drake #4)
Brothers in Arms (Matt Drake #5)

Chosen (The Chosen Few trilogy #1)

The Razor's Edge (Disavowed #1)

Walking with Ghosts (A short story)
A Whispering of Ghosts (A short story)

Connect with David on Twitter - dleadbeater2011

Visit David's NEW website – davidleadbeater.com

Follow David's Blog - http://davidleadbeaternovels.blogspot.co.uk/

All helpful, genuine comments are welcome. I would love to hear from you.
davidleadbeater2011@hotmail.co.uk

For my family.

CHAPTER ONE

THE PRESENT

Alicia Myles was not the kind of person to look back on her life. In fact, the only time her old life caught up with her was when she slept. If, when awake, she could look upon her seven year old self, she would not recognize a single scrap of the person she was today.

That was before she'd been forged.

Aged eight, she remembered sitting up in bed and hugging her knees to her chest, bathed in the silvery glow of moonlight that filtered through the broken blinds; a wraith or an angel, barely formed, the promise of the future still fresh, pure and alive in her mind. The terrible, unfamiliar sounds had only recently started. Her father shouting. Her mother – at first – answering back. The sound of a glass smashing. The sound of the fridge door crashing open and, no doubt. the sight of her father reaching in to grab another one of those cans he'd started drinking – the ones he seemed to like even through the day.

Drink and crush. Drink and crush.

The awful noise of those cans being crushed in anger still reverberated through her memories. It was the sound of her innocence being taken, the sound of her family life being torn to shreds.

So she sat, huddled in bed, trying desperately not to hear, but at the same time dreadfully curious to understand what her parents were angry about. Were they mad at each other? At someone else? At the world outside their locked doors? Then she heard her mother start to cry. She felt her heart beat faster, the anxiety making her temperature rise. She gritted her teeth together in an attempt not to cry herself.

The fridge door smashed again and then, faintly, she heard her father consoling her mother. That was the start of it.

It would get much worse.

*

She woke in the dark, bathed in sweat, and sat up in bed. Alicia immediately hugged her knees to her chest in unconscious imitation of the girl she used to be. Tatters of old memory stirred smoldering ashes in her soul. In less than a second she had shrugged them off. She took a moment to evaluate where she was. So much had happened lately.

Naked, in bed, with a man beside her. That was nothing new. The first difference was that she knew exactly who this man was. He wasn't just a body to numb away the night terrors. This was Lomas. The man she'd left Drake's new team to be with. At least until the journey curved her away in another direction.

She slipped out of bed and moved soundlessly over to the window. A finely sculpted, tree-lined eighteen-hole golf course stretched away from her, nothing but a clump of shadows in the full moonless dark. Alicia shivered slightly. She had never been comforted by the dark, nor by the bed sheets or the solitary act of sleeping. Bad memories died hard. She heard Lomas's breathing change and knew in that moment that he had come awake.

"Go back to sleep," she said, tonelessly. "I'll join you soon."

Darkness shifted outside, trees stirred by the breeze. The biker gang had decided to enjoy a few days of R&R at Uncle Sam's expense, part of a small package Drake had managed to secure through Jonathan Gates and his new agency SPEAR.

What the hell did it stand for again? Alicia couldn't remember. She'd seen more than her fair share of action lately, and it was time to let the alertness slip a little and relax. Not that she ever could. Her dreams reminded her of that. At the age of nine she had sat up every night after her lights went out, attentive, prepared, waiting for the shouting to start.

And it always did.

Chasing away the anxiety, Alicia rushed back to the bed and jumped on Lomas's prone figure, straddling him. She laughed, forced at first, but then slipped quickly into the person she had become. Lomas grunted and tried to push her off, but she pinned him with her knees.

"Not a chance, biker boy. Just lie there and enjoy the ride."

She began to move on him, the pleasure forcing away the memories, her noise scaring off the old fears. Her hair whipped back. Her hands clutched his big shoulders, gripping painfully. Time, life, decisions, the past and the future all ceased to exist. This was her freedom, her true release.

When they finished, she rolled off. Lomas immediately rolled on top of her. "Now, how about we do this *my* way?"

Alicia held his gaze. "So long as you take your time. I'm no Ducati, to be ridden nought to a hundred in seven seconds. More like your luxury Harley chassis."

"I think I know that." Lomas bent his head to kiss her.

At that moment Alicia's cell phone rang. She whispered, "Don't stop," to Lomas and picked it up from the bedside table.

"Hello? Not the best timing, Torsten."

"Alicia? It's Dahl." The big Swede spoke rapidly as if he hadn't heard her. "We need you . . ."

"Oh yeah? I heard—"

"It's about Drake, Alicia. The Russians have taken him."

Alicia sat up, ungraciously flipping Lomas' body away in an instant. "*What?* Taken him where? What happened to Mai?"

"*Russia.* Where the hell do you think? Meet us there, Alicia. We'll let you know the exact location. And . . . be quick . . . it's not good."

Dahl ended the call. Alicia closed her eyes for a moment and sighed inwardly. Then she whispered, "For fucksake, Drake."

CHAPTER TWO

3 HOURS EARLIER

Matt Drake would later look back and wonder why on earth Mai and he hadn't been better prepared. Any rookie would have seen that the only chance the Russians had of abducting him was at sundown, when the two of them made their nightly sojourn to the Little Fountains Café on 18th Street. They made some of the best pulled pork sandwiches Drake had ever tasted, and offered them an anonymous romantic meal. The price was leaving the heavy cordon of security that surrounded their CIA-owned hotel and driving a few miles north.

Maybe it was the comedown after defeating the arms dealer, Shaun Kingston, and his North Korean accomplices only two days ago. Maybe it was because Jonathan Gates hadn't secured them a new HQ yet, and they had no job to focus on. Or maybe it was just because Mai and Drake were a little lost in each other . . . for the second time in their lives.

As it was, the team were all taking a few days. Drake didn't know the details, but Hayden and Kinimaka were working some things out, Karin and Komodo were at it like rabbits, and good ole Torsten Dahl was spending most of his days talking to his wife and kids via his laptop's video link. Until Gates could acquire a new HQ, their options were somewhat limited. Homeland wanted them. The CIA wanted them. But those agencies would use the team for their own ends and means. Gates wanted SPEAR to retain its elitist image, determined to retain them as the best of the best, required only for the most critical missions.

And by critical, Drake thought. *The Secretary meant crazy and desperate. Something verging on the apocalyptic.*

He already missed Alicia and her odd, slightly unhinged wit. He wondered when he would see her again. Not soon enough, probably.

But Mai filled his days and nights with her inexplicable mix of tenderness and toughness. He barely remembered most of their previous relationship but, as they joined together again, some of the more complex elements came flooding back.

Like her insomnia. And how she hardly ever relaxed her guard, as if always afraid someone from her past was looking for her and would eventually find her. This was arguably true, but extremely unlikely.

Drake was driving one of the CIA pool cars. It was the third time they had made the trip in as many nights. The traffic, as always, crawled along like a snake stalking its prey, so Drake engaged the satnav and punched in the 'previous address'. The machine began its monotonous directions.

The in-car phone bleeped. Drake answered, "Ay up."

Hayden's voice reminded him of work, taking him away from the moment Mai and he were sharing. "Just some info to pass along. Gates came through with the new HQ. It's opposite the mall on Pennsylvania Avenue." She coughed. "Could be worse."

"When do you want us in?"

"It'll take a few days to get the comms up and running, but most of the infrastructure is already there. It's an old CIA secret ops hole."

Mai grunted. "It sounds charming."

"Today's Tuesday. Let's say Thursday. I'll let you know the address."

Drake disconnected and looked out the window. "Wonder what's gonna kick off next? Between Odin, the Blood King, the Shadow Elite and North bloody Korea I don't know which is worse."

"The Blood King," Mai whispered without pause. "No question."

"And those latest Russkies weren't exactly Care Bears," Drake assured her. "Especially that Zanko. Big hairy bastard."

"How is Romero?" Mai asked. "Have you heard from him?"

"Nope. Not a thing. Guess he's back at Delta. Why, you heard from Smyth?"

Mai smiled. "All the time."

"Want me to . . . y'know . . . take him out?"

"Why? Are you jealous?"

"A little."

"He's just flirting. He thinks he loves me. He'll get over it."

"He'd better," Drake said tetchily, but it was all a game. Both Drake and Mai knew how much they owed the Delta soldiers. Drake turned the wheel as the satnav directed them away from the main arteries and through some quieter back streets.

"I think you should call Ben. See how he's getting along."

Drake nodded. "I will. Soon as I find the time."

"Well, don't stay out of touch too long. He was one of your best friends."

The words stirred up memories Drake wanted to stay dormant. And lately, any memory of Kennedy Moore sent a barb through his heart. *Have I fallen for Mai too soon after Kennedy's death?*

"I'll do my best."

Mai changed the subject. "So, are you going for that pork thing again tonight? You really should try the seared Ahi, it—"

A car pulled out in front of Drake. He swerved hard to avoid the collision.

"Christ!"

He jammed on the brakes and skidded broadside across the road, the hood of the car narrowly missing a parked minivan. The car in front of them, a black Escalade, had stopped dead.

Mai said, "I don't like—"

A second Escalade pulled out behind them, swerving across the road, effectively blocking them in.

Drake reached for the glove box, finding only a single Glock. "This thing bulletproof?"

"I doubt it."

Drake tapped the phone. "Better call out the whole nine yards," he told the CIA tech who answered. "I think we're being ambushed."

Both Escalades erupted with black-clad bodies. Men literally spewed out of every door, holding small devices that looked like tasers in their hands and shouting. Drake's car was quickly surrounded. All the men wore full-face balaclavas with the eye and nose holes cut out, their body language screaming that they were being held on a very tight leash.

"Stay in the car," Drake said and revved the engine. "We can—"

A man stepped forward and placed a small black box on their pool car's hood. Then he held up a remote control and depressed his thumb. Instantly, the engine's note became a low burble, then died. Drake stared at Mai.

"What the . . ."

"You go nowhere!" a voice screamed. "Except with us. Get out now!"

Drake showed them his hands, dropping the Glock into his lap. Mai gently clicked open the door. "They have tasers, Matt. We have a Glock."

"But they just killed our car."

"Be ready."

As soon as Mai put a foot out of the door, the men ran forward. She moved fast, flinging the door viciously at the first two to arrive and smashing them aside. The next she kicked in the head and scooped up his fallen taser. More came at her. Mai turned sideways on to meet them.

Drake flung his door open, bringing the Glock around. Men ran at him from all sides. He turned toward the back of the car, the quicker target, and fired three shots. Three men collapsed, but the rest were on him. Drake took a punch in the face to evade another man's taser, then broke the second man's arm, relieving him of his weapon. The first man tried another punch, but this time his fist met hard taser. There was a sudden crackle and the flash of a lightning bolt. Thousands of volts surged through the man, making him scream and dance before finally slumping at Drake's feet.

More men leaned in. Drake fired his gun again. He ripped at one of the balaclavas, seeing a glimpse of a rough, pock-marked face and colorful neck tattoos. He could hear them all grunting curses in a guttural tongue. One of the fists that struck at him and missed had painful looking, self-inked tattoos inscribed on the knuckles.

Russian letters, Drake knew, even if he couldn't turn them into English. He threw a man against the side of the car, smashed another across the bridge of the nose with his now empty gun, used the taser again and then flung it aside when he realized it was out of charge. He stayed behind the car door, limiting his enemy's angle of attack.

If they survived for a few more minutes, the CIA would have men here.

A gap opened up as his opponents fell over each other. Drake leapfrogged them and raced for the back of the car. There would be more weapons in the trunk. But before he could even lay a hand on the metal, they accosted him again, facing up to him and striking with fists and legs. Drake blocked and backed away. There was a clear escape route past their enemy's rearmost Escalade, but he couldn't leave without Mai.

He chanced a glance around her side of the vehicle. Mai danced and leapt amidst a heap of the fallen. With every blow she broke bones, ruptured organs and crushed windpipes. She held a taser in each hand. Drake saw the assembled Russians gather and launch a six man attack at her, but even then she killed four with lightning quick reflexes and leapt back, making space between herself and the remaining two.

"Mai!"

His shout caught her attention. He indicated the escape route, still blocking and fending off his attackers. He was being driven toward the sidewalk where he'd have to slip between parked cars, then there would be a high fence at his back. He could see occupants of the nearby houses looking out of their windows and leaning over balconies, some of them filming the fight on their cell phones. He shouted, "Call 911!" more in an attempt to unnerve the Russians than to get help.

"Hurry!" The leader of the assault party sounded agitated now. "We must leave!"

Drake backed up until he felt Mai behind him. "Ay up."

"One day," Mai flipped an assailant, guiding his flight so that he landed hard and struck a colleague on the way down. "You're going to have to explain that crazy Yorkshire dialect to me."

They broke for the escape route, leaving their attackers momentarily bewildered. The gap between the rear Escalade and the sidewalk was big enough for them to squeeze through without slowing down. Suddenly free, Drake chanced a look back.

"Why the hell are they using tasers? They could have had us . . . oh shit!"

Their attackers hadn't given chase, because they had been joined by two men carrying oversize, outlandish guns. The lead Russian screamed at them. Drake saw them kneel, take aim, and fire . . . then the pain kicked in and the road rose up to strike his face. The last thing he heard was a murderous whisper close to his ear, something about '*prison food*'.

CHAPTER THREE

It was Wednesday 30 January when Matt Drake woke. He was aware of lying on his back on a rock hard surface, of the pitted concrete ceiling above him, of the piercing chill in the air, of the stone walls that surrounded him, and of the headache that pounded his brain. He was aware of a distant commotion. His last memory was of running from the Russians, Mai at his side.

Mai!

He sat up too quickly. Lightning bolts of pain struck like blazing chaff inside his head. A sense of nausea made him sit stock still for long minutes, struggling to repress the urge to throw up. As he sat there, he studied the metal toilet bowl and adjacent sink that had been bolted to the far wall. When he managed to swivel his head more than an inch he saw the heavy bars that lined the front wall.

Jail cell. He was in some kind of prison. And now the distant commotion swam into better focus. It was the sound of many men together. A prison population.

Fear gnawed at his heart. Men had been known to disappear forever in the world's worst prisons. Back in his SAS days, he had put several there himself. More recently, Dmitry Kovalenko had vanished into an American one.

How long had he been here? Where was he? Questions lined up like captives led in front of a firing squad. Tentatively, he jumped down off his bare bunk, little more than a long concrete block, and padded toward the bars. Gradual illumination stung his eyes, reviving the headache. He still wore the same clothes he had been abducted with, but his pockets had been emptied. No cell phone. No receipts. No wallet. When he approached the bars he slowed, inching his way onward until he could touch them.

Directly outside his cell ran a walkway, bordered by a thick iron railing. A great space lay beyond that, so deep that he saw nothing but air. Across stood a row of cells, no doubt a mirror to his own row. Over there, though, all the doors stood open.

The noise of an angry crowd echoed up from below.

Drake looked around. There was nothing he could drag over here, nothing he could use as a platform. The bunk was one big concrete slab, the toilet and sink were firmly bolted to the wall. He knew there were men who could actually extract those bolts and use them to dig an escape tunnel, but they were paid $10 million a movie in Hollywood.

He turned back to the bars and gave them a shake. Nothing rattled. Then a figure crossed his field of vision and blocked out all the light.

Drake backed away.

Zanko!

The cell door rattled. The giant squeezed inside, closely followed by another man. Drake recognized him as the starey-eyed individual he had briefly seen sitting in the back office when Romero and he had assaulted the timber yard.

"Little man!" Zanko greeted him with open arms. "I have brought the armpits! As promised, yes? And," Zanko sniffed the air. "They have not been washed." The Russian, as before, was bare-chested, the thick black hairs hanging limp.

"Where am I?"

"What? The famous Matt Drake doesn't know? James Bond would know." Zanko turned to his compatriot. "Wouldn't James Bond know, Nikolai?"

The eyes remained wide and staring but the mouth spoke at last. "Welcome to our . . . concrete jungle, my English friend." His voice was soft, menacing. "We reserved the five star suite just for you. In gratitude – for killing my men."

"They attacked me," Drake said evenly, watching the giant's every move. "And Mai. Where is she?"

The other man showed no signs of recognition. He stepped forward, holding out a veiny hand. "I am Nikolai Razin."

Drake studied him up close. The man was past his best years, probably in his early sixties, but still looked fit and healthy. His unnerving gaze was both severe and searching, the eyes as emotionless as a corpse's. The knuckles of the hand he held out were twisted and badly callused, as if he'd spent a lifetime hitting things. But the suit he wore and the watch that dangled from his wrist both spoke of wealth.

Drake ignored the gesture. "So what happens next?"

Razin stepped past him and went to sit on the bunk. Zanko stayed by the door, still grinning.

"I run this jail," Razin said. "I own it and the guards who work here. I own the government official who oversees it. I own the official who oversees him. You see?"

"So I guess I'm in Russia."

Zanko again spread his arms wide. "Welcome home."

"Now, I own you." Razin studied him. "What do you think about that?"

Drake shrugged. "It's been said before. Yet," he smiled a little, "here I am."

"Ah, yes, of course. Well, if you answer some questions, I'll make your stay less unpleasant before your inevitable death."

"I thought I was here because I killed your men," Drake said. "After hitting your timber yard."

"Not exactly."

Drake thought back to that day. "Babylon then. You think I saw your operation, is that it?"

Razin pursed his lips. "Babylon is only part of the puzzle."

"The Tower of Babel?"

Razin watched him closely. "How about the Tomb of the Gods?"

Drake didn't feign the surprise that swept across his face. "What?"

"The *third* tomb, to be exact. I want you to tell me all about the third tomb, Mr Drake, and about the device inside it."

Drake thought for a moment. He could buy time if he explained a few meaningless details. "The device was Odin's path to Armageddon. He could resurrect Ragnarok any time the thing was set off, survive it, and return. The thing with Odin's shield is what set it all in motion. This time."

"But how does the device work? What energy does it feed off?"

Drake frowned. "No idea."

"Was it ever turned on?"

"Are you crazy? Why would anyone ever switch the bloody thing on?"

"To harness its power. To switch if off again. To see if it works. To have their finger on the trigger. The Americans weren't interested in this?"

Drake flicked his mind back over Jonathan Gates' actions. He didn't think the Secretary of Defense wanted any further investigation of the device, but Gates wasn't the only big dog out there. "I don't know," he admitted. "But why would someone turn it on if they weren't sure how to turn it off?"

"Men with too much power sometimes believe they themselves are gods."

Drake started to feel disconcerted. He sat in Razin's jail, a prisoner, with the monster Zanko beside him, and was starting to think that the Russian actually made sense.

"The Shadow Elite," Drake said. "They would switch it on in their arrogance."

Razin motioned rapidly. "As would the Chinese. The French. The English. Perhaps even the Russians. Do not think our governments are any better."

"Still," Drake said. "It's all conjecture."

"Conjecture, yes. You said it, Mr Drake. Did you see the device or the place where it stands?"

"No. But I *was* in the tomb."

"Did you feel . . . an energy . . . to the place?"

At first, Drake pulled a face, sure Razin had blown a fuse, but then he remembered. "Actually, yes," he said, surprised. "The whole place felt *charged.* We thought it was because it was filled with evil gods. We felt *chills.* Unaccountable fear. We put it down to some kind of evil resonance." He shrugged. "Too many vampire movies, I guess."

"Earth energy," Razin said, almost to himself. "So our professor knows what he talks about, dah."

"What?"

"It seems there may be another way to turn the device on."

Drake's body went cold as if he'd been drenched in ice water. "Are you joking?"

Razin met his eyes. "The gods had a failsafe. They must have. Because if everything ever written about the seven swords tells us that they can always *stop* the device, then there must be more than one way to turn it on."

"Wait." Drake shook his head. "Swords? What swords?"

Razin blinked, as if realizing he'd said too much. "Oh, I'm a rambling old man." He sneered, clearly not believing his own statement enough to back it up. "We'll talk more tomorrow, Mr Drake. That is . . . if you are still alive."

He nodded at Zanko.

"Let him join the population. Then leave him. We'll watch on the monitors."

"There's lots more to tell about the tomb," Drake tried.

"Ah, I'm sure. But the prisoners are waiting for you. They're looking forward to welcoming you to the Motherland. I am sure a few broken bones will not phase a man like you, dah? Now, Zanko."

The monster Russian grabbed Drake's arm and thrust him through the cell door. "Don't die too soon, little man. I want my time with you."

CHAPTER FOUR

Mano Kinimaka stood back and watched as the world went crazy around him. His heart went out to Hayden as she juggled Gates on the phone with Dahl firing questions on her other side, and tried to cope with Mai in her face, all at the same time. The small but deadly Japanese woman had been left in the road, face down, no injuries except those done to her deep sense of pride. The Russians had clearly been given a single mandate – to snatch Drake. They probably hadn't even known who Mai was. They had clearly expected an easier time of it though, using tasers instead of guns to minimize the backlash. They had planned it well – even down to using a localized mini-EMP to kill Drake's car engine, and long-range taser guns to stop a getaway.

But they hadn't figured on the illustrious team of Drake and Mai. The Russians had lost twelve men in the attack. The rescue teams had missed them by minutes. As soon as Mai came round she identified the attackers as Russian and remembered the last comment she had heard before passing out, a threatening sentence whispered to Drake.

"Zanko sends you a message, 'Little man, you will enjoy our prison food'."

Kinimaka watched as Hayden, at Mai's request, put Gates on speakerphone. The Secretary was assuring them he would clear a plane to fly through Russian airspace and land near Moscow. This despite the current cold relations over the Syrian problem, but then Gates would know the man in charge of the man in charge.

"I'll talk to them," Gates was saying. "And explain the situation. They remain extremely grateful to your team for taking out the Blood King. His organisation has all but vanished from the streets. And, as you know, there's nothing like a past good deed to foster a future favor. Agent Jaye." His voice rose commandingly over her next question. "Just get going."

Kinimaka moved out of the corner and, conscious of his size, threaded a careful path through a disarray of tables and chairs and half-unpacked gear. His size was a constant sensitive point for him. It was why he had been in the corner to start with – there was more room and less chance of bumping into something he hadn't seen. He was proud of his size; proud of his physique, but it could also be a nuisance.

"Big lad coming through," he said. "Watch yer scrawny backs."

He saw Hayden glance up as he walked past, stared at her and walked straight into Komodo. "Hey."

"Put your tongue back in, Mano. Listen." Komodo leaned in. "You and the boss lady seem awful close these days. You . . .?" He let it hang.

Kinimaka was fiercely loyal and would never divulge. "I don't gossip about family, friends or girls, Trevor. You know that."

"Hey, it's jus' Karin who's asking, man. She's *English.*" He whispered the last word as if that explained the gossip request. "Me, I don't care."

"Good." Kinimaka strode past, finally reaching his gear. The team had raced quickly to their new HQ on Pennsylvania Avenue, oblivious to the bare rooms and barren walls, knowing only that they needed to get together, form a plan, and save Drake.

Dahl was doing the work of two. "If these are the same Russians that Drake and Romero pissed off, then we know they're based in Moscow." He packed his gear as he spoke rapidly to Mai and Hayden. "Can we be sure?"

"What other Russians has Matt pissed off lately?" Mai asked.

"The *Blood King,*" Dahl said pointedly, shaking his head.

"Bull. That was months ago. Plus, Kovalenko's in jail. And you just heard – his organisation has vanished."

"I heard," Dahl assured her. "And that's what worries me."

"The message included the name *Zanko,*" Mai said softly. "That's the name of the Russian they encountered in Moscow."

"Right." Dahl nodded. "Right. Then we need to find the jail. And we have a place to start looking."

Kinimaka felt his cell vibrate. He fished the small device out of his pocket, wrists as usual stretching the material to breaking point. The screen flashed with a single name, *Kono.*

"Damn," he whispered.

"Hope you ain't thinking of texting," Hayden's voice whispered softly at his side. "With them big jumbo fingers you'd either break the phone or spell out one of those long Scandinavian names Dahl likes so much."

"I've done that before," Kinimaka admitted. "I was trying to text, *cool.* Came out as *abdojaminn.*"

Hayden laughed. "You gonna speak to her this time? Might be your last chance for a while, Mano."

"Damn. How can you hate someone and love them so much at the same time?" Kinimaka slid the screen to answer. "Hi Kono. How are you?"

"Okay, baby brother. Okay. Hey, I need—"

"You know something, Kono. That's how you always start your calls. *I need.*"

"Sorry. But Mano, are you anywhere near me?"

"California? I'm in Washington DC, so that's a big no. Why?"

"You said to call if I needed help. Well, I always need help. I know that. I'm a fuck-up, Mano. I fucked it up for you and Mom and Dad. Sometimes – I even think someone's following me."

It had been his sister's way of getting his attention when she needed it in the past, but had always been just a ruse to wangle money out of him.

Kinimaka was very conscious of the team speeding around him, urgency firing their every movement. "I have to go, Kono. I'll call when I get back."

She started to talk, but Kinimaka ended the call. He ignored Hayden's look and glanced at Dahl.

The mad Swede was hefting his pack, anger and determination written across every solid inch of his features. Kinimaka almost pitied the enemy who would have to face that.

Dahl spoke. "Well, we managed almost two days off! Now, let's go and teach these bastards a lesson they'll never forget."

Kinimaka said, "I wonder how big this prison is."

"Who cares?" Dahl muttered. "One thing's for sure – it won't be big enough to stop us."

Hayden turned to the team. "Karin and Komodo will stay here and set up the new HQ. They'll work the technology magic that we might need in the field. Now, let's finish tooling up and go get our man back."

CHAPTER FIVE

Drake was led along the walkway and toward a set of stairs. The tumult below grew louder as he approached. Zanko padded along at his side, a gleeful gorilla, promising even worse endings to Drake than the dreaded unwashed armpit smothering. The boss, Nikolai Razin, came last, saying nothing. Drake wondered what the man had been fishing for. His only hope here in this bleak and hopeless place was to play for time until the team arrived, which he had no doubt would happen. It was just a question of when.

"So how do your seven swords figure in with the history of the Tombs of the Gods?" He paused at the top of the stair.

"Ah, do not worry about that. We will talk again later if you can still function. Eight hours is a long time to be alone in a Russian prison, my friend."

Zanko patted his head, almost breaking his neck. "Tough man like this? He'll be giving the orders by tonight." His guffaw rang out stridently. "Now get moving, little man. Or maybe you need the toilet first?"

Drake felt himself pushed, and flew down three steps before managing to stay his fall. As he descended, the prison mess hall came into view and, closer by, the makeshift gym. Big men sat around on low benches, pumping iron, lifting loaded arm weights, toweling off, or psyching themselves up for the next big lift.

As Drake approached the ground floor, every hooded pair of eyes lifted to take a look at him. A thick wave of loathing arrowed across the spaces between them, drenching him in revulsion. This was so much more than intimidation. Despite all his training, Drake found it almost impossible not to show fear.

Do not look away. He repeated it to himself as a mantra. The trick was to not look directly into their eyes, which would give the impression of a challenge, but also not to let his own eyes turn downcast, which was a sign of weakness and submission. Although here, in this jail, none of that would make a difference.

Men stood up. Zanko came to a stop and motioned Drake onward. "Go on! Meet your new cellmates. This is where we leave you. We have a great deal of business to attend." The big man's muscles flexed as if eager to get started.

Razin eyed Drake one last time. "You made a mistake, killing my men, shutting down my operation. You see, even a small abduction ring like that has its benefits. Some of these men though—" he gestured at the packed mess hall. "They broke bread with Kovalenko. Others – they were his comrades."

The two Russians turned and walked away along the corridor between two rows of cells. An arched, heavily barred gate lay at the far end. Guards were stationed outside, watching.

Drake turned back to the mess hall. The tumult had certainly lessened, most of the inmates craning their necks to get a glimpse of the fresh meat. Drake decided standing alone in the middle of nowhere like the new kid in school probably wasn't the cleverest approach, so he made for the food bays. A big clock, set high above the mess hall, told him that the time was 1800 hours Russian time. *That puts it at what?* he thought, *1000 hours, Washington time?* Of course, he didn't actually know how long he had been out. Could have been hours. Could have been days. Still . . . the team would hopefully be on their way.

A great bulk blocked his path, craggy sweat-streaked face leaning in until their noses were inches apart. A hand was laid deliberately on his chest and shoved him backward. The man spoke in Russian, harsh guttural, vicious Russian.

Drake shook his head. "No speakee da Russkie."

He had processed this scenario already. There was no winning option. If this were an American or English jail he would take this man down and then the next, at least try to stave off any further challenges. But here? There were about five hundred men watching him, at least half of them probably wanted to take his head off.

Playing for time remained his only option.

The man stood up, making himself look big. Drake was treated to the sight of his six pack and rippling arm muscles. When the haymaker came Drake evaded it, slipping out of reach.

"Look. I don't want to fight you. Your boss – he needs information from me." Drake tapped his head. "Important. Information. Dah?"

The prisoner roared and steamed forward. Drake met him head on with an elbow that whipped the man's head back hard, then sent him crashing to the ground. Immediately he skipped away, holding both his hands up.

The prisoner struggled to his knees. Now, behind him, Drake saw a row of men approaching from the gym area, dumbbells still clutched in sweaty hands, nostrils flaring, and eyes wide with anger. He backed away, circumventing the mess area and angling toward a far wall where he saw a series of open doors. As he slowly sidestepped, the group of men kept pace. Drake saw a trio of guards, positioned around the eating prisoners, watching with interest. They carried batons. Other guards, situated in sealed off balconies above, carried automatic weapons. He wondered if he might be able to reach one of them.

The first room he reached was empty save for a bolted down table. The second room led to what looked like a visitor's room, the third led to the showers. Maybe not. It was the second room that interested him most. It had other doors leading off it. Maybe they led to the kitchens and laundry room. Maybe there was a place he could hole up.

Then a hooter sounded and the mess hall began to empty out. Even so, several more interested parties drifted toward Drake. One of them shouted at him in English, another scooted across the floor like a monkey. Yet another started to literally rip his vest away in shreds and pound at his chest, bellowing until spittle flew from his lips. The hostile environment lay heavy with the intent of violence. Faced by over a dozen enraged Russian inmates, Drake had reached the end of the line.

CHAPTER SIX

Mai Kitano struggled through a storm of emotion as the fast jet touched down just outside Moscow. Would the adversities of her life never let up? Having fought clear of her conflict-laden past and her demanding government employers, she had now rediscovered the man she had once loved, only to lose him again.

The life of a . . . she paused her thought. *What the hell was she anyway?* Ex-ninja. Ex-member of one of the most notorious clans in Japanese history. Trained assassin. Yakuza infiltrator and destroyer. Cosplay champion. Sprite.

That last description entered her head when the face of Alicia Myles popped around the corner of the open airplane door. Myles didn't look happy.

"What the fuck, guys? I'm gone two days. In Alicia-time, that's eight shags. And you can't even hang on to my favorite team member? *Fuck!"*

Dahl approached her. "We have a few bits and pieces to catch up on." He motioned her back down the steps. "Shall we?"

"Oh, we shall," Alicia mimicked the Swede's accent. "But it's a bitch of a day out here, Torsty. Better bring your long johns."

Mai rose from her seat and grabbed her pack. Kinimaka lumbered along before her, barely able to squeeze down the aisle, following in Hayden's footsteps as ever. She drifted patiently in their wake. Once outside, the sharp air whipped her face and stung her eyes. The group wasted no time in hurrying inside, traversing a drafty corridor before Hayden led them into an enormous hanger. A gleaming black Chevrolet minivan stood before them, doors flung wide.

"This is it," Hayden said. "We have the timber yard's address. We go in hard, fast and without mercy. This is not an exploratory mission, guys, this is search and destroy. Are we ready?"

Everyone nodded. Alicia quickly suited up. Dahl had one last thing to say, “And when we grab one of these bastards, you do anything necessary to make them talk. Anything.”

Hayden pocketed two Glocks and hefted a bigger gun. “That's one of our own out there. Let's go send these assholes straight to hell.”

CHAPTER SEVEN

Drake ran at them, trying to utilize the dining hall's vast space for his own ends. He leapt as he approached the first man, sending him sprawling with a heavy kick to the chest. He spun immediately on landing, catching the next with a flying spin kick. The third hit the next kick as Drake doubled up the spin. As the horde got too close, Drake stepped back and leapt on to one of the mess tables. He picked up a plastic plate and sent it skimming at a prisoner's head, then grabbed the tray it had rested on. When another man came forward, Drake smashed him across the head with it, leaving a deep imprint in the hard plastic.

"It ain't worth it, guys."

But they were grinning, even the ones with blood dripping form their mouths and noses. They loved this. It was what most of them lived for. The one who thought he was a monkey alternatively squatted and leaped into the air, screeching like a banshee. The rest formed an ever decreasing circle and tried to hem him in.

Drake saw the move instantly. Trouble was there was nowhere to go. He jumped back on to a mess table, conscious now of the nearby guards and seriously considering relieving one of them of their batons. He ran the length of the table, jumped across to another, now nearing the food bays. Maybe there was something he could use as a weapon behind the counter.

It shouldn't have surprised him, but when the three guards suddenly raced at him he blinked in shock. He was caught between them, a mouse in a very severe trap, and they were on him before he could even think.

Drake went down, the three men above him. He did his best to block their kicks and punches, but several found a way through to the backs of his legs and spine. When the first baton strike landed, he squirmed in reflexive pain, making a slight gap for himself between one of the guard's wide open legs. Quickly, he scrambled through, rising instantly. The guards turned fast, but not nearly fast enough.

Drake throat-punched the baton wielder, grabbed the weapon as it fell and smashed it across the next man's face. Then, with the ease born of a lifetime's training, he killed the third whilst making sure the first two were incapacitated forever. A baton in each hand, he faced the oncoming prisoners.

"You might get me," he breathed. "But you'll pay fuckin' dearly for it."

The prisoners came in a group. The first ended up with a broken wrist, staring at it stupidly as it dangled before him, clearly unable to process what had happened so fast. The next lost teeth, but pushed on anyway, spitting them to the ground in a spray of blood. Drake slipped to his left, wielding the batons in both hands, a constant scything flurry of pain. A Russian dropped to his knees, holding the top of his head, blood welling up between his fingers. Drake sent a baton spinning at his jawbone, broke it and moved quickly on.

He sensed another at his back. The safe-zone was shrinking by the second. He spun and took the man out, but the forced action gave the others time to move in closer. When he spun back again, they were just feet away.

Drake dropped the batons, resorting to hand to hand combat. As the inmates struck at him, he reared up, and saw a strange sight at the other side of the room.

Another inmate, waving at him, beckoning that he follow. He mouthed the words *I can help you.* Drake knew it might be a trap, but it could hardly get any worse. He nodded and used the great burst of strength he was saving for a last stand to smash through the surrounding men. The inmate disappeared into what Drake remembered as the second room, the one with several exit doors. Drake leapt into space and ran hard, legs feeling as though they were on fire. Angry grunts filled the air behind him. How dare he spoil their fun?

Drake swerved around the doorframe and into the room. The inmate stood across from him, peeking out from behind another door.

"This way," the man said in English, only slightly accented, and vanished. The second door led to a storage room, left open for the inmates presumably with Razin's consent, piled high and racked out with spare blankets, overalls, boots and even coats. Drake followed his savior through the small room and out into a white-washed corridor.

"Quick!"

Several doors lay ahead. The inmate ran straight for the third on the right, slipping in without breaking stride. Drake hightailed it after him, ready for anything. But when he entered, all he saw was a pair of boots disappearing up into the ceiling.

A face popped out. *"Come on!* Crazy Russians aren't as slow as you think."

Drake took the proffered hands and allowed the man to pull him up into a narrow space. Then he crouched in the dark as a ceiling tile was replaced. Close together, they could barely see each other's features.

"Don't move."

After only a few minutes, Drake heard the sound of pursuit. He saw nothing, but heard men shambling about below, searching the room. After a minute they moved on.

"I think we're safe now."

"Thank you. Why did you save my arse?"

"Let us say I seized an opportunity when I saw one. I know your name. Mine is Yorgi."

Drake could make out little of the man in the gloom, but knew he was tall, thin and rangy. Most probably a lot stronger than he looked, and certainly a lot more resourceful. Drake sensed something small being pushed toward him. "Take this. But use it only as a last resort, my friend."

He took the improvised shiv, knowing full well that Yorgi could have gutted him in the dark with it. "Cheers."

"Hide it in your sock. Razin and Zanko will not search you again."

"Okay. Do you know how long I've been here?"

"Not long. Razin brought you in today."

"So is it Wednesday?" Drake counted off the hours. "Bollocks. I'd hoped I might have been out longer."

"That Zanko," Yorgi breathed. "He don't like you. Not one bit. And that man's a very bad enemy to have."

Drake just nodded. He didn't need to be reminded. "And why are you hiding in the dark, Yorgi?"

"Out there." Yorgi's body moved, signifying a nod. "They don't like thieves. They think you're going to steal their toothbrush or their mama's picture or something. It's easier to get lost in a rat hole like this. Plus, I'm still relatively young and very good looking. It's best to stay hidden."

"So you're a thief? And Russian? You speak good English, Yorgi." Drake didn't know the man well enough yet to wonder aloud where his small bristle-ended shank had come from.

"I studied when I was young. I was made to study." A loaded sigh, full of regrets. "Wealthy parents."

Drake wanted to ask how he had ended up in here, in Razin's prison, but again it was too soon to risk upsetting his new friend. Instead, he switched the conversation to something he needed.

"Razin and Zanko," he said. "Who the hell are they?"

"Nothing," Yorgi said. "They're just bullies with money. Razin runs a big organisation that is into almost everything illegal you can think of. His lieutenants, Zanko, Maxim and Viktoriyah enforce his rules and watch his back. They're ruthless, totally ruthless."

"Are they in to some kind of *mystery?*" Drake pressed. "They were asking me about some swords when they came into my cell."

"It's no mystery. Razin's men are always coming and going through here. They talk. I listen." Yorgi appeared to motion past Drake. Maybe there was a network of ceiling space around here. "It's how I knew you were here. And why I took a chance."

"You're hoping that when I escape I'll take you with me. I figured that. What I haven't figured yet is how you *eat.*"

"I have friends out there. I do favors for them, they bring me food and water. It is the way of our prison."

"God, Yorgi. How long have you *been* in here?"

A heavy silence followed. Then Yorgi sniffed. "I don't know."

Drake abruptly closed his mouth, the words he was about to speak lost forever, as they heard voices below. Two men conversing equably in Russian. Drake listened until they went away and then stretched his aching joints.

"Yorgi. If you can, I'd like to hear about the swords."

"I know a little. Razin is looking for the seven swords of Babylon in the old ruins. Once he finds them they will make him leader of the world, or something." Yorgi laughed quietly. "He's a nutcase. But he's our nutcase."

"Where did he come across this information?"

"Well, I suppose it must be from that professor guy. The one he abducted."

"Abducted?"

"Story goes that one of Razin's lieutenants, Maxim I think, got the call that some American professor was digging around the old site of ancient Babylon and asking some very leading questions. He would go into the bigger towns and cities and talk about Alexander the Great and his golden swords, about some powerful towers, and ramble on about earth energy. He was looking for any information he could get. Now anyone who knows about Alexander also knows there's a great deal yet to find relating to him, including his body, his tomb. Anything relating to him could be worth a fortune. So when the Russians got wind of the professor's investigations, they nabbed him."

Drake whistled. "He stood out further than Posh Spice's ribs. And he's *American?"*

"They say."

"Do you know where they're keeping him?"

Yorgi stayed quiet. Drake sensed a trade coming on. "Yorgi?"

"Why are you so interested? I have heard a little more, yes. But I do not want to spend the rest of my life rotting away in this place."

"You have my word, matey. If I escape, I'll take you with me."

"Okay. I heard them complaining that they have to escort him daily through Red Square. So it must be close by. I will try to trade for more information."

"Good. But be careful—" Drake managed to stop himself by gritting his teeth hard. Why the hell was he telling a Russian thief to be careful in prison? *Old habits die hard*, he thought. *Even in this hellhole.*

"I will. I do have plenty to trade." Yorgi laughed. "But you have to go back now. If you're quiet you'll make it back to your cell. It's after lockdown. Tomorrow—" Yorgi shrugged. "I may not be able to help you."

Drake frowned. "Won't they have missed me at roll call?"

Yorgi grinned. "You really think they care about that kind of thing in this prison?"

Drake shrugged and looked around. "I can't stay here?"

"Razin would tear this place apart looking for you. There are more men than me who use this rat hole as a haven. And at least some of them are worth saving." Yorgi sighed heavily. "I am sorry. You must go."

Drake nodded. "I think we'll need another day, Yorgi. But be ready. Be ready when it all kicks off."

"How will I know?"

"Oh. You'll certainly know when *my* friends arrive."

CHAPTER EIGHT

Mai held on tight as Dahl swung the minivan around a final corner and powered hard toward the battered gates that fronted the Russian timber yard.

"Bastards!" he cried as he burst through, hyped up to the max, as they all were at the thought of one of their friends being held behind enemy lines. There would be no respite, no quarter given, until Drake was safe.

The gates smashed apart, crashing against the side walls of the building and buckling. These were most likely the same gates that Drake and Romero had breached, bent and damaged even before Dahl sent them to a rusty heaven.

The minivan screeched to a halt in the middle of the yard. Dusk was setting behind the high, overladen timber racks, but there was still enough light for the strike team to see their way. A cabin stood in front of them, spilling bright light, the only door at the top of a set of concrete steps. Dahl raced ahead, gun held high. Even Mai and Alicia had to hurry to keep up with him.

The door was flung open. Dahl didn't hesitate. He shot the man who stepped through in the stomach and waited a moment as he tumbled down the steps and hit the yard, face first. His groans of agony told them he was out of the fight, but still useful for torturing information out of. Dahl stepped over him, Mai now at his back. She had experienced no after-effects from the tasing, at least not physically. The actual knowledge of being beaten and losing Drake had hurt far more than any electrical charge or bullet.

"Move, little sprite!" Alicia said, at her back. "Stop dawdling!"

Around the corner of the cabin came the sound of gunfire. Hayden and Kinimaka stayed to take care of that, whilst Mai sped after Dahl. The Swede had cleared the counter in a single bound, wounded the man crouched beneath it, and was advancing on the main cabin. He slowed at the arched entrance. A bullet crashed into the big frame.

Mai planted herself against the wall opposite him. They counted to three, then peered through the doorway, firing twice, once to confuse and once to kill, at the same time evaluating their enemy and the room.

Alicia crouched beside them. "How we looking?"

"Two at my side, both under cover," Dahl said.

"Two at mine. Exposed," Mai whispered.

They counted to three again and fired. Dahl cursed, "Still two."

Mai turned back, smiling. "One left."

"Damn, we aren't playing that bloody game again are we?"

"Not if you can't keep up, Torsten."

Mai fired blindly around the corner. The sound of a man groaning, and the crash as he toppled to the floor brought another tight smile to her face. "That'll be zero."

Dahl sniffed. "Well, mine are hidden behind desks."

A man suddenly appeared behind them, coming through an inner side door that had to lead to a storeroom or toilet. Alicia swiveled her aim with godlike reflexes, spraying his knees and double-tapping the top of his head as he hit the deck.

"Ah, bollocks to this," Dahl said, and let the gun rip on full auto as he stepped around the frame. Mai backed him up, springing to the opposite side of the main cabin in one bound and presenting a different deadly target. Bullets slammed into the desks, ripping splinters away from their edges. Timber, plastic and hot lead exploded across the rear of the cabin in a devastating mushroom cloud. One man screamed as shards of wood speared his face. Another had his head so close to the floor his ass was visible over the top of the table. Mai winged it, just once.

Dahl ran forward, staying low, and kicked the table aside. At that moment another man popped up from the office beyond, but Mai took him out like a tin duck at a shooting gallery. His body flew back against the cabin's rear window, shaking the whole structure.

Alicia stepped in, closely followed by Hayden and Kinimaka. "All good?"

Mai nodded. "We should interrogate them separately. Make sure they're telling us the truth."

Alicia produced a steel hammer. "On it." She crouched beside the nearest fallen Russian, brandishing the weapon.

"What's your name?"

"V . . . Vladimir." His eyes were wide with fear, hands creeping automatically to his scalp.

Alicia eyed him closely. "You been hit by one of these before, Vlad?"

Mai watched as the man shuddered. She vaguely remembered the name Vladimir from Drake's report. Wasn't he the one running around with a hammer sticking out of his head? She left Alicia to her work and walked to the back of the cabin, finding the Russian she had winged in the ass.

She crouched down, whispering in his ear, "I don't need tools. I can make you scream and die with only my hands in less than a minute. Would you like to try?"

The Russian shook his head vehemently, rolling on to his side and groaning with the pain. Mai took hold of his windpipe between two fingers and gave it a little squeeze. "Alright then. I want the address of the jail. The one connected to Zanko. You have five seconds."

Kinimaka stayed with Hayden, watching the cabin whilst Mai, Alicia and Dahl completed their work. It only took a moment for Hayden to notice the charts and maps pinned to the nearby wall; the same ones Drake had momentarily scanned.

"Mano," she said, pointing. "Take a look."

Kinimaka followed her example. He still couldn't quite shake Kono's disturbing phone call from out of his mind – she was vulnerable living in LA – and he did know some people who lived out that way and would be willing to look out for her. But for how long? He couldn't seriously ask colleagues to watch over her indefinitely. Besides, he was sure Aaron Trent would have better things to do.

His contact with Kono, and the occasional calls, were always kept a secret from their mother. Kono had walked away from the family home years ago, brash, rebellious and disrespectful, not the way the Kinimaka family had been brought up. The split had almost put his mother into therapy, especially coming so soon after the unexpected death of his father.

Now Mano tolerated his sister because, deep down, he loved her. Any layer above that was still raw, exposed and full of hate.

"Mano?"

"Sorry." He squinted at the place where Hayden was pointing. It was an ancient map of the city of Babylon, complete with the eight gates, including the Ishtar Gate – the main entrance – with an added notation – *Ishtar* was the Babylonian Goddess of sex and love – the assumed site of the enormous Ziggurat and the Tower of Babel, the mound of which can still be seen today, and a very interesting highlighted sentence at the bottom.

Babylon literally means, 'Gateway of the Gods'.

Hayden stared at Kinimaka. "Oh no."

"I thought we were done with those freaky tombs. They're so small, you can barely swing a cat inside one."

Hayden shrugged. "Not while they're still translating most of the gods' language. Not whilst the doomsday device still exists. You gotta remember, Mano, they're discovering new stuff nearly every day."

"The Ishtar gate seems to be a prominent landmark," Hayden said. She snapped a few photos on her phone. "Look. Here's a map of how Babylon looks now."

Kinimaka studied it. "Big difference."

"And what's this? The Dance of the Seven Veils. The Saber Dance. Sounds kinky. Want me to learn it for you?"

Kinimaka tried to pretend he hadn't heard. He respected his new girlfriend too much to talk that way within earshot of others.

"And the pit of Babylon. Wow, it's the original foundation of the original city. Quite the landmark."

Kinimaka let his eyes wander over a few more details. He hadn't realized Alexander the Great – the man said to be the greatest king and one of the wisest men of all time – had died in Babylon. He mentioned the fact to Hayden.

But his girlfriend wasn't listening. She was staring, eyes wide, at a third map. "Crap."

Kinimaka leaned forward. It was a map of Germany, marked by a big red circle and a set of coordinates. "Shit," he echoed. "That . . . that's Singen."

"The location of the third tomb. What the hell's going on?" There was a thick red line linking tomb three to the pit of Babylon.

Mai listened hard as her prisoner whispered the location of the prison to her. She had to listen hard because his voice was croaky due to a bruised windpipe. But the address still came, eventually.

She looked over at Dahl. "Got it?"

"Yes. It's just outside the city."

"I have the same." She shifted to Alicia. "You?"

The Englishwoman grunted. "Damn, Vladimir, you really want this hammer back where it belongs? You do? Okay." She brought the hammer slicing down, claw end first, halting a millimeter from the man's skull, so close the curved blades parted hair.

Vladimir screamed out the address.

Mai smiled. "They all match. We know where Drake is."

Dahl jumped to his feet, face like thunder and fury. "Let's roll."

CHAPTER NINE

Drake spent a night in his cell, unmolested. Not daring to sleep, he rested his eyes and allowed his mind to drift, whilst keeping his senses attuned for any sound of unwanted company. Most of all, he missed Mai. Keeping company with her lately had made his whole existence more upbeat. A bright future existed with the Japanese girl and the rest of the new team. It was time to embrace his newfound fortune.

There was just the small matter of escaping Razin's prison and deciding if this 'Babylon thing' needed further attention, to deal with first.

A loud klaxon sounded the call to breakfast. Drake's door slid open with the rest. He wondered if he might get away with staying put, but a guard soon began to rattle the bars with his baton, quickly joined by two more.

A barrage of Russian swear words proved that cursing was a universal language.

Drake followed them out of the cell, along the walkway and down the steps into the mess hall. Half the benches were already occupied, and the other half of the inmates queued up for food. The gym area was empty, but Drake immediately spied several of last night's opponents eyeing him from a far table.

No doubt downing their porridge, he thought. Fuelling up on energy for a big day of Drake-bashing.

He sat down at an empty table, at the end of a long bench, watchful. Hunger pangs played on his stomach like an orchestra, but he ignored them. No way was he joining that queue to find minced rat and chunky coleslaw waiting for him at the end.

Nothing happened, but the atmosphere grew steadily more charged. He watched the clock, seeing it jump past 0900 hours. No way could he expect an extraction in the next twelve hours. If the team did try, it would be without sufficient planning – maybe Dahl's style, but not Hayden's. She would ensure sufficient, superior resources before making her move. At 0930 a side door opened and sunlight flooded through. The inmates began to file toward it.

Exercise yard.

He watched the guards watch him. They were waiting for something. Half smiles ghosted across their faces. Itchy fingers twirled batons. There was a reason he hadn't been accosted yet, and it wasn't to let the prisoners' food settle.

The last man to rise, he drifted slowly toward the open door. The sounds of raised voices and a bouncing ball indicated at least one game was underway. When Drake stepped outside, he quickly shielded his eyes from the sun, not that it was overly bright, but he'd been dwelling in interior gloom for a few days.

A row of long, stepped benches stood off to his left, like the bleachers at an American football game. Men stood and sat along them, the higher their position the higher their standing in the prison. King of the hill mentality. A wrought iron outdoor gym sat in the far corner. A basketball court come football pitch in the center. Many inmates lounged or walked around the exterior fence, staying away from the melee in the middle. Drake looked up and saw two occupied guard towers and a balcony attached to the prison wall, where more guards could patrol or lounge, as they did now. He walked to the right, staying close to the prison fence.

The football game continued, the men ignoring most of the rules. Groups congregated together on the bleachers, gangs designated by their prison tats. Loners circulated around the edges, staying watchful or handing out tiny plastic packets. Money changed hands. Drake was surprised to see Yorgi lounging up ahead and slowed down when he passed the thief.

"Tonight?" Drake mumbled, face pointed at his toes.

"Watch your back," Yorgi whispered. "Something will happen. Watch the guards. When they move away, get ready."

Shit. Drake had been right. The prisoners *did* have something planned. He quickly made another reconnoiter of the area, identifying possible weapons, areas to fall back to, certain inmates who held themselves in the way that said they were actually dangerous rather than just muscle-bound and deranged.

The sun rose higher. The football game ended. Some of the men sneered at Drake and challenged him by raising fists and grinning. Drake saw the chance of a little payback.

"You want me to play? Well I—"

A guard vanished from his field of vision, slipping back indoors. Another stepped down from a watchtower. The balcony guards turned away and vanished through an unseen door. Total silence descended over the exercise yard.

A half-naked figure walked out through the door, into the light. Drake turned to study him and breathed, "For fuck's sake."

Zanko.

CHAPTER TEN

Kinimaka watched as Dahl paced impatiently.

"Are they ready yet, Hayden? We can't wait all bloody day."

Hayden cupped the receiver. "I'm talking to them now. Gates already made the call. It shouldn't be long."

Alicia came up to Kinimaka. "What's the deal, big boy? Karin set up that new HQ yet? Ready to watch our backs."

Kinimaka nodded. "She's almost there. The only thing they've had time to do is set up the comms and the total surveillance systems. Very high-tech."

"Don't give a fuck. So long as it helps get us an escape route, it can be Captain Jack's spyglass for all I care."

"You've watched Pirates of the Caribbean?"

Alicia gave him a saucy wink. "The first ten minutes. Then the middle ten. Then the last ten. Besides, ain't no movie gets by me starring the Deppster." Alicia moaned. "Should call him Johnny Viagra."

Kinimaka choked. "That's more than I need to know. Jeez."

"True. But I never disappoint, Mano. You should know that by now.

Kinimaka thought over the heart-to-heart they'd had, what seemed an age ago now. Back in that hotel in Vienna, the night before they charged the terrorist battlefield like the veritable Light Brigade. Alicia had revealed a part of her past, a tragic part, and secured a place in his heart forever.

"Of course I know, Alicia. You can say anything you want to me."

"Well, I did want to check something with a real man." Alicia leaned in close. "Y'see, Lomas has this problem down below. He keeps on—"

"No!" Kinimaka yelped and danced away. Alicia laughed. Mai had to physically grab hold of Dahl's shoulders to stop the man's frantic pacing.

Hayden replaced the receiver and turned to them. "We've been allocated a chopper from a local base. Plus ammo. But they're not risking any men. We're on our own."

Dahl headed straight for the door. "Not a fucking problem."

CHAPTER ELEVEN

Drake sensed rather than saw the crowd of inmates melt away. His full focus latched firmly on the man-mountain stalking toward him. Zanko flexed enormous chest muscles as he walked, pecs beating away like a base drum. The hands, spread wide, made him think of Mai's relatively small hands when she placed them in his.

And Mai could probably kick his arse to hell and back.

Drake moved sideways, aiming to give himself space, placing the gym and its well-used equipment at his back. Zanko increased his pace.

"Now we tangle, little man. Let's see if the famous Matt Drake is made of the same shit as the rest of them."

Drake slipped away as the great, growling bear reached for him. A light drizzle began to fall across the exercise yard as the clouds obscured the sun. Zanko lunged. Drake ducked and stepped in before delivering a stinging blow to the giant's ribs and then his kidneys. The Yorkshireman ducked under another wild, swinging blow, came back around to Zanko's front, and delivered a push-kick to the chest with all the strength he could muster.

The Russian coughed and shrugged, but didn't waver. "My grandmother can hit harder than that! And I really do mean it. Come on, fight me!"

Drake lunged, struck, then danced away. Zanko took another blow to the ribs, grinning. He mimicked Drake's movements stride for stride, slowly pushing him back. Drake caught a flicker in Zanko's eyes and suddenly realized—

The other inmates had formed a cordon at his back. Half a dozen more steps and he would be close enough for them to fling him straight into Zanko's arms! He skipped quickly among the gym equipment, lifting a small set of dumbbells and pacing warily behind a heavy lifting frame. There was only one way this fight was going to end.

Zanko roared and charged, stopping only to heft the big frame and fling it to the side. Drake slammed the dumbbells against the side of his head, arm vibrating with the impact. Zanko staggered and went down on one knee. Drake brought the dumbbells down again, this time aiming for the Russian's exposed skull.

Zanko tore his legs away with an arm sweep. Drake suddenly saw sky and landed flat on his back, the air rushing out of his lungs. He held on to the dumbbells, legs already scrambling to get away. But Zanko landed on his lower body like a beached whale, sending jolts of agony shooting around Drake's nerve clusters. Quickly, he brought the dumbbells overhead, using every ounce of strength to heave them at Zanko's head.

The Russian threw up a massive forearm, blocking the blow. But even he grunted in pain when they hit. Drake withdrew the dumbbells and tried to move. Zanko righted himself and sat on Drake's legs, practically crushing his knees. With his right arm, Zanko blocked Drake's next blow and ripped the dumbbells from his hand, then threw them away so they landed hard against a far wall.

Zanko leaned forward, head the size of a rhinoceros suddenly blocking all the light. "It seems you lost."

Drake struggled, twisting beneath the immense weight. With a speed that surprised Zanko he sat up, striking his forehead against the bridge of the Russian's nose, then struck with both elbows, twisting his torso each time to deliver a more brutal blow. Zanko grunted again and appeared to flinch. Blood streamed from his nose and over his lips. Drake heard the inmates' collective gasp.

The hammer blow came out of nowhere, stunning Drake, causing so much instant pain his whole body froze upright for a second as it tried to process. Stars exploded in his brain. Clouds obscured his vision.

Zanko had smashed a fist into his stomach. Drake found himself holding on to the Russian's shoulders as he gasped for air, even the barest slither of breath eluding him.

Zanko laughed, blood spattering everywhere. Drake wheezed in his face, still unable to breathe. Zanko jumped up, then hefted Drake above his shoulders, holding him like a powerlifter grips a barbell.

Drake wheezed in an ounce of breath, stomach convulsing, then hit the ground hard as Zanko threw him across the yard. Still conscious enough to tuck and roll, Drake lay still for a few precious seconds as Zanko stalked up to him. He thought about using the shank in his sock, but decided that might put the fight on a whole new level. Zanko moved in closer.

"Time to—"

Drake came up groggy, but with an aim born of experience. His left fist swung hard into Zanko's groin.

"Dahhhhhhh!"

Zanko doubled over, hands clasping, eyes bulging. "Not . . . fair," he managed to gasp.

"And you think this is?" Drake indicated the yard, the inmates, the lack of guards. He stood with his hands on his knees as Zanko moaned, recovering slowly from the immense stomach blow.

"You pack a punch like a fuckin' jackhammer on acid, Zanko."

The Russian's face twisted into a feral grin. "I know, little man. You should meet my grandmother, Zoya."

"Maybe next time." Drake launched a knee-strike, slamming into his opponent's forehead. Zanko tumbled back, losing balance, and crashed to the ground. The inmates, raucous until now, went quiet, some of them staring at Drake with sudden awe.

Drake spied Yorgi still attached to the side fence. The thief was watching carefully, chin resting in his hands.

Zanko struggled to one knee. Drake decided against the top of the skull attack this time, not wanting to break an elbow, but moved to the Russian's back. The thick neck looked like a corded tree trunk. He moved in to deliver a swift punch, but at that moment Zanko swiveled and caught the blow in a huge fist. With a burst of strength, he yanked Drake off his feet and brought him sprawling into a face-plant. Drake's head exploded for the second time in five minutes.

But this time Zanko didn't give Drake any respite. A double blow to the stomach sent the Yorkshireman to his knees, head hanging; a punch to the side of the skull sent him toppling on to his side. Drake's head grew fuzzy as the concrete came up to meet him.

Then Zanko's mouth was at his ear, even as the Russian delivered more blows to his body. "Every day, Drake. You get this every single day."

Pain seared from Drake's abdomen to his brain, more pain than he could stand.

"Until you die."

The last thing Drake saw was the much promised armpit, dripping with sweat, a tangled mess of matted black hair, and then the putrid stink as the foul mass closed over his face.

CHAPTER TWELVE

Several hours later, Drake came to. A heavy stench hung in the air and it took him a moment to realize it was Zanko's stink, plastered across his own face. With that knowledge, Drake gagged, jumped down from his bunk and ran over to the sink. SAS training had never included being smothered into unconsciousness beneath a crazy Russian's armpit. *Though it had included similar*, he mused, splashing his face and scrubbing it with a bar of old soap. Luckily, his breakfast stayed down. He began to wonder what time it was. The bastards had taken his watch when they first threw him in here. That was twenty quid's worth of Casio he'd probably never see again.

He walked to the front of the cell, grabbing the bars. If he leaned far enough to the left he could see the door that led to the yard. It was closed. He glanced up then, toward one of the guard perches. Above that was a grimy window. Drake saw daylight, but of the waning variety. It was near sundown.

Good. Wouldn't be long now.

He needed another chat with Yorgi. There were still unasked questions and, since he couldn't absolutely guarantee taking the inmate with him if he managed to escape, he wanted every ounce of information he could glean. Drake stepped back and stretched warily. His stomach felt like it had been hit by a pile driver, his limbs throbbed in time to the flow of his blood. He had been taught to compartmentalize pain, but this was a whole new level.

Nevertheless, he stepped out of his open cell door and moved to the railing, peering down at the level below. He was wondering how he might find Yorgi, when the man drifted into view, catching his eye. All the other prisoners were occupied, playing cards, or wrestling, pumping iron or maybe discussing who might be worth shanking that day. The gangs all had their heads together. Drake tried to peer into every corner, but saw no sign of Razin or Zanko.

Ignoring the pain, he darted for the steps and walked fast across the dining hall, entering the meeting room and the corridor beyond a few seconds after Yorgi. Even though there were no sounds of pursuit, the two didn't slow down or talk until they were hidden again inside the roof space.

"A good fight," Yorgi said first. "Earlier. You put up a good fight against Zanko. I've never seen him even bleed before, let alone be knocked down."

"Fat lot of good that did me."

"Eh?" Yorgi didn't understand the saying.

Drake rubbed his ribs. "I still lost."

"Ah, but now the gangs respect you. They won't harm you again, not unless Razin orders them to."

"Small mercy."

"The American professor," Yorgi said. "I have not yet found him. But I know another way."

Drake half smiled. "Let me guess. It involves you being on the outside?"

Yorgi shifted. "You see how the world works quite well, my new friend."

Drake said nothing. Chances were, Yorgi already knew where this professor was being kept, or at least the street name. Razin's men weren't being exactly secretive with their information.

"I'll see what I can do," he said at last. "But come tomorrow – any time – keep a very close watch on me."

Yorgi nodded in the dark and offered a bottle of water. Drake drank thirstily. "Damn, that's good. Have you heard anything new about Razin's project?"

"The Babylon thing? The swords? No. But if he hasn't found them yet, he will soon. The man is obsessed and he can throw all his resources at this."

"That's what I feared."

Yorgi went quiet. Drake sipped half the bottle and handed it back. The two of them sat there for a while in silence. With time on his hands, Drake found his thoughts wandering. A question popped into his head – one that burned away at his heart and mind like the searing face of an iron, one that he wished he had the time to fully address.

"Yorgi," he said, hesitant. "In your travels, during your life, have you ever heard of an agent . . . or an assassin . . . called Coyote?"

The Russian thief almost choked on his water, spitting some of it on to the Styrofoam roof tiles. Then he went very still.

Drake waited.

Yorgi cleared his throat. "What kind of name is that?" He laughed nervously.

Drake shrugged. "A memorable one."

"Well, I don't know that person. No."

"Are you sure, Yorgi?"

"Why should I?"

"People in your line of work. They . . . know many things. They hear everything. It's part of your job."

"Why do you say that?"

Drake sighed. "I knew a very good thief once. He . . . died recently."

"And did he not know this Coyote?"

"I never got the chance to ask him."

"I am sorry. The name means nothing to me." Yorgi's voice was firm now, resolute. Drake let it drop.

"Fair enough."

Yorgi held out a bar of chocolate. "Let us hope for a good tomorrow, my friend."

Drake unwrapped the thick block. "I'm counting on it."

CHAPTER THIRTEEN

It took all day Thursday for the team to prepare. Dahl constantly chomped at the bit. Hayden worked wonders through Jonathan Gates with the Russian government. Having already acquired a chopper and weapons, she further smoothed the path by getting the Russians to admit they would rather see the jail obliterated off the map than not – it would rid them of part of the blight that was Nikolai Razin.

But the chopper had to be American made. The arms had to be American. It was all to guard the Minister of Defense's back, and it wasted valuable time, but was extremely necessary. Karin kept in touch and watched several areas via satellite feed, all the time fine-tuning her tech from Washington, preparing to be their 'all-seeing-eyes' when they assaulted the jail.

Alicia was ready within minutes of their arrival, and spent the next several hours texting Lomas and keeping herself upbeat by insulting almost everyone who came within three feet of her. The only person she gave a pass to was Mai – the Japanese woman seemed uncharacteristically anxious not only about Drake, but about something from her past too. She mentioned it briefly to Alicia – *the clan is looking for me* – but Alicia didn't know enough about Mai's life to heed the first signs of onrushing calamity.

Kinimaka watched it all from the back of the room, offering advice where he could. When Hayden started to look overburdened, her jaw clenched and shoulders tense, he eased over to her and took her outside for a break. When Torsten Dahl appeared a few feet away, phone to his ear, saying what sounded like a 'hope to speak soon but can't be too sure' speech to his wife and kids, Kinimaka moved away. When Alicia beckoned him over he listened to her talk about the biker gang as if they were her newfound family – and he smiled. It was good that she had found a semblance of home; at least until she decided it was time to move on.

And when the phones were dumped into their cradles and all calls ended; when the quiet of anticipation fell like a soft, frayed blanket; when the team – the family – looked to each other and prepared for one of the biggest assaults of their lives, Mano Kinimaka took a second to send his mother a last simple text.

Love you.

CHAPTER FOURTEEN

Drake heard the sound of approaching helicopters as he lay waiting atop the concrete block that was his bed. It was early morning. His eyes were closed, but sleep had never been so far away. He was waiting for this moment; that sound.

The *whump whump* of the approaching choppers took him back a few months to the start of all the current madness where, in York, he had simply been photographing models at a catwalk show. *Those were the days,* he mused.

But now Mai was back in his life, the beat of his heart restored, and even now she was on her way to pull his arse out of the mire. He jumped up, checked that the shiv was still down his sock, and moved next to the bars. Somehow, he didn't think this was one of those prisons that would stay locked down during a raid. The inmates would be called upon to help defend it.

Razin's rules.

The noise increased. Prisoners across the aisle from Drake leaned out of their cell doors, arms waving, faces pressed between the bars. The choppers drew closer. The men began to shout. Drake thought the team might breach through the exercise yard wall or the kitchen area. They wouldn't risk blowing out any wall that ran anywhere near a cell. They wouldn't go through the front door. This was strictly smash and grab.

Which brought him to his first problem. *Yorgi.* He hoped the waif-like thief had heard the tumult by now and was standing ready, maybe even using the roof space to creep nearer to Drake's cell, but he couldn't be sure of it. So when the cell doors opened with the sound of a large bolt shooting back, he waited a moment for the aisle to clear, then slipped quickly away from his room. Following silently in the wake of the last man, he descended the stairs and circumvented the gym area whilst trying to ignore the shrill complaints of his bruised body. Rotor blades thudded just beyond the walls, the sound unmistakable now to even the oldest and most inexperienced ears. The team was landing.

Drake ran. Gunfire sounded from outside the walls. Inmates ran to the exercise yard door, but it was locked. Someone shouted for one of the guards to open it. A man recognized Drake and stepped in front, but ended up on his back, nose askew, to sleep out the rest of the day. Drake's eyes unceasingly sought his target, but Yorgi made no appearance. He raced into the meeting room and beyond into the bright corridor. Two men stood up ahead, blocking his way, a guard and a prisoner quietly conversing.

"Here he is," the guard said in English. "His friend. Get him."

Drake never slowed. He used his momentum to drop and slide across the polished floor, swinging his legs as he got close to the prisoner, sending him crumpling to the floor. When he landed, Drake had already relieved the guard of his baton. He spun once, taking the guard out with a blow across the forehead and the prisoner out with a strike to the back of the neck.

Then he was speeding off again, approaching the end of the corridor. He ran down to Yorgi's room and saw the destroyed roof tiles, pipes and aluminum framing scattered across the floor.

Someone had found Yorgi and pulled him out of his secret home.

Drake swore. Where would they take him? Was he, Drake, to blame? He searched the floor for any sign of blood or something he could use as a weapon. He picked up one of the steel pipes – a prison weapon if ever he saw one. Footsteps thundered by outside the door, guards rushing so fast that they didn't see him. Drake walked to the frame and listened.

Muffled shouts reached his ears, the sound of a man begging for mercy behind a closed door. *The standard prison echo,* he thought, but this voice sounded a lot like Yorgi's.

Drake rushed out, listening hard, pinpointing the noise as coming from behind the fifth door down. A rushing sound accompanied the screams, a sound Drake had heard before.

Oh shit.

He barged into the room, letting the door smash back against the wall. Three men whirled at the sound, one of them holding a wide, industrial hose. Yorgi sat against the rear wall, drenched, whimpering, gasping for breath. They had been trying to drown him standing up.

Drake ran hard. The hose whipped and exploded with a thick stream aimed at his legs. Drake jumped through the torrent, bringing the pipe down on a man's nose before lashing it left across a second man's mouth. Both screamed and bent double, holding their heads in their hands. Drake dropped the pipe and grabbed the hands of the man holding the hose, forcing the brass handle down between his legs. He let go and immediately the hose, unconstrained, began to skip and jerk like a ferocious snake. Drake jabbed the man in the solar plexus before finishing him with a rigid windpipe strike. He ran across to Yorgi.

"Hey, hey, you alright?"

The saturated man looked up. "I have had worse beatings."

"Bloody great." Drake extended a hand. "Trust me. I do keep my word."

They sprinted back up the glaring corridor, Yorgi squelching and shivering with every step. Drake slowed as they reached the far door and put an arm out to stop Yorgi.

"Wait."

He peered into the room. It was empty, but through the open door at the far end he could see right into the mess hall. Pandemonium reigned. Prisoners scurried haphazardly past the opening; shouting, gesticulating and fighting each other. A great huddle of them suddenly fell backwards, tripping over feet and twisting to crawl away. Drake heard a loud explosion before brick dust and shrapnel flew in a razor-edged cloud across the mess room.

"Now!"

Drake pulled Yorgi along. The sound of gunfire exploded from ahead. Prisoners twisted, spurting blood, as they charged forward. Drake paused for a second at the entrance to the mess hall, then walked out into full view, hands in the air.

Don't shoot me, he silently intoned. *Please . . .*

"Matt!"

Mai's shout came on the heels of Dahl's cheer and just before Alicia's expletive. The three soldiers knelt among a pile of rubble, rifles tucked firmly into their shoulders, a ragged, crumbling hole at their backs where the door to the yard used to be. Some of the prisoners recognized Drake and charged at him. The guns bucked and men skidded to his feet, already dead.

Drake ran hard, pulling Yorgi along. Mai and Alicia covered his sprint as Dahl turned to check their own retreat. A shout sounded from somewhere behind Drake. He whipped his head around and saw a spectacular sight. The whole crowd of prisoners – mostly Razin's men – hurtling toward him in a rag-tag wedge. Not a man amongst them wanted to have to explain to Zanko why they hadn't tried to prevent Matt Drake's escape.

Drake reached his friends. Mai and Alicia, and now Dahl, fired around him, felling prisoners with leg and body shots so that they tripped up the men following behind. Some hurdled their fallen comrades, brandishing an assortment of weapons from plastic trays to improvised shanks; others swung knotted bed sheets full of rocks.

"Go!" Drake shouted.

"Nice to see you too!" Alicia shouted back, carefully squeezing shots off as the mob closed in. Drake ran through them, letting them cover his back, out into the exercise yard. A crazy scene met his eyes.

A military chopper had landed in the yard, amidst prison vehicles and storage sheds. The rotors were still spinning, as was the barrel of the nose cannon, having fired a burst at the prison's main entrance where most of the guards were situated. The fence was down, a clear escape route showed right to the helicopters door. But the guards in their towers and their wired-off perches still took pot shots.

Drake whirled. "You guys bring me a gun?"

Dahl skidded to a halt beside him. "This is a quick extraction. We have no intentions of inducing a shoot out!"

"You're taking the piss." Drake pointed at the guard towers. "They're all yours, Dahl."

He ran hard, staying low, heaving Yorgi firmly behind him. At first, bullets peppered the dirt around his feet, but, after a few well-placed shots from Dahl, the volleys soon stopped. Drake exited the fenced area. Both Mai and Alicia backed out of the ragged hole. Alicia threw a small device back into the prison and shouted, *"Run!"*

Drake put his head down. An explosion sounded behind him, and, when he slipped a glance that way, he saw a cloud of fire stretching up and billowing out, Mai, Dahl and Alicia framed by the flames, sprinting hard, guns still firmly at their shoulders and searching for targets, faces set as grim and hard as he'd ever seen.

The chopper came up quick. Hayden and Kinimaka stared down at him. Gunshots peppered the windshield and bounced off. Drake saw Hayden finessing the cyclic stick as he clambered aboard.

Yorgi made a wet sound as he plumped down on to the seat beside him.

The chopper lifted off, barely giving the other three enough time to jump aboard. Dahl was the last, making an athletic leap to grab hold of one of the skids, then crouching and leaping again in an instant, gun swinging, like a world-class free runner.

Drake stared. "Nice."

"New hobby."

"I meant the rescue."

"Oh, well, you're welcome. Couldn't leave you out here on your own to be horribly tortured."

"Dahl," Alicia said, "hasn't stop pacing up and down since we got here. I think he loves you, Drakey."

"Bog off."

Dahl reddened.

"And thanks to you too, Alicia." Drake let himself relax for just a moment as the chopper continued to rise.

"You know, they just had to say words like *guns* and *explosions* to get me here."

Drake turned to Mai. "Hey—"

Just then Hayden screamed, *"Oh no, dammit! They've got a fu—"*

A massive explosion shook the chopper as the rocket propelled grenade struck the chopper's undercarriage. The helicopter immediately spun out of control.

Kinimaka shouted out what was already clear, *"Hold on! We're going down!"*

CHAPTER FIFTEEN

Drake grabbed hold of a restraint strap with his left hand, and pushed Yorgi firmly back into his seat with the other. He saw Hayden fighting the collective, Kinimaka leaning across to help by adding his own strength, as the sky flicked around and around like a crazy kaleidoscope.

"Ow!" Drake smashed his head against the bulkhead. Aware that the ground was rushing up, he held on even tighter and yelled, "Where's the spare guns, for fuck's sake!"

The chopper slammed down hard, the sickening crunch of its buckling skids giving them a millisecond to prepare before the belly of the machine struck concrete. The impact sent Alicia tumbling, smashing her head against a seat back. Mai and Dahl held on, but crashed into each other. Drake protected Yorgi with a grip like a band of steel.

As the chopper came to rest, Hayden immediately unbuckled and climbed out of her seat. "Hurry!" Both she and Kinimaka took up weapons and opened the cockpit doors, quickly establishing positions as guards came running forward.

Alicia groaned as blood seeped from her scalp down her forehead. Drake crouched beside her. "Can you focus? Can I borrow your gun?"

"Piss off!"

Dahl threw open the side door, reaching into a lockbox as he did so. "Spare weapons and mags in there, Drake. Help yourself. You might want to arm your new friend, too."

The Swede jumped down, followed by Mai. Drake delved into the lockbox. Alicia jumped out the other side, backing up Hayden. Guards ran at them from the entrance of the prison building, using the cover provided by several sheds and vehicles along the way. Prisoners had crossed over the breach in the wall by now and were again massing for a charge.

"We don't have much time!" Hayden yelled. "Anyone got a plan?"

Dahl shouted above the din. "This way!"

Drake picked an M4 assault rifle, slightly out of date perhaps, but a great weapon, and handed Yorgi a SIG Pro semi-automatic pistol. "Make sure it's loaded and grab some spare ammo." Drake readied himself at the door, prepping the M4.

"Ready?"

Yorgi nodded.

Drake jumped, landing a foot behind Dahl. Bullets fizzed all around the stranded chopper, even skimming off the concrete and the tiny spaces underneath the machine. Yorgi landed awkwardly and Drake steadied the man before he tripped headlong. Mai sent sporadic bursts at the walls over the prisoner's heads, shattering the concrete and showering them with hard shards. Dahl made sure they all saw where he was pointing.

"There."

He took off, staying low. Drake quickly searched the inmate crowd for signs of Zanko or Razin, but saw nothing. He waited as Mai slipped past him and he saw Hayden, Kinimaka and Alicia running their way. He turned and followed the mad Swede, making a bee-line for a big, green Ukrainian built KrAZ truck. The behemoth was a six wheeler, with an open back partly covered with a tarpaulin that strapped into hooks situated all along the trucks high, steel sides.

Perfect for deflecting bullets.

Dahl clambered up into the high cab, whooping with delight when he found that the truck was already idling. Drake reasoned that his team's helicopter arrival had interrupted some kind of delivery and the driver was long gone.

The team climbed aboard, two in the cab and the rest in the truck bed, sitting with their backs against the solid sides. Dahl pumped the accelerator and shifted gears, wincing as the mechanism made a deep, angry grinding sound.

Alicia sat beside him. "It ain't your wife, Dahl. You can't smooch the damn thing into submission. Give it some fuckin' wellie."

Dahl rammed the gear lever home and stepped on the pedals. The truck roared and lurched forward. Diesel smoke belched from the exhausts. Bullets pinged and bounced off the sides as the guards rounded the stranded chopper. Dahl trod on the accelerator and turned the wheel, aiming for the prison gates.

He slammed the back panel. “Gatehouse!”

A trio of guards already stood outside, aiming their weapons as the truck roared toward them. Mai and Drake stood up in the back and let loose on full auto. Two of the guards twisted and fell, the third ran like a spooked rabbit. When the truck slowed, Drake jumped to the ground and ran, using the enormous wheels as shelter, before smashing his way into the gatehouse where he searched a wall-mounted, gray console. The commands were written in Russian, but there were only two significant buttons. One red, the other green.

He hit the green one, heard the satisfying crunch and saw movement as the gates swung inward, and climbed back into the truck as it began to pick up speed. As he paused atop the sides he cursed. “Bastards are chasing us.”

The heavy truck rumbled and roared as it bounced and crashed its way through the prison gates and on to a rough-and-ready road. Dahl fought the wheel at every turn. Alicia checked the side mirrors to gauge the pursuit.

“Three trucks, a little Land Rover type thing and a kind of mini-pickup. Drake would probably know the makes, models and street value.” She smiled tightly.

Dahl was wracking his memory. “You remember the map? If we branch off up the road ahead we come to Zalinsk – the empty town?”

“Yeah.”

“Good.” Dahl swung the wheel hard when the turn came up, sending the truck jouncing along an even bumpier road and his teammates sprawling across the truck’s bed. Through the subsequent yelling, Dahl uttered the quiet words, “Apologies people.”

They crested a muddy rise. The town of Zalinsk lay in a shallow depression, nothing more than an unsystematic jumble of buildings, many now open to the elements as the place had been abandoned for so long. With the pursuing vehicles only a half mile behind, Dahl set off down the slope only a little faster than was safe. When the truck hit the bottom he aimed it at the middle of two of the nearest buildings and hauled on the brakes when it had effectively blocked the road.

"Pile out!"

Dahl hit the dirt first, Alicia a step behind. Drake scaled the truck's sides and flipped himself over the top, then waited for Yorgi. Mai landed deftly beside him.

"Who is your new friend, Matt?"

"Prisoner. Thief. Informer. Entrepreneur. It's good to see you, Mai."

"It will get even better when we reach civilization." Mai smiled demurely, then raced off through the open door of a nearby building, heading for the roof. The pursuing convoy was already thundering down the slope, some of the guards taking hopeless potshots. Drake followed Mai as Hayden and Kinimaka aimed for a nearby structure, the big man as usual ensuring he was the screen between his boss and the line of fire. Drake thought that Hayden was so used to his routine, she barely noticed it anymore.

Gunfire cracked from the rooftop. Drake saw the lead truck's windshield shatter and had an idea. "Yorgi, wait behind me." He pointed.

Sinking to his knees, he took aim with the sturdy M4. The sights lined up and he squeezed off a flurry of bullets. The lead truck lurched and swerved as the driver-side tire exploded, veering off the road and bouncing rapidly down a sharp hill. Drake imagined the men being flung around inside the truck bed much more vigorously than he had been, and saluted with the rifle when he saw two of them thrown so high they were tossed over the side.

His teammates all opened fire. The second two vehicles ground to a halt, their occupants scrambling out and either finding cover or rushing around the back. Drake stayed where he was for the moment.

Then, four guards poked their heads into sight. One exploded out of sight instantly, a splash of red being the only testament that he'd been there at all. The other three leveled rocket launchers.

Drake ducked and threw himself into the dirt as missiles flew at them.

CHAPTER SIXTEEN

Russell Cayman wandered through the chaotic, dust-thickened ballroom, an eerie wraith in the dark. Otherworldly, the stench of death and human flesh clinging to him like a thick, toxic miasma. His step was sure and he had eyes for only one thing.

The bones of Kali, Goddess of Evil.

She hung before him, wired to the wall in all her glory. Cayman had rebuilt her skeleton full-size and then used iron wall hooks and industrial wire to keep her in place, spread magnificently across the wall and looking down on him from a superior position.

On them.

Cayman dragged the half-dead body of a local man behind him, fingers wrapped in his long blood-matted hair, the slithering sound of his last passage punctuated only by the occasional tattoo of his boots striking the floor in response to intense spasms of agony. Cayman stopped when Kali loomed over him, the sight of her dirty gray bones a soothing balm to his scorched eyes.

"My Goddess." He knelt. Around him tiny shadows shifted – the denizens he lived with, all squatting in the dark like creeping Gollums – in the once-empty mansion that had belonged to the secret group known as the Shadow Elite. The ballroom was where most of them had so painfully died, so Cayman found it fitting that Kali should reside here, pressed up against the dried patches of their life blood.

"I bring you . . . a sacrifice."

He threw the body at her feet, watching as the twitching man bled out. He enjoyed taking and killing the locals in this area of Vienna, sometimes offering them to Kali, other times feeding them to the rats and adding their tenderest pieces to his saucepan.

He had grown into a culinary genius.

When the man stopped twitching, Cayman moved forward, kneeling in the pool of still warm blood, and supplicated in front of his god. He leaned over and kissed Kali's feet, held the cold bones against his cheek. At last he felt whole again, nourished, part of a family. Cayman's real mother had dumped him into a ditch and driven away when high on drugs. Kali would be his guardian, his overseer, for life.

His cell phone rang for the first time in weeks. He wasn't happy, but he wasn't surprised. In most ways he was fully expecting the call. Cayman kissed the cracked bones one more time before standing and moving away to a far corner, at the center of a sticky network of spider webs.

"Yes."

"Have you been expecting me, Russell?"

"Yes, sir, I have."

"Good. Where are you now?"

"The old mansion."

"In Vienna? How excellent. Then you must come to me at once."

Cayman acquiesced. He had always known there existed one single man, one indistinct figure who ruled them all. The true leader of the Shadow Elite. "I'll set out as soon as it's light, Mr Block."

"And Cayman?"

"Yes, Mr Block?"

"Make sure you bring the bones of Kali with you. With her help . . . we will once again rule the world."

Cayman was in no position to argue with the once and future king of the world. He softly agreed and finished the call, staring up one more time at the immense skeleton wired to the twenty-foot high wall.

"We have one more night, my Goddess."

CHAPTER SEVENTEEN

Drake shielded his eyes as the rockets exploded. Sheets of flame burst upwards and outwards, detonating like a fire bomb. He saw the entire building to his right literally sag as walls were blasted away – the same building Mai, Alicia and Dahl occupied. He could only watch as rock and stone cascaded down and the entire structure began to crumble.

"Look out!" The warning felt way too late.

Mai, lying in wait on the flat roof, had ducked behind the stone parapet when she saw the missiles swinging in. Their impact sent an ominous vibration through the structure beneath her, one she felt through her own body and understood immediately. At first there was only the groan of heavy foundations shifting, but then the entire roof area lurched and sagged. The front end slumped, bricks and mortar cascading away, crashing to the ground below. Mai scrambled backwards, catching the eyes of Dahl and Alicia.

The Englishwoman shook her head. "Building's collapsing with us on top?" She sighed. "Must be Friday fuckin' morning."

Dahl rose and nodded at Mai. "You ready?"

"I know there's only one way off this roof."

The entire building dropped another inch, the front part of the roof falling away to leave a rough and ragged precipice. Dahl strapped his weapon over his shoulders, and Mai followed suit. As the roof sagged again, they saw the prison guards situated ahead of them jump into their vehicles and advance. When the collapse accelerated, Dahl roared and ran straight at the disintegrating edge. The whole building rumbled and shook. Cracks exploded across the roof's surface. Mai ran at his heels, Alicia close by. The roar of adrenalin pumped like a thrash band in their ears. Their sprint suddenly turned into a *downhill* race as the top of the building sank even lower. A mushroom cloud of dust and smoke billowed ahead.

Dahl reached the edge and hurled himself into space, pushing off hard and using the still slightly elevated roofline to get extra lift. Mai leaped beside him, arms and legs still pumping, as the bulk of the building caved in behind them. The roar of shattering brick and rock hurt Mai's ears. Her eyes sought the ground through the smoke, hoping they had jumped far enough to clear—

They landed hard, hitting grass a second before debris burst across it in a tumbling tidal wave of rubble. Mai felt her legs clipped by rock as she landed and rolled, her momentum keeping her ahead of the wave. Still, fragments of rock flew around her, compressed, then fired out by the rolling mass. At last they stopped; the clouds and the dreadful noise behind them, the onrushing vehicles before them.

Dahl, kneeling, legs covered by a mound of rubble, unstrapped his rifle and took aim. "Blow the bastards' tires out."

Drake told Yorgi to stay put and ran up to them. "Bloody hell! Are you lot okay?"

Bullets flew past his head, but fired from behind. Hayden and Kinimaka were still snug on their rooftop and following Dahl's lead. Mai checked her body quickly, but saw no signs of blood. Nothing vital screamed at her. She joined the rest of the SPEAR team and took aim. Her first shot shattered a windscreen. The vehicle veered wildly, speeding closer. Her second shot took out the second vehicle's front passenger tire. It swerved to the left and clipped the rear end of the first vehicle.

"Shit!"

The team scattered as the first vehicle tipped and crashed on to its roof, momentum sending it tumbling toward their position. Five tons of metal bounced past them, coming to rest amidst the ruins of the house. Dahl groaned. The rocks piled on his legs had slowed him up and the truck's front bumper had come within an inch of his skull as it whipped past.

"I'll finish 'em." Alicia scrambled after the battered vehicle.

Mai squeezed her trigger as men jumped from the second vehicle. One fell backwards, slamming hard against the bodywork before slumping lifelessly. Dahl uttered a satisfied grunt as he took out another. Then a third stepped around the hood, RPG cradled across his shoulder. As he pulled the trigger, Hayden or Kinimaka took his head off with a double-shot – the RPG aimed straight up as its operator fell – the grenade screamed high up into the air like a flare before falling down through a small arc and exploding against a rocky outcrop.

Mai heard more shots and much cursing as Alicia dispatched the guards still trapped in the second truck. That left only two remaining. "They'll be radioing for help."

Drake pulled a face. "I doubt they can have many more guards to send. They still have to run the jail."

"I meant from *other* connections," Mai explained carefully, making Drake feel a little foolish. "Razin clearly owns part of the Russian government."

"If they did, they'd have told him you were coming to free me," Drake said.

"They didn't have enough time," Dahl said with a wicked grin. "Hey, good to see you, ya bloody Yorkshire terrier."

Drake took the proffered hand with a grin of his own. Alicia slapped him across the back of the head as she returned.

"How the hell did they snatch you in the first friggin' place? Did you stop sleeping with a gun under your pillow?"

Drake thought back to the abduction. "It was our fault," he admitted. "We got complacent."

"Too much Mai-time?"

"Is that possible?"

"I wouldn't know." Alicia sniffed. "But you sure interrupted me at a delicate moment."

"Delicate? You?"

"Well, if you must know, Lomas was just—"

Hayden ran up to them, Kinimaka a step behind. "We should go. Now."

Mai indicated the truck slewed across the road ahead. "There are two still alive out there."

"Makes no difference. If they return to the jail we've got 'em off our backs. If they follow our asses we can ambush them. Main thing is – let's get the truck outta here." She pointed at the vehicle they had arrived in. "That truck."

Kinimaka laughed. Alicia scowled at him. "Mano. What the hell have you done to her? Though clearly not English, she at least used to *seem* human."

Within three hours they were installed inside one of the CIA's Moscow-based safe houses. The last of the prison guards hadn't bothered to follow them, leaving the rest of their getaway uneventful. Drake had asked that all questions be delayed until they were safe and could relax a little, so, after showering, eating and spending a few moments with Mai, the team gathered in various poses around the front room. Curtains were drawn against the dark and prying eyes. All exits were locked and watched over by a central CCTV system. Alarms were activated.

Kinimaka stood by the window. Through the gap between the material and the plaster wall, he had a good view of the street outside. The big man didn't take any chances at safe houses. He still had nightmares about the one assaulted by Boudreau and the Blood King's small army.

He listened as Drake described his first few hours of captivity. The Russians, Razin and Zanko, sounded like the type of men their team had been assembled to deal with. When Drake introduced Yorgi, Kinimaka studied the whip-like man with new eyes.

A thief. An escaped felon. A resourceful procurer of goods. A sly, clever man with secret agendas.

Alicia stated the obvious out loud. "So you helped Drake so he'd drag your sorry carcass outta there? What now?"

Yorgi bit hard into the burger he'd been handed, clearly savoring something other than prison fodder. "Now? I have not thought so far—"

"Balls," Alicia said. "You thought very well."

Yorgi shrugged. Drake stepped in. "Give the guy a chance. He has information we can use. Don't forget, this was Razin's prison, full of his men."

Yorgi nodded, still chewing. "He owned the men, the guards, everything."

Hayden spoke up, "We saw something of Razin's research when we hit the timber yard. Ancient Babylon, the Tower of Babel, the

Dance of the Seven Veils. Singen." The last word was directed at Drake with some poignancy.

The Yorkshireman caught on. "Come again?"

"They found some kind of link between Singen and Babylon. And Babylon, translated, means *Gateway of the Gods.*"

"Razin did ask a shedload of questions about the third tomb," Drake remembered. "It was pretty much all he was interested in." He proceeded to relate everything Yorgi had told him about the seven swords, Razin's proclamation that they would turn him into a world leader, how they were searching for them in the old ruins, and of the American professor who was helping them against his will.

"They're holding this professor somewhere around Red Square," Drake finished. "Though I do believe Yorgi sniffed out a little more before our departure?"

Yorgi stepped in, eager to help. "I did give up over half my stash for this. He's on Tverskaya Street."

Kinimaka felt a tendril of shock squirm in his stomach. The rest of the team looked, understandably, disturbed. "An American professor being held here?" Hayden nodded at the window. "In Moscow. Are you kidding?"

"Razin nabbed him when he blabbed too much about his bloody research," Drake told her. "And Red Square's twenty minutes away . . ."

"We need to prepare," Hayden said. "Speak to Gates."

Mai agreed. "Maybe we should get the Russians involved."

Alicia laughed. "Little sprite, you losing your mind as well as your edge? They've been about as useful as an old Skoda so far."

Mai shot the Englishwoman a hard look. Kinimaka knew what was behind that cloud. The ex-Japanese agent blamed herself for losing Drake. And something else was going on with her, an event that had ties to her hidden past, and Mai Kitano was clearly stressed.

They talked until the small hours and when they were all about to retire for a few hours, Dahl's cell phone rang.

The Swede eyed the screen uncertainly. "This is odd."

Kinimaka watched him as he listened to the caller. The Hawaiian had been expecting a call of his own tonight, hoping for one from home and dreading one from California. The business with Kono was going to have to be resolved one day.

Now Dahl put his phone on the table and sat back, looking troubled. "That was Olle Akerman. You remember? My man in Iceland who's translating the language of the gods? And my friend—" he added.

"What is it?" Hayden prompted.

"Well, he says he'll explain all when he sees me. But something's happening over at the Icelandic tomb. Three dead. One presumably missing. And . . ." Dahl paused, shaking his head.

"What?"

"Olle had to run for his life. He was being chased out of the tomb. By Russell Cayman."

"Cayman?" Hayden echoed. "He's back?"

"Something very nasty's going on," Drake said, glancing around the group. "Something that involves the tombs, these swords, Cayman, and God knows what else. And we need to get up to speed before it's too late."

Dahl jumped to his feet. "And that's why I'm heading to Iceland," he said. "On the next flight out."

CHAPTER EIGHTEEN

Russell Cayman had finally come face to face with the true leader of the Shadow Elite. The man's real name was Zak Block and he welcomed Cayman into his home, explained himself thoroughly, and truly communicated with him as an equal. Times were hard indeed for the Shadow Elite.

The last remaining member of the secret society that ran the world had called in every favor he had ever been owed. His power had been diminished by the loss of his figurehead – the Norseman – and the other members. Many of his contacts had chosen the opportunity to melt away, to cover their tracks, but Block had reached out like never before, reconnecting with the most powerful, the most vulnerable, clawing in every sinner he could find like a devil reaching up from the lowliest pits of hell. His resources were still almost bottomless, enabling him to find many willing partners to walk the jewel-encrusted path to purgatory.

This empire would rise anew. It would be bigger than the first. He would not let it fail again.

On Wednesday, Cayman had sat opposite him, having first deposited the many bones of Kali, carefully wrapped, in an adjoining room. "She has watched over me."

"As have we." Block showed no prejudice at Cayman's words. "We never went away, Russell. We delved ourselves even deeper and returned armed with much more than a chest full of treasure."

"I need no treasure."

"Oh, I know. But I could give you the Singen tomb to make your home. What do you think of that?"

Cayman stiffened. It was all he would ever need.

"The doomsday device is the fastest way to regain control of the world," Block said. "For that I need you, Kali, and one other man of *like mind.*"

"The pieces of Odin were destroyed," Cayman said. "Along with the Norseman. What can I do?"

"You will walk the path, Russell. I will see to it. You and Kali will prepare the way."

"How?"

"We will activate the device, then shut it down. We will show the world our intent and make it squirm at our feet."

"You sound like one of the Singen gods," Cayman pointed out.

"I know." Block grinned agreeably, completely missing Cayman's meaning.

Cayman had lost none of his investigative prowess during the last few months. "So you're saying there's another way to activate the device?"

"Isn't there always? Of course. Russell, I have men everywhere, you know that. My network of informants, of paid lurkers, of *inside men,* is wider and far deeper than that of the intelligence agency you once worked for, and any other you could care to mention. Previously, I used the Shadow Elite to help cloak my dealings. Now," he shrugged, "I no longer have that luxury. But I can rebuild."

"You have a spy inside the CIA?"

"I have half a dozen. But that is not where my information came from."

Cayman knotted his brow. "Ah, the tombs themselves?"

"The horse's mouth is, as ever, the richest procurer of information. My experience has always been – if you need to know something important, go straight to the source, don't waste your time buying third parties or paying off spies. But Russell, I find myself troubled. I am used to being the man in charge, the man who supervises the supervisor, not the worker and doer of deeds."

Cayman nodded. He knew a little of this man's past and his overwhelming passion. Zak Block had spent many years studying people, all types of people, and cataloguing their reactions to different scenarios, by living amongst them. He had engineered life-altering events for ordinary people just so he could observe how it affected them. His study of human nature had come to an abrupt end when the Shadow Elite fell, dragging him away from his latest and last premise in faraway Blackpool, UK.

"I understand, sir."

"Well, we will all have our roles." Block shrugged. "You. I. The third man. The cells I am setting up even now to help safeguard our venture. But to help me, you must first understand what has happened. As I mentioned, I have several informers scattered amongst the three tombs of the gods, covering the many skillsets being employed within. My thoughts are that the tombs are being discovered anew every single day, thus giving us the endless potential for new revelations. This view is also held by many of the free world's governments. They are all over this like carrion worrying at a carcass. My men are experts in their fields, true leaders, thus giving me the edge, I believe."

Cayman nodded at the pause, wondering if Block's new found penchant for anxiety stretched to reassurance too. He sipped from a bottle of water, casting a furtive glance toward the room where Kali lay in pieces. It had been hours since he had last admired her.

"With that in mind, it should come as no surprise to learn that my translator of the gods' languages working inside the Icelandic tomb made an enormously significant discovery a few days ago." Block licked his lips and smiled icily. "A discovery that he brought straight to my attention."

"And only he made this discovery?" Cayman tried hard not to make his voice sound skeptical.

"They have four translators working shifts in there. It's a substantial job. Once they have passed the security checks, these professors and super-geeks are trusted and left to work as they prefer."

"Alone?"

"Yes, Russell, alone. Mr Jakob Hult always works alone, for obvious reasons." Block was starting to sound annoyed so Cayman let him speak, moving slightly to keep Kali's bones within his line of sight.

Block closed his eyes and started to recite from memory, the slight smile on his face showing he savored every single word, "*'And though Odin's device shall need His nine pieces to activate'*." Block stopped there. "Activate is the wrong word, but my translator assures me it is the closest alternative. *'There shall remain one more way, this being a double failsafe for Odin and his Gods. And so . . . place three like minds in three separate tombs with three separate parts of the same God. And thus, this way too, there are nine parts. Do this, and the device shall activate, joining the vortexes, and burning the world to ashes'."* Block stopped expectantly.

Cayman thought it through. "Why is it a double failsafe?"

"Because it's a *second* way to activate the device and we also need *three* men, separated, all with like minds. I guess it's like not allowing one man to have his hands on the nuke codes."

"And the vortexes?"

Block pulled a face. "That's one thing we haven't fathomed yet."

Cayman stared at Kali's bones. "You want to divide her up?"

"It's the only way. I don't want to start smuggling gods' bones out of the tombs, not when we have one right here. And Cayman, you will be a big part of this. A big, bright shining part. Think of the reward."

Cayman *was* thinking of the reward. The rest of his life, in solitude, living amongst the vile and sinful, immorally infused old bones of the worst gods in history. "The end justifies the means, I guess."

"Oh, it does." Block's smile widened. "Imagine our power. Mightier than ever before. Once we hold the key to the device we will own *everything*."

CHAPTER NINETEEN

Cayman saw one more hole. "You mentioned three men?"

"Three men. Three tombs. Three parts of Kali. In truth, I do not see how us all having *like minds* makes a difference, but we'll do that anyway."

"Perhaps it has something to do with these vortexes?" Cayman suggested.

"Perhaps. But now we must prepare, Russell. Your task, as I'm sure you know, is to secrete one of Kali's bones in each of the tombs, then wait at Singen until the appointed hour when we shall join our minds. Presently, I will go to the Hawaiian tomb. Our third man will be present at the Icelandic tomb."

Cayman again found his gaze drawn toward the bags of bones. "Then I'll get started." He walked past Block, dismissing himself, and entered the far room. It was only Wednesday. He would visit the Icelandic tomb first, since he knew its layout and security measures. For a moment he stood upright, clearing his mind, then fell to his knees and unzipped the bag.

Her scent drifted out, ancient malevolence mixed with overwhelming greed and lust, sloth and wrath. All the seven deadly sins infused into a set of dusty old bones that would never quite be just that. Cayman thought his mind may have been a little bit warped before he met Kali, but she had changed all that. Now he could function. Now the way forward was clear.

His future crouched in festering anticipation, waiting for him in the beautifully wretched tombs of the gods.

Zak Block allowed himself not an ounce of judgment. To pull off this gargantuan task he needed Russell Cayman, and now was not the time to form an opinion. Now was the time for action.

The Shadow Elite, whilst no longer having any kind of major army at its beck and call, still employed many insanely-capable cells in all parts of the world. Mercenaries. Ex-soldiers, disgruntled by low pay and officious officers. Warriors unhinged by all they had seen and done. And the plain crazy – the killers. A small, scattered army remained at Block's beck and call.

He called each and every one now, using prearranged code words and promising an influx of funds. He told each one where he needed them and dispatched them immediately, to await his call. He asked an expert cell to travel shortly to Iceland to deal with his translator – Jakob Hult – with extreme prejudice. The man had completed his task and had now become a liability. He knew far too much about Block's new master plan.

Each cell would guard a tomb, both covering Cayman's back and awaiting the hour when three men would turn from mortals into gods and truly rule the world.

The new game was on.

CHAPTER TWENTY

Torsten Dahl arrived in Reykjavik, Iceland, around Saturday lunchtime and immediately called his friend, Olle Akerman.

"Where are you, Olle?"

"What? No greeting, my old friend? I am with your wife. Ha!"

Dahl waited patiently.

"Alright, alright, I am nervous that is all. I have been nervous since I saw that Cayman pig sneaking around the tomb. Thought I would never see him again."

Dahl knew that Cayman had taken charge of the Icelandic tomb's operations when everyone still thought he worked for the DIA. "You escaped him, Olle. Remember that. Now, where are you?"

Akerman gave him the address of a coffee shop. "I have read that Reykjavik is among the safest cities in the world. That is very good, ja?"

Dahl left the airport and jumped straight into a taxi. The driver took him straight into the heart of Rejkyavik. Dahl studied the blocky buildings and the ever present looming spire of *Hallgrimskirkja*, the mountains across the water in the distance. Rejkyavik was a pretty place and, lacking the bustle of Stockholm, always seemed appealing whenever he visited. Johanna and the kids would love it here. Only trouble was, he only ever visited as part of an ongoing mission. Johanna might not even know he was here.

Akerman waved from outside the coffee shop as Dahl's taxi pulled up. Dahl shook his head, paid the driver, and ushered the older man back inside. "Low profile, Olle. Low profile."

"Ah. You soldiers and your missions. It is a good job you have people like me to keep your heads in the real world, ja?"

Dahl directed him to the back of the shop, next to the fire exit. He then ordered drinks and sat down lightly on the edge of a comfortable seat. During the last two hours of flying he had evaluated all the information Drake and Yorgi had conveyed. The only clear move they could make was to try and liberate the professor.

The team over in Moscow had agreed with him and an operation was even now under way.

Dahl watched the front doors. "So Olle. Tell me all about it."

"Well, first I hear that something has been translated. Something huge. And by one of my colleagues, Jakob Hult. News like that, it is a big thing for us. The process of translation is very boring, Torsten."

"Understood. Go on."

"So, of the four of us – all translators – suddenly two have had accidents and are dead. And then Jakob, he vanishes. That leaves me. Just me. Very scary." Akerman shook his head.

"And then you saw Cayman?"

"No. Then I decide to investigate." Akerman grinned. "Jakob's sector, it is sealed off, but not very well . . ."

Dahl sighed. "Oh, Olle."

"I am very good at this, Torsten. Do not worry. I go over there and have a sneak around. Sadly, I find nothing. Just the same boring translations I am dealing with. But I do see that a small part of the rock is broken away."

Dahl made a motion. "As if someone had smashed it off on purpose?"

"I think so, yes. To hide what they found. And only one person could do that – Jakob. But then the security come around and I am forced to leave, but decide to return the next night."

"Of course you do."

"And that is when I see Cayman. He is sneaking around, heading up the ladders toward Odin's tomb. The man carried a rucksack and weapons. It is then, unfortunately, that I sneezed . . ." Akerman hung his head in embarrassment.

"Cayman saw you. Did he say anything?"

"No. He just looked at me. A . . . a horrible stare, Torsten. A dead soul. I knew then that if I didn't run I would die. So run I did."

Dahl placed a hand on Akerman's shoulder. "I am sorry."

"It is not your fault. But then, the next day, I *see* Jakob. He is not hiding. I am walking through Reykjavik to get the shuttle to the tomb and Jakob is heading to the seaport. I follow him . . . ah, it's not so difficult, no matter how much you spies and soldiers like to puff your egos up about it, and see him with money. A lot of money. He is purchasing a boat. That is when I called you, Torsten."

"You think Jakob was paid off and is trying to leave by boat?"

Akerman shrugged. "I am academic. I leave the grunt thinking to you, my friend."

"Well if that's the case." Dahl hurriedly finished his coffee. "We should find Jakob now, before he has chance to leave, and persuade him to talk to us."

"My thoughts exactly."

"Really?"

"I would have already done it if I hadn't known someone more suited to the manual labor." Akerman paused. "That is you."

"Thanks. Now, drink up, Olle, we have a rogue translator to catch before someone else gets to him."

CHAPTER TWENTY ONE

Drake and the team made ready. As the dawn's gray light began to illuminate the eastern horizon, they were already driving steadily toward Tverskaya Street. Yesterday, they had observed the place, noticing how difficult access would be. The building itself was close enough to Red Square to get away with the extra security machinations, but also fronted by a private car park and surrounded by civilian offices and a few shops, not to mention the main thoroughfare that was Tverskaya Street. But this was the weekend. Many of those places would be unoccupied.

The traffic was sparse, most of the citizens and tourists still snoozing at this hour. Drake had spotted Zanko twice yesterday and two other men, but there had been no sign of Razin, although the man would most likely have a legitimate business or two in the area. The backpack between Drake's legs was full of guns and ammo. It would not do to get stopped by the police at this point, even though the team's ultimate purpose would explain everything away. The Russians were hardly known for their tolerance.

The professor was being held for the purpose of providing information indirectly linked to the tombs of the gods. That in itself was enough for Drake's team to make a move, never mind that the information may have relevance to the doomsday device.

With this being a sensitive target, a dawn raid, and one that would undoubtedly meet resistance, they had decided to limit the strike force to three members. Drake, Mai and Alicia. The Englishwoman parked the car across the street. The three of them watched the door of their target building for a while, and the windows to either side.

"Yorgi," Drake said over the car phone. "You had better be bloody right about this."

"I will stake my reputation on it."

Alicia grumbled, "Reputation? You're a thief."

Drake glanced her way. "So was Belmonte. And he died saving our lives."

Alicia nodded. "So he did."

After a moment, Drake hefted his pack. The three of them exited the car and shouldered the bags. They were dressed in jeans and large-size jackets to help hide the padding of a Kevlar vest. Alicia voiced their concerns as she negotiated the wide road.

"Do we look like tourists or undercover police officers? Cos I can never tell the difference."

Mai gave her a fleeting look. "All you need is your mask, Myles. Drake and I will hold your hand."

Alicia snorted. "Yeah. Right after you let go of each other's."

Once across Tverskaya Street, the trio moved quickly into the car park that fronted Razin's building. Ducking behind a pair of parked cars, Mai took out a small but powerful, hand-held spotter scope and studied the building.

"No movement," she reported. "And sparse furniture. The front is likely a façade. The real action goes on in the back."

"Helps the plan." Drake stayed low as he ran across the car park, pausing briefly between another small group of parked cars to slip a balaclava over his head. "Ready?"

"It itches." Alicia complained, rubbing where the material stretched across her forehead.

"I thought you would be used to them," Mai said slyly. "Don't Lomas and you . . ."

"Piss off, sprite."

Drake caught their attention with a cough. "Ready?"

He moved before they could answer, weapon at the ready. They ran around the side of the building, hugging the wall, and stopped three feet short of a side door. Drake lacked the tact and subtlety that might have led him to investigate ways of bypassing the low-tech magnetic strip alarm system, and simply leaned forward, took aim, and fired two muffled shots into the lock. The mechanism twisted and dropped to the floor; the door inched open.

Shouting sprung up from inside.

Drake pushed his way inside, immediately surprised to find that the back of the house resembled a police holding area. Each one of the mini-cells was empty, but two more rooms attached to the back wall were spilling out tough-looking Russians. Drake heard distinctive American tones coming from the furthest room, then a sharp slap and a cry.

"He's here."

Drake fired constantly. Mai and Alicia fanned out behind him. The first Russian fell at their feet, the second pinwheeled into a row of bars, crushing his nose. The next two came up together, trying to overwhelm the attackers, but Mai and Alicia took them out from the sides. Drake threw a small flash bang grenade, then instantly hit the deck, hands pressed firmly over his ears. Even then the explosion, when it came, was louder and more effective than those he remembered from training. He blinked hard, fighting the disorientation, stood up, and was immediately hit by a body. Arms wrestled the gun from him. His sense of survival kicked in and he abandoned the weapon – if you allow an opponent to concentrate on his strongest point he will quickly reveal his weakest – and scrambled out from underneath. His attacker lay, a gun in each hand, unable to defend himself as Drake crushed his windpipe and his nose, then broke both wrists. He recaptured his weapon, whirling through the mayhem.

A man burst out of the nearest room, machine pistol firing. Bullets pinged and zipped off every wall, bouncing away from the solid steel bars and even ricocheting through his own men. Drake ducked low, raising his own gun and firing blindly in the man's general direction. A rake of holes appeared in the ceiling, signifying that Drake's effort had paid off. He raised his head, trying to peer through the second room's open door.

So far, there was no sign of anyone he knew. Several men lay groaning or disorientated, some crawling across the floor, clearly at a loss as to which way was up or down. Alicia leapt for the door, hiding to the side with her back against the wall. Mai drifted toward Drake.

"Soldiers!" a voice cried out, all but quaking. *"Soldiers stop! If you come further I put bullet through his head. You hear me? You have come for American, no?"*

Drake motioned at Alicia to wait. He squinted hard. The flying bullets had punched several holes through the room's plaster wall. If he could just . . .

A shot rang out. Drake's heart sunk. *No!*

"That was warning. The next goes through brain! Now back off."

"Alright," Drake said. "Just cool yer engines, mate. We're leaving."

Through the holes he managed to piece together a patchwork puzzle of the scene inside the room. A man stood holding a gun over the professor who was seated, possibly even chained to a desk, but the man was standing *beside* the professor, not behind him.

"Just one thing. Look to the window behind you."

Drake signaled to Mai, who raised her weapon. He pointed to the external wall, held up three, then four fingers and pointed to his head. He watched the man turn briefly, the gun swinging away from the professor's head.

"I warned you—"

Mai fired three times, aiming between three and four feet from the exterior wall. Drake watched his body fly backwards, the gun drop, and the professor jerk against his bonds. He signaled to Alicia.

"Go."

He and Mai covered the retreat as Alicia dragged the struggling professor out of the room.

"He's a feisty one," Alicia spoke up, grimacing slightly.

"You don't understand," the professor shouted. Drake saw signs of torture on his face and etched into both his arms.

"They have my wife! The bastards have my wife. They will kill her if I don't cooperate." The man burst into tears, still trying to drag Alicia back.

"Where?" Drake scooped up his other arm and took some of the weight.

"Pittsburgh."

Drake stared at Alicia. "You're kidding? Pittsburgh, America?"

"Please. Please save her. I will do anything you want. But my wife, she doesn't know anything about this."

Drake dragged the professor into the streets. "We'll do our best to save her."

CHAPTER TWENTY TWO

Dahl and Akerman made their way down to the old harbor, scanning the various sized vessels moored to their right. The inner harbor was home to dozens of small boats and larger ships, some owned by Reykjavik residents, others visiting from near and far. The two men parked near the entrance and proceeded on foot, Dahl keeping a surreptitious watch on every angle. The real danger, if indeed there was any at all, would come after they met Jakob Hult.

A harsh wind blew in from the sea, carrying with it the sting of spray and salt. They passed a myriad of different colored signs, each one promising 'Sea Tours' or a 'Festival of the Sea' or 'Whale Watching' and, especially, 'Sea Angling'. The Atlantic looked like an undulating gray swell beyond the sea walls, and out on this spit of land Dahl saw it on three separate horizons. He imagined how different a story it would be if, like Drake recently, you found yourself swimming out there, adrift, lost.

He shook it off, looking off to the eastern horizon in the direction of Sweden. Somewhere over there his wife and two children were going about their day, oblivious to his location. *A blissful ignorance,* he thought. He wondered what Johanna was doing at that exact moment.

Then Akerman spoke, "Are you thinking what I'm thinking?"

Dahl shot him a suspicious look. The translator was also gazing wistfully to the east. "I bloody well hope not."

"I miss her terribly, don't you?"

"Olle—" Dahl's voice carried a warning tone.

"Stockholm," Akerman said innocently. "Why? What were you thinking of?"

Dahl stopped. They had reached the area where Akerman had seen Jakob purchasing the boat. The older man pointed to a relatively small vessel, white hulled, with a high rail at the prow and a single blocky cabin in the middle. A ladder ran up the side of the cabin and the mast stood behind it, a curved area of wooden deck leading aft.

Dahl started down the quayside, coming to stop at the mooring post in front of the boat. Through the grimy window at the front of the cabin he could just make out some movement. At that moment, the glass shattered and a man's head came part of the way through. Dahl then heard another man's malicious laughter. He cleared the quayside and landed on the boat, sprinting hard. Within seconds he had reached the cabin. Through the wide-flung door he saw an older man who could only be Jakob Hult falling to his knees, looking up at a much younger, fitter man. The second man wore a black t-shirt that emphasized his bulging muscles, had a grim set to his face and a bearing that screamed military.

Dahl moved in fast, coming close to the military man. "What's going on here?"

The youngster's eyes went wide. Clearly, he had been enjoying himself too much to even notice the Swede's approach. "Who the—" he began, speaking with an accent. *Something mid-European*, Dahl thought. *Hard to pinpoint.*

"Walk away," Dahl was told. "Leave now and you won't get hurt."

The Swede could barely keep the smile from his lips. "*I* won't get hurt?"

"Don't fu—" ended up being the last two words he was going to speak for a while as Dahl smashed the bridge of his hand under the guy's nose. His eyes rolled up and he slithered to the ground like a set of falling curtains.

"Oh, thank you." Jakob Hult breathed a sigh and moved so that his back was against the bulkhead. "I don't know—"

"Cut the crap," Dahl said quickly. "I know what those men were doing here and I know what you did. Now, speak to me. Fast. There's no way he was acting alone."

As he spoke he heard a whisper of sound at his back and spun. The man there – another military figure – was actually leaning around Dahl's bulk, pointing a weapon at Jakob.

"Stop!"

The gun went off, the bullet shattering Jakob's collarbone. Dahl used the seconds at his disposal to lunge and take hold of the gun hand, shatter it against the door frame, and twist it first to the left then right, dislocating the shoulder. Before his opponent could even scream, Dahl slammed his face into the ship's side.

Akerman was screaming. Dahl looked up to see the translator running down the quay, a man in black chasing him. Dahl cursed. He looked to Jakob, took in the gray pallor and pouring blood. Hult was dead, but wasn't quite there yet.

Damn.

Dahl scooped up a handgun and fired at the figure chasing Akerman. Within a moment he had pulled up and backed away, giving Akerman precious moments to hide. Dahl gritted his teeth, put his feelings aside, and ran to Hult's side.

"Tell me," he hissed. "Tell me what you know."

Jakob's mouth worked, his eyes wide. Blood flew from his lips. "I . . . can't—"

"They *killed* you," Dahl spat. "For what? Tell me. There is no man better equipped to avenge you better."

The eyes closed, life slipping away. Dahl leaned in as sound flitted through the torn lips. "Found a translation . . . relating to . . . about the device." His head lolled. Dahl held it steady between his hands.

"There shall remain one other way to activate . . .two failsafes . . ." Jakob sat up a little, suddenly stronger. His eyes flew open. "Three minds, three tombs, three bones. Do you see? Do you see?"

Dahl was silent for a heartbeat. Then, "Not really."

"And Cayman." The translator's head sagged for the last time, his entire body now going limp. "He . . . he too knows . . ."

Dahl cursed loudly. Hult was dead. With no time to spare he lifted his head and looked out the window. The last remaining merc was still casting about for Akerman. Time for Dahl to pay him a visit. He grabbed another weapon and exited the cabin, making sure he could be seen on deck.

"Hey!"

The black-clad figure turned and took in the situation. He would know Dahl had taken out his two mates. He fired. Dahl didn't move. The shot ricocheted off the boat's white railing. Dahl ran forward, taking aim. He needed to wing this one and draw some answers out of him. He fired once. The merc half turned, looking surprised, and stared at a ragged, red streak that had just been made along the top of his shoulder. Close.

In another moment he was turning, running back up the quay. Dahl pocketed the guns and took off after him, breathing easy, conscious of their surroundings and what lay further ahead. If the merc continued in that direction, he would head toward an outdoor market. Dahl increased his speed, but the soldier was pretty fast, maintaining the gap. They passed several gawping locals and two fishermen, who just shook their heads in bemusement before casting another line. Dahl yelled at the man to stop, but may as well have saved his breath. They darted across the harbor, cutting across to the left toward the market. Maybe the merc thought he could lose Dahl there.

The merc barged through the pedestrians, pushing them aside and into the wooden stalls. Dahl closed at first, but then found his way hampered. He hurdled several rolling individuals, one injured, and leapfrogged over a damaged stall. The merc charged on, heading for a set of stairs. He glanced back, his look of surprise apparent as Dahl got closer. Up the steps he dashed, at the top rebounding off the side wall, using it to jump higher and attain an almost unreachable ledge.

Then he ran across the narrow ledge, arms out for balance, forty feet above the market, until he managed to grab on to a rail at the far side and leap over, accessing another level.

Dahl emulated him with ease, using the side wall to give him lift and landing feet first on the ledge without needing to steady himself. Five seconds and he was across it, leaping atop the rail itself and then leaping again, instantly breaking into a sprint.

The merc stepped out from behind a corner, launching a series of hand strikes which Dahl deftly blocked. The Swede used elbow and shoulder to catch the blows, then struck back. When the merc started kicking up close, Dahl stopped him with a raised knee, jabbing constantly and snapping his opponent's head back every time he landed a blow.

It didn't take long for the merc to realize he was outclassed. With a last flurry, he managed to break free and dart away, rushing toward a far set of steps that led down to the street.

Dahl hurried after him, unable to keep the grin off his face.

The mad Swede hadn't had this much fun since he'd been forced to give back that Shelby Mustang.

CHAPTER TWENTY THREE

Dahl slipped down the handrail that bordered the steps, rapidly gaining on his quarry. At the bottom he managed to deliver a boot to the man's spine, sending him flailing head first, but through skill or pure blind luck, he managed to arrest his fall and keep running.

Dahl's phone rang. He fished it out. Akerman. *Bollocks.*

"Are you okay? What is it?"

"Just wondering how you were doing."

"Make your way back to the café, Olle. I'll meet you there. And stay out of sight!"

Dahl ended the call as Akerman started to question the aptitude within those last few sentences. The merc loped straight across a road and over a big roundabout at its center. Cars swerved and honked horns, a driver leaned out and waved a fist. Dahl followed in his wake, finding the way blocked by two cars that had ended up so close together they were literally touching bumpers. He leapt feet first, slid along a nicely polished bonnet, and hit the road even faster. The roundabout was bordered by block paving, enabling Dahl to get a good grip. At the top he hopped from upraised block to block, hitting the slope hard and skidding part of the way. The merc caused havoc again, crossing the next road before he rushed into a border of thick trees.

Dahl burst through seconds later and took a moment to catch his breath. This might be a good place to pause and stop the chase with his handgun. But no. The merc darted into a skatepark, quiet at this time of the day but still populated. Dahl ran hard, clearing a raised wedge formation with a narrow top ledge for BMX's, then barreling down a set of steps. Another recreational wedge stood before him, sprawling the length of the park. The merc jumped from foot to foot up the vertical surface. Each leap raised him that bit higher until he could clamber over the top. Then he turned, a triumphant grin on his face.

If Dahl had had his weapon free he could have shot him then, but instead ran hard, aping the merc's movements, finding the ascent easier than he had imagined. Up above, he heard a gasp, and figured the merc was probably thinking the same. Dahl reached the top. The merc had shown good sense and hadn't stopped to confront him. He leapt over the edge, still running in freefall, landed, tucked and rolled, then came up without losing stride.

They skirted a wide, sharp depression in the ground, darting around its edge after each other like storm waters circle a whirlpool, then burst out of the other side of the skatepark, back on to the civilian streets. The chase continued, neither man flagging nor losing ground. Then a huge space opened up ahead.

Dahl stared. The sign was clear: FC REYKJAVIK.

A bloody football stadium, he thought. *Shit.*

Sure enough, the merc was on the same wavelength. Here was a place big enough in which to lose his pursuer. He arrowed toward it, scaled the fence around the main gates like a monkey, and simply flipped himself over the top, avoiding the razor wire with several inches to spare, then landed adroitly on the other side. Dahl stopped and reached for his gun. The merc took off like a terrified rabbit. Dahl fired once, the bullet kicking up concrete shards from around the man's feet.

The last thing he wanted to do was willingly enter a rival's football stadium, but Dahl stayed his quaking heart and shot out the locks on the fence. *Ahh,* he thought, feeling marginally better, then rushed on through.

Distance and time focused into a narrow tunnel for Dahl as he hotfooted it after his target. The figure leaped from a car bonnet to a low balcony and then up further still to the second floor, swinging his whole body up like a trained acrobat. For a second, his hand lost purchase and he scrambled desperately, all the while allowing the Swede to close the gap, but then he steadied his grip and took a firm hold. Once there, he broke a window and disappeared inside. Dahl made the same leaps, paused as he crossed the broken threshold, then dashed inside. He saw black clothing only a few feet ahead, racing along a corridor, and then the man veered away. The sound of gunfire preceded the even louder sound of exploding glass. Dahl entered the same room and, through the shattered high, wide, box seat picture-window, saw the merc leaping from seat back to seat back, going deeper into the stadium.

Dahl jumped down from the window, feeling his feet strike the hard plastic of the chair backs and then hopped forward, repeating the move again and again. In tandem, they bounded down the rows of seats, the harsh sea breeze helping to keep them cool, the sense of the wide open football field ahead serving only to disorient them. Dahl was three rows behind his quarry. With one crazy leap he knew he would be able to catch the man in mid-flight, but worried about the landing. Too many variables even for him. As they reached field level the merc must know he had nowhere else to go. He used his last jump to launch his body as far as he was able, flying high across the outer track, landing on the edge of the green field, rolling, and coming up with a handgun clasped between two hands.

Dahl stood, legs apart, on top of the last row of seat backs, aiming his own gun. "Drop it."

"I've trained in this shit my whole life," the merc gasped. "Who the hell are you?"

Dahl said nothing. The merc's gun wavered just an inch. The Swede needed no other opportunity. He fired instantly, watching as the bullet struck his opponents upper chest and sent him sprawling backwards, red blood spraying across the newly mown green grass.

He jumped and ran forward. "Who sent you?" he shouted as he ran and knelt by the merc's side. "What is it you want with the tombs?"

The eyes swam with pain. "Fuck you."

Dahl mashed the barrel of his gun inside the gushing bullet wound. "Easy or hard way, wanker. Which do you want?"

Back arched, the merc roared for Dahl to stop. "You think they tell us that? All I know is that professor guy gave my boss some vital information. So vital, he had to go."

"What sort of information?"

"Some kind of message they found in the tomb. The kind that makes powerful men sit up fast."

Dahl caught that one. "Powerful men?"

“The guy I work for.” The merc grimaced and slumped back down. “Makes you look like a fuckin' pussycat. He's the devil and all his demons in a fucking truck and he's driving us all straight to hell. Now, either shoot me or get the fuck away from me, you English arsehole.”

Dahl backed away. He didn't correct the man. Something told him he should make all haste and get back to Moscow. Something told him that time was rapidly running out.

CHAPTER TWENTY FOUR

Drake didn't relax until they had the professor tucked away inside the safe house. He threw down his pack and weapons, and took a bottle of water from the fridge, drinking it quickly. He watched Mai carefully place the man at the round table and take an inventory of his wounds.

Hayden said the word and Kinimaka fetched the first aid box. Only this one was more like a *suitcase*. The CIA catered for everything. Mai set about tending his wounds.

Drake motioned to Hayden. "Says his wife is being held by the Russians. In *America.*"

"What? Christ. Where?"

Drake told her and listened as she made the call to Karin. He took another bottle of water from the fridge and set it down in front of the professor.

"We work for the American government," he said. "Tell us what you know."

"None of you guys sound American," the man said. "Except her." He nodded at Hayden.

"But we did just save your ungrateful Yankee ass," Alicia growled. "And we'll try to save your wife's too."

Drake pushed the bottle closer, watching the man sweat, smelling his fear. "We're most of the team that found the three tombs of the gods. Talk to us. We can help."

Mai cleansed one of his wounds with gentle dabs of a swab. "Why not start with your name?"

"Sure. I'm sorry. My name's Wayne Patterson. I'm a professor of historical archaeology at the University of Pittsburgh.

"Why are you in Moscow, Wayne?"

"That Razin asshole and his goons. They made me work for them. Abducted me in Iraq and brought me here. When I wouldn't cooperate they found out my address back home and . . ." he took a breath, "kidnapped Audrey. Please, you have to help her."

"We will," Drake said. "Why were you in Iraq, Professor Patterson?"

At last the man began to unwind a little. "Can't you guess? A professor of archaeology in Iraq? Babylon, of course. That place is . . . *was* my passion."

Drake nodded and settled back. "We know something of what you found. Why don't you tell us the long story."

"They say Babylon was the first place where evil amassed in this world. I'm talking about evil men, vile groups. Evil deeds. The city of heavenly sin. Always, it has had a connection to evil. From the days of the bible to the time of Hussein. It's fitting then, that Babylon might now in fact save the world. Sit back and grab a glass, this is the mystery story to end all mystery stories."

"Babylon was the largest city in the world – twice. Ringed by eight gates, the largest of which was called the Ishtar Gate. Alexander the Great, the man who once ruled the majority of the world, lived and died in Babylon, ending his days at the palace of Nebuchadnezzar. On his deathbed a dance was performed – the Saber Dance, or the Dance of the Seven Veils. Alexander often referred to himself as the son of Zeus. Now, all of the above is pure fact, recorded in history."

"Babylon translates as the gateway of the gods." Yorgi spoke up from his seat on the couch. "Is that why Alexander settled there?"

"I think Babylon *drew* him in. Other than that, it's some major coincidence that the man everyone at the time believed to be a son of the highest god ended up there. He founded over a dozen Alexandrias. The most extensive library in ancient history. He knew Egyptian pharaohs, emperors and queens. He's been called the greatest king and the wisest man who ever lived."

"Probably all bullshit," Alicia cut in, breaking the spell. "Legends always improve over time."

"Maybe you're right. But back to Babylon. The Etemananki Ziggurat was built inside the city, accidently demolished by

Alexander, and said to be the first ever Tower of Babel. Its foundation mound was so enormous it can still be seen today."

"Wait." Drake said. "The first Tower of Babel. I thought there was only one."

"Oh no. There are hundreds of towers, all built for the same purpose, erected all over the world. But that's another story. One I will get to later. The Babylon we all know was actually built over the site of an even more ancient city, also called Babylon. This original city was razed, destroyed in much the same way as the cities of Sodom and Gomorrah, wiped off the map by God's holy fire as punishment for their abhorrent sins. Now, it is said that men later dug a pit and removed the dread remains of that city and reburied them *within the foundations of the new city.* So we have the enduring legend of the pit of Babylon – a terrible black hole, devoid of all light, where nothing will ever exist again save for the sludge of death and destruction."

"I know a few places like that," Alicia said. "They're called night clubs."

"Babylon was the center of the world. Alexander its greatest king, surrounded by fierce warriors and the most learned of all men. It stands to reason that he would be the possessor of many secrets. And if he heard tell of something that might end the world, would he not take note?"

Drake sat up now. Suddenly, the professor was talking his language.

"Would he not make provision?"

Drake knotted his brows. "You're saying . . ."

"That if a man like Alexander could, he *would* find a way to save the world."

Now even Alicia leaned forward. "And did he?"

"Oh yes."

CHAPTER TWENTY FIVE

"But why would a man like Alexander believe in some kind of world-ending device?" Hayden questioned, stepping forward. "Would he not question its authenticity?"

Professor Patterson smiled. "Ah well, he knew all about earth energy and the vortexes. Sacred places that hold shattering power. Truth be told," he sighed, "the learned people of those times actually knew a lot more about them than we do today. Now, it's all classed as . . ."

"Bollocks?" Alicia offered.

The American blinked. "Not sure what you mean there, little lady, but I have to say the notions that earth energy exists are today seen mostly as fanciful at best. It's never been proved you see. Not officially, though several well-funded agencies are secretly investigating the possibilities. The idea that the earth had a deeply buried current of power running through it. No one wants to hear about it."

"What does earth energy have to do with the end of the world?"

"Well, I will ask you this. Do you think the destructive power of the elements could destroy it?"

"Yes." Drake remembered something. "An element overload that causes destruction, chaos, rivers of fire."

"And what do you think is the best way to describe the four elements?"

"They're energies," Mai said quietly. "Provided by the earth."

Patterson smiled. "Sure enough. The ancient civilizations knew all about earth energy. Many of them worshiped it in some form or other. Now, the most obvious signs of earth energy appear at an earth energy vortex. Basically a place of great power. A focal point, possibly a convergence of currents. Think of sites like Uluru-Kata Tjuta – Ayers Rock – in Australia. The Great Pyramid. Glastonbury Tor. Haleakala Crater in Hawaii. If you've ever visited these places, you'll understand what I mean. Have you ever stood at the edge of the Grand Canyon, lost in its silent, overwhelming vastness, and wondered as to how much latent power a sacred place like that can hold? Or Waimea Canyon on Kauai. The Meteora Rocks in Greece. The Reflecting Desert in Bolivia. Death Valley, Nevada. Crystal Caverns, Mexico. The Fairy Chimneys of Turkey. The Great Blue Hole of Belize. I could go on."

Drake interrupted, "Do you think the three tombs were positioned purposefully at earth energy vortexes?"

Patterson nodded. "Undoubtedly."

"Excuse me." Kinimaka walked through from the kitchen area. "This kind of history lesson certainly has its place, but as far as we know the world ain't in danger. Now, how does it lead to Razin abducting you and using you to find these swords?"

That seemed to snap Patterson back to the real world. He stared at Hayden. "Have you found my wife?"

"The call's gone out. We're waiting to hear."

"The seven swords of Babylon were made to Alexander's instructions. Formed of a special material they were each inscribed with a different message which, when read whole, would allow a man to wield the unlimited power of the gods." Patterson looked each person in the eye in turn. "They were said to be mystical, powerful, and possessed of a tremendous secret that could shake the world to its very foundations."

"How?"

"That, I don't know. As I said the message – the instructions, if you like – are inscribed into the swords."

"I wonder what Cayman has to do with all this," Drake mused, staring at the pockmarked table. "I'll take a wild guess, Professor, and say that Razin wants the swords only to bargain with. He's not interested in the tombs."

Patterson shrugged. "I don't know. He does know about the tomb at Singen, though. When they found the first sword they found what they later knew to be the layout of the tomb at Singen."

"They've already *found* a sword?" Hayden gasped.

"Oh, they've found four. I'm good at my job, miss."

"Four?" Hayden sounded like she was choking.

"The first four were buried in the pit of Babylon. That's where Razin searched first. The safety of my wife depended on my accurate research and I could not disappoint. The remaining three swords – they were buried at the Tower of Babel. The *original* tower."

"This message inscribed on them," Hayden said. "Can you be more specific?"

"I haven't read it. Actually, I can't read it."

Drake swirled his water. "Why not?"

"It's written in this new language they've found." Patterson looked depressed. "The language of the gods."

No one moved. Drake assumed everyone else was as stunned as he. "Alexander knew the language of the gods?"

"Like I said—"

"Yeah, yeah, son of Zeus. Wisest of them all. Etcetera." Alicia pushed away from the table.

Drake eyed Mai, then turned to Hayden. "This mission isn't over. We need to recover those swords."

Hayden was checking her phone. "That was Dahl. He's on his way back. Says 'with crucial information'. We'll wait for him and then go to Iraq. My guess is – Razin's already there."

CHAPTER TWENTY SIX

Drake used the downtime to allay at least one demon. He made the call to Ben Blake, the one he'd been promising himself to make for the last few weeks. A careful, profound conversation was long overdue, but, even as he dialed the phone, Drake knew this call probably wouldn't go well. In some ways, he still partly blamed Ben for Kennedy's death, but that was the solider in him unable to accept that the kid hadn't made at least some attempt to save her. On the other hand, he had dragged Ben into this from the very beginning and, at first, it had just been the two of them. Not even six months had passed since they'd begun their quest for the bones of Odin, and an awful lot of turbulent water had passed under the bridge since then. Ben himself had gotten blood on his hands and faced death many times. And now that Drake was at least starting to move on with Mai, a few things had attained a clearer perspective.

Ben Blake had been his best friend before all this began. Ben had offered his friendship and his help for free before, and after, he knew what kind of man Drake was. The poor kid had lost Hayden Jaye, possibly the best catch of his life. He deserved better than being shunned.

"Hello? Matt?"

"Hey, Ben."

"I can't hear you. Matt? How you doing?"

"Good. I'm good!" Drake raised his voice. The noise coming from Ben's side of the phone was horrendous. "What the hell's that? The frog chorus?"

Ben groaned. "In a manner of speaking. It's the band."

"The Wall of Sleep. I hear you haven't improved much then."

"I just got back a couple of weeks ago. Give me chance. What have you been doing?"

"Ah, not so much. Kidnapped, tossed into jail. Almost got to play a game of footie with the inmates, though, before God-Zanko fell on me."

"Eh? Which god now? You went to jail? I thought you were fighting the North Koreans."

Drake snorted. "That was last week. This week it's the Russians and maybe someone else. You know the drill."

"Russians?" Ben sounded scared. "Is the Blood King—"

"Nah. Don't worry about that bastard. He's away for life. Even his men have vanished now. This is another set of nasties. Anyway, enough of that bollocks. How's it going with you?"

"Mum and Dad were happy to see me, but they miss Karin. How's she doing?"

"She misses you, Ben."

"I'm okay. And . . . and Hayden?"

"If you spoke to them when they called you, then you'd know."

A powerful guitar riff drowned out Ben's reply. Drake heard the guys calling him in the background. Ben heaved a sigh. "Well . . ."

"Alright, mate. But Ben, the next time I'm in England, we need to talk."

"That would be good."

Feeling as though he'd accomplished nothing, Drake finished up. Next he rang Sam, his ex-SAS buddy and the man who had helped him take down the terrorists in the Czech Republic not so long ago. He asked that Sam and Jo, his other great army friend, keep their eyes on Ben whenever they were able. Sam told him it would be tough, but promised to do what he could. Drake couldn't ask for more.

As he dumped the cell phone on the bedside table, Mai walked into the room. Her shoulder length, black hair was drawn severely back, her dark eyes troubled. Drake knew she would speak her mind if she felt the need, so said nothing.

A little while later, she sat beside him on the bed. She placed a hand on his knee, but not in a sensual manner, more of a comforter.

"Matt." She stared at the floor. "I don't lose often. And to get beat and lose you . . ." she shook her head. "I'm not used to it."

"It's not your fault. Hey, I got beat too. Twice, actually, if you include my jail-yard brawl with King Kong's big brother."

Mai's expression put him in his place. "You *do* lose, Matt. I don't. And this is the worst possible time for me to start failing."

"Why? Because of Cayman and the Babylon thing?"

"Of course not. Something else is in play, Matt. Something that leads all the way back to my childhood. You know about that of course."

"Fuck me, Mai. That's huge."

"I know. I just can't lose my edge now."

Drake relented. "We got complacent. We took a few days off. We shouldn't have to be on our guard twenty four hours a day, but," he shrugged, "that's the job. And, Mai, I'm always here for you."

Mai stood up. "It won't happen again. Look, when this is over I want to go and see Chika. Visit her in Tokyo. Maybe the two of us?"

Drake grinned. "Sound idea. Bloody sound. I haven't visited Tokyo since the old Coscon days."

Mai looked wistful for a minute, remembering. "Those were the best of days."

Drake framed her face with his hands and leaned in to kiss her. "And so are these."

CHAPTER TWENTY SEVEN

Mai Kitano watched Drake sleep from her perch by the window. She couldn't relax. The endless, sleepless nights had not affected her yet, but would soon take their toll. Even here, in Russia, in this safe house, with CIA protection, she knew that she was far from safe. Mai was not afraid, fear did not live in her, but she was anxious and worried about her friends.

The clan is looking for you.

Just a one line message, received on a personal email address that nobody except a few of her old contacts knew. But devastating. Truly dreadful. The past that she thought she had left behind was catching her up, a looming freight train full of horrors, and she had no option but to meet it head on.

Now, she thought. *Just when I got him back.*

The events of the past few days had put the very real mortality of Mai and her family and friends into perspective. Reality had checked in with a vengeance.

Without any more deliberation she dialed Chika's number. Her sister answered on the third ring.

"Moshi-moshi?"

"It is me Chika."

"Sister! I have missed you."

"And I you, Chika. It is good to hear your voice." Mai proceeded to ask her sister about her job, her friends, and whether any men had appeared in her life of late. Chika reacted a little cagily to the last question, but confirmed that all was well, and Mai started to relax. She laughed a little, talked of the few good times they had shared, but then, near the end of the conversation, Chika finally came out with the one thing Mai had been dreading all along.

"Two days ago," she said. "Some men visited me at work. They were asking about you Mai. And about your past."

"Did they threaten you?"

"Oh no. They were very nice. Why would you say that?"

"Because of my past, Chika. That is why."

"I don't know much about your past. I told them that. And I told them I didn't know where you were. Which I don't."

Mai glossed over the rest, quickly alleviating any alarm Chika may have felt by saying it was most likely something to do with her old job at the government. She waited the required time and then told Chika to be safe.

"Goodbye, Sister."

Her next call was to Dai Hibiki. "Where are you, Dai?"

"Wow, Mai. No contact for years, then you wrench me out of deep cover and now ring me whilst I'm servicing the girlfriend. This had better be good."

"Correction, Hibiki. I *saved* your feeble hide from being flayed to bits, and then your *girlfriend's* from two minutes of skin on skin that doesn't really measure up, if you know what I mean."

"Ah, you remember me well."

"Never forget." Mai owed her life and more to Dai Hibiki. "But I need to ask you something—"

"Don't bother. I know what you're going to ask. I gave them nothing, Mai. Nothing."

"What? Then they came to you also?"

"Also?"

"Some men visited Chika recently, asking about my past."

"Then yes, they visited me too. But at work, Mai. They showed no signs of malice. No ulterior motive."

But the clan wouldn't, Mai wanted to scream. They moved in the highest circles, taking every head they fancied and smiled whilst they did it. Once, she had been a part of that.

"Please. Do your best to look after Chika for me. Until I can get there."

"Already on it."

"What?"

"I mean yes, way ahead of you. As soon as you mentioned her name I started planning a visit."

Mai knitted her brows. There was something in Hibiki's tone, something that told her he was keeping a secret. She wondered briefly if it had to do with Chika.

"Okay, Dai. I'll speak to you as soon as I can."

She terminated the call, still staring out the window, searching the shadows for the returning ghosts of her past.

CHAPTER TWENTY EIGHT

Drake met Torsten Dahl at the door, patting the big man on the back, and then shook hands with the diminutive-by-comparison professor, Olle Akerman.

"Bit of an adventure?"

Dahl wrinkled his nose. "Nothing special. Just practicing my free running." As usual, the Swede wasn't boasting. To him, the Iceland jaunt had been standard fare.

Akerman still looked a little shaken. "I had to run for my life whilst Torsten here was playing 'boats' with a couple of thugs. Frightful."

Drake bolted the door behind them, listening carefully as the triple locking mechanism kicked in. The CIA manned CCTV would also be surveying the surroundings for as far as a mile in every direction, but, not wanting to solely trust the CIA, Hayden had put Mai on patrol as back-up.

The boss of SPEAR pointed Dahl and Akerman to a seat. "We've waited for you. Please tell us what you know." Smiling, the blond haired agent sat down next to Akerman, the worry lines of the last few months all but gone from her face. Drake thought that Kinimaka was shaping up nicely for her.

Dahl went quickly through the story that Akerman had told him in Iceland. "One of Olle's colleagues discovered some kind of ancient message in the tomb, written in the language of the gods. Something significant, apparently. This man – Jakob Hult – sold his findings to the kind of ruthless individual we seem to keep on coming up against. They killed Hult and tried to kill us."

"But they didn't succeed." Hayden smiled again.

Dahl shrugged. "There were only three."

"Whatever this message was, Hult took it away from the tomb," Akerman told them. "He smashed off part of the rock where it appeared." The older man looked angry. "Such disrespect for our history."

"For proof," Drake said. "He needed proof."

"Yes," Dahl carried on. "Well, then, my little friend here, he bumped into Russell Cayman. What that crazy bastard was doing at the tomb we don't know. But Olle escaped and called me. That's it."

Hayden sat back. "That's it? You said this was good information, Dahl."

The Swede nodded. "Later, as Jakob died, he revealed a few things relating to the translation, particularly the doomsday device. First he said, 'there shall remain one other way to activate . . . two failsafes'. And finally he said, 'three minds, three tombs, three bones. Nine parts. Do you see?' Just like that."

Drake feigned alarm. "Just like that?"

Dahl growled at him. "Don't start."

Alicia helped herself to a beer. "Alright, Torsty. Well, I guess your trip wasn't a total washout. It's certain now – there's another way to activate that device, and you can be damn sure Cayman's on to it, as well as whoever's controlling that fruit bat. But the nine parts were all destroyed." She stared at Dahl. "Weren't they?"

"Absolutely. Blown to hell."

"Well, we don't know where Cayman is. We don't know who or where his boss is. We don't know the rest of the translation," Hayden said. "I say we stick to the plan and go after the swords."

Drake stood up. "Ready an' willing. Let's thrash this out."

CHAPTER TWENTY NINE

Russell Cayman was flown by private jet to Honolulu, landing on a rough airstrip somewhere north of the city. As the airplane banked over the famous shoreline of Waikiki Beach, he stared down at the wealth of hotels; the rainbow-striped ones, the pink ones, the high-rise ones, and, beyond them across the golden sands, all the way to Diamond Head itself. The old crater jutted out from the landscape as if proclaiming its importance. Deep rooted in Hawaiian legend, none could have guessed as to the shocking significance of the ancient myths buried within.

Cayman was alone on the plane. Alone apart from the pilot and a small rucksack that took pride of place on the seat next to him. The rucksack was well-padded and the item within carefully wrapped. Cayman sat with his left hand resting atop it, his fingers within, touching the outer packaging of the object.

Kali's smallest right hand finger, whole. The pinkie of her left hand he had already hidden within the Icelandic tomb. He had slipped in and out, posing as a translator and using the dead man's ID, coming unstuck only when a chance meeting occurred with someone who knew him. Cayman couldn't even remember the old man's face, but saw the recognition and fear in those eyes. He gave chase, but the old man knew the tomb like the back of his hand. No way could Cayman find him and maintain his ultimate cover, so he planted the bone and left. Zak Block would never know.

Now, as the plane skidded to a bumpy halt, Cayman made ready to disembark. He had seen no sign of Block's mercenary 'cells' in Iceland, but the leader of the Shadow Elite had recently assured him that *two* cells had now entered Honolulu, and were just getting into place. They would help Cayman if they could, but their chief directive was to infiltrate and wait for Block.

Cayman drove toward the city. Diamond Head grew larger ahead, the ocean to his left sparkling and dotted with swimmers and surfers as the sun began to set, swelling across the horizon. He circumvented the extinct volcano, finally parking the car out of sight near one of the fenced off entry points to one of Oahu's many lava tubes. They all led to Diamond Head, but this one especially had been pinpointed as leading indirectly to the trap system below. Cayman strapped Kali to his back, picked up another bag full of the tools he would need and set off. Neither of the Hawaiian cells had been in touch yet, so he had to believe he was on his own.

Cayman cut through the wire at the back of the compound, the most unobtrusive place, then fixed it back up with wire ties. Not perfect, but good enough for the time he would need. He climbed on to the roof of the small building and carefully swiveled the CCTV camera until its lens pointed away from the door. Again, not perfect, but kids and youths broke into these places all the time, and Cayman only needed a few hours. He jumped to the ground and within seconds was inside.

Not bothering with the light, he switched on his own torch and made his way to the lava tube. In this facility it was a smooth black hole in the ground, but one that sloped gently downwards instead of descending into a pit. He slipped inside, careful to adjust Kali's pack, and began to slither down on his backside, now holding the Maglite between his teeth.

The darkness down here was comforting, not slithering with unknown horrors like the one in Singen, but profound and menacing nevertheless. He wondered what manner of creature might survive down here, what subterranean terror, and felt a sudden longing for Kali's old tomb. Soon, he would return. Soon, it would become his home.

Cayman traversed the length of the lava tube, dropping gently until he sat with his legs dangling, forty feet up and looking out over the first trap system. Wrath – the first level of Hell.

The carved face of the Devil stared hard at Cayman, the fires that had once given life and meaning to the trap now extinguished. Cayman took a moment to study those hollow eye sockets, the hooked nose and cavernous mouth, and broke out into a smile. This was going to be a much more pleasurable evening than he had ever imagined.

And then on to Singen.

CHAPTER THIRTY

Drake listened impatiently as Hayden set up a conference call with Karin and Gates. Their genius computer-come-communications operative sounded in high spirits now that the new HQ was shaping up, but the Secretary of Defense seemed very preoccupied, despite the levity of the situation.

"The swords link to the device and the gods," Gates said. "That much is obvious. I want those inscriptions – they should tell us more. And Cayman is acting because of the translation, but on whose orders?"

"Could the Shadow Elite be back?" Hayden suggested, eyes fixed firmly in the middle-distance, taking in every word her boss said.

"Anything's possible at this point. Rule nothing out, Hayden. One thing's for sure, the person who paid for that translation and killed Jakob Hult will follow this through to the end."

"We're fully up and running," Karin broke in. "We can help you from this end."

"Secure those swords," Gates said. "Yours is the team to do it. Time is of the essence. And I want someone researching this earth energy vortex subject. If Professor Patterson thinks it's a genuine phenomenon, then we need to know. I don't want any last minute surprises."

"I believe he *is* the expert on that," Hayden said. "But I'll check."

Professor Patterson walked up to the table. "I can help you. But, sir, what news of my wife?"

"That's me." Komodo's deep voice came over the airwaves. "We're putting a team together right now, Professor. Our friends, Romero and Smyth, are en route."

Drake approved. "Good choice." He watched Mai as she sat by the window, seemingly preoccupied with something outside. Was there a distance growing in her lately? Ever since he'd been taken. He knew she criticized her own abilities on that night, but also knew there was no way to convince her it hadn't been her fault. It could happen any time, to any one of them. Even Dahl. Drake smiled at the big Swede, who was shepherding Akerman around. Dahl caught the look and checked his flies.

Drake looked away, listening.

"I have my own situation at this end," Gates was saying in a resigned tone. "Some men – they think they're too important not to be heard. And they are seriously disturbed if they think—" The Secretary stopped, as if suddenly realizing he had gone too far. "Never mind. It's my problem. Is there anything else, Jaye?"

"I think that's everything, sir." Hayden waited for Gates to sign off, then addressed Karin. "Do you know anything about that?"

"No. It's news to me."

Hayden pursed her lips, clearly worried. Drake read her mind. They were all worried about Jonathan Gates, the real power behind SPEAR – the man had barely taken a breath since his wife was murdered. And he had some fierce enemies up on the Hill, rodents that would be only too glad to gnaw the ground from beneath his feet.

"Alright, Karin. Keep an eye out for Cayman, and if he pops up anywhere in the world tell us immediately."

"And my wife?" Patterson pressed.

Drake touched the man's elbow. "With Komodo, Romero and Smyth on the case, it won't be long. Try to trust us." He bit the words back, but they were out of his mouth before he could stop them. "No one will have a better chance," he added, a bit lamely.

Patterson stared at him. "You're a real comfort."

"I'm not here to comfort you." Drake walked away and across to Mai. She greeted him with a smile.

"Ready to hit Iraq, go kick some Russian arse and grab us some swords?"

"I'd follow you anywhere, Matt."

Drake stopped his spiel. Mai's reply hadn't sounded quite right. "Are you okay?"

"The clan's looking for me," she said softly. "They will never stop."

"Listen," Drake sat down next to her. "You're not alone in this. It's not even just you and me." He pointed at the assembled team. "Every one of those guys. Every single one will fall in and help. We'll get this Babylon thing out of the way and then—" he squeezed her hand. "Sort you out."

Mai's expression, if anything, darkened. "You don't know them, Matt. You just don't know them like I do. Nor who their leader is . . ."

CHAPTER THIRTY ONE

The team were transported to the nearest American base, and then on to Camp Adder in Iraq, a tight hub of military operations and communications. From there, the terrain was rough and dangerous, negotiable only by the onboard computer that led them unerringly to the preregistered coordinates. Drake stepped out of the big, uncomfortable army vehicle, seeing the lights of Camp Babylon in the distance. Whoever had decided to place a military base atop one of the world's greatest ancient ruins had certainly been hitting the monkey juice hard that night.

Unless the Americans were looking for something, he thought. *And the base was a smokescreen.*

Their own destination was a little way off yet, across the pitch darkness of the desert. The team made ready, donning night-vision goggles, arming up, and checking coordinates. This was to be purely a reconnoiter, thus everyone was going, including Patterson and Akerman. Patterson would have knowledge of the dig site. Akerman was in it for the excitement.

"Stay close," Dahl warned the energized translator. "And keep quiet, or I'll have to gag you."

"You and your wife," Akerman said. "Both sound just the same."

Alicia sidled up to the Swede. "You can gag me any time, Torst."

"And what would your new boyfriend think of that?"

Alicia's mouth opened, but no words came out. Even Mai sent her a sly smile. Drake pondered the fact that there were no secrets anymore in this team. He looked at Yorgi. "You got any more secrets to tell us, pal, before we move out?"

"About the Russians?" Yorgi shook his head. "No."

Drake caught the nuance. "What about anything else?"

Yorgi hesitated. "We will talk. Later."

Drake moved out last, Mai at his side. Hayden and Kinimaka led the way, followed by Alicia and Dahl, the civilians amongst them.

Dueling currents of air picked up bits of sand and flung them at the interlopers. Tangles of scrub grabbed at their ankles. A high sandbank rose out of nowhere, making them scramble to the top, and, once down the other side, the distant lights of the American base disappeared altogether.

Still they walked, guided only by the handheld satnav. After what seemed like an hour, Hayden held a fist up and the team came to a stop. Drake heard the click in his ear.

"Target dead ahead. Absolute silence now unless it's essential."

Drake peered hard. Even this close, it was hard to make out what they were looking at. A small circular winch, maybe six feet high, rose out of the desert ahead, insignificant amongst the many higher mounds that surrounded it. No doubt in daylight, it would even appear abandoned. There was nothing else. No huts. No vehicles. No Russians. Drake stared.

The Bluetooth connection clicked again. "I see a camouflaged area to the right." It was Mai, eagle-eyed as ever. Now that she'd said it, Drake discerned the slight swaying of a camouflage net in the steady breeze. Blocky shapes stood underneath it, no doubt vehicles, crates and some kind of shelter. "Got it."

A faint light emanated from the middle of the gantry, silvery lights shining up from whatever lay within. The glow was swallowed by the night as soon as it cleared the man-made apparatus, carefully regulated.

"I'm guessing that's a hole," Drake whispered. "Must be the pit."

Professor Patterson's connection clicked several times before he managed to make himself heard. "I can confirm that. It's where Razin will have found the first of the swords, according to Alexander's histories."

"How do you know so much about Alexander?" Mai asked.

Patterson blinked. "What can I say? Of the literally thousands of texts, accounts and histories written of him, I have read about ninety percent in my time. The Pittsburgh University acquired for me a few works written by people who actually knew him, such as Ptolemy and Callisthenes. And of course there are the accounts of Aristotle – his teacher."

"Aristotle?" Mai's eyebrows raised. "I did not know that."

"Oh yes. It's difficult to question the fact that Alexander became one of the wisest and greatest Kings of all time, if not *the* greatest, isn't it? I spent years studying the histories of Macedonia – his homeland. Did you know his empire covered three continents? The story of the swords and seven veils is well-known, but the cross reference that they were buried in the pit and the tower, rather than in his tomb, came from some more personal accounts."

"You said the other swords are buried at the Tower of Babel?" Hayden interrupted.

"Yes. Over there."

Eight pairs of goggles turned to see where he was pointing. "Sorry. To the North."

Even in the murk Drake distinguished a wide knoll, rounded at the top and surrounded by steep slopes. A sudden sense of ancient mystery swept over him. Here was the Babylon of old; resplendent with plundered beauty, wicked sin and eternal pleasure. Here was the capital of the old world, once a city of splendor, but now a crumbled ruin. But under these eternal shifting sands, who knew what unlimited wealth of ancient riches awaited the courageous treasure hunter?

The clatter of metal on metal sounded in front of them, and a swaying bucket rose into sight. A man clambered out of the hole; clothes and face filthy, curses flowing from his mouth, before he wandered off in the direction of the camouflage tent.

"They're still checking out the pit," Hayden pointed out.

"Probably searching for more artifacts." Alicia said. "The few megalomaniacs I've known were nothing if not consumed by greed."

Professor Patterson hadn't taken his eyes away from the distant mound. "Though the seven swords were made to Alexander the Great's blueprint, including the inscriptions, he never actually used any of them. Amongst the seven, there was one called the Great Sword, the principal weapon. Its inscription was critical in understanding the rest, so I believe. Unfortunately, we don't know in what order they were buried."

Kinimaka shifted uneasily, his odd bulk not exactly suited to lying still for long periods of time. "Feels like there's a friggin' scorpion up my ass."

Alicia grunted. "Try high kicking whilst wearing a G-string. Then you'll know real pain."

"Mano," Hayden whispered. "You're *vibrating.*"

"Oh." Kinimaka reached into his pocket and turned his cell phone off. "Kono again, no doubt."

"That sister of yours is worse than the scorpion," Alicia commented before turning back to Patterson. "So, Prof, what's the lowdown on this dance? The Saber Dance. Sounds kinky."

"Ah. Performed once only at Alexander's death bed. Also called the Dance of the Seven Veils. The dancers performed with the swords wearing very little other than diaphanous gowns.

"And that pit?" Drake indicated the dimly lit hole that lay before them. "That's the site of the *original* Babylon?"

"Not exactly. *That* site remains unknown. The pit is where the last remaining dregs and ashes of the city were buried, out of sight of human eyes and minds. The city's vile waste; from burned humans to charred artifacts to scorched bricks and soil, were all deposited in there, buried forever, never to be seen again."

"Because it was evil?"

"In the same way as Sodom and Gomorrah was seen as evil in the Bible, yes."

"I'm just thinking that evil connects well with tomb three at Singen. We were constantly reminded that all the evil gods were buried there."

Patterson nodded, barely discernible in the dark. "It's been called everything. Supposedly bottomless, it was described as the lair of Ctulhu. Remember HP Lovecraft and his fantastical demons? The entrance to Purgatory. The source of the Black Death, plague, and every other major disease of the last few thousand years. I would not want to descend into that filth, my friends."

"It's just a hole in the ground," Kinimaka pointed out.

"But it has . . . something."

"Earth energy? Is this one of your vortexes?"

"I think so. Yes. Can't you feel an inexplicable stillness, a marvelous awe?"

Drake frowned. He had visited some of the places Patterson mentioned earlier. It was true that when a person stood and gazed at something wondrous, it felt like more was at work than simply Mother Nature's plan. Something deeper.

"When we have time, you might want to explain this earth energy theory of yours in more depth, Professor."

"Be glad to."

Hayden shuffled back in the sand, dragging at Kinimaka's belt to give him a start. "We have what we need," she whispered. "Let's go and plan how to storm this place."

CHAPTER THIRTY TWO

Jonathan Gates hurried into the crisis meeting, still dazed and unable to fully grasp the absurdity of the situation he currently found himself in. Twelve men sat around the enormous table, stern gazes reflecting either the precedence of their station, the gravity of their concerns or the depth of their desperation. These were powerful men – undoubtedly some of the most powerful men in the world – but they were still only men, fighting to be heard.

President Charles Coburn nodded toward him. "Jonathan, sit down. We can get started."

Gates took his seat, seeing the Vice President, the Secretary of State, the Assistant to the President for National Security Affairs, the Chairman of the Joint Chiefs, the President's Chief of Staff and the Counsel to the President all assembled along with Directors of the CIA, FBI and Homeland, plus two five-star generals.

President Coburn indicated the latter two. "General Stone and General Edwards. You should start at the beginning."

Stone took the lead. "We believe the three tombs at Iceland, Hawaii and Germany represent the biggest threat to America's freedom and security since the cold war. Forget Al-Qaeda, the potential threat inherent through ownership of Singen's doomsday device is unprecedented. And now," he half turned toward Gates, "with the latest revelation that a *second* method of activation probably exists, I feel – *we* feel – that America should take the initiative."

If possible, the expressions at the table grew even more severe, but it was still impossible to gauge where everyone's view would land. *Or better,* Gates thought. *On which side everyone's agenda would be best served.*

"Go on." Coburn leaned over as his assistant whispered briefly into his ear.

"The only way to be safe and sure is to activate the device, see what it does, then deactivate it, either making it unusable or burying it in a deep hole somewhere."

Gates saw an immediate head shake from the Director of the CIA and counted him as a potential ally. "It's already in a deep hole," the Director said. "And a German one at that. How do you propose to pull that one off, General?"

Stone pursed his lips. "Any way we can, sir. This is the country's wellbeing at risk." He was clearly pursuing the security and vulnerability angle which, Gates imagined, was the main reason he hadn't been kicked straight back to base. A clever angle, more important to the people assembled in this room right now than anything else.

Especially to the President. "What makes you think you can turn it off again?"

"NASA send men into space. MIT train supercomputer engineers. We surely have enough learned minds between us to disable an archaic device. It might not even work."

"But we need to know," the other General spoke up.

President Coburn turned to Gates. "Your team is pursuing this one, Jonathan. Assuming we can talk the Germans into cooperating, what's your take?"

Gates studied the President. Though in his mid-fifties he looked more like a fit young man of forty, with the face and physique of someone who looked after himself and worked out regularly. Gates had heard it said that Coburn only slept three hours every night, not because of the demands of the job, but because that was all he needed. The President's face was now open and expectant. Gates had never taken him for a fool. That said, he still decided to appeal to the man the President used to be and, deep down, undoubtedly still was.

"You were once in the field, sir. You know the importance of letting the team do its work. Eyes and boots on the ground are crucial and need paying attention to. They will come through."

"How can you possibly know that?" The President wasn't blustering or complaining, or even drawing on past experience. It was a sincere, viable question. And not a man in this room really cared that the President had once fought with honor for his country.

Since he had signed that oath of office he had become, by necessity, a very different man. One who was sometimes forced to bend, like a tree amidst a hurricane.

Gates tried a different tack. “They've never failed us before, sir. They did, in fact, discover all of these tombs. They captured Dmitry Kovalenko—”

“I'm aware of the team’s accomplishments, Jonathan,” Coburn interjected. “But unless you can give me a concrete reassurance that your team will stop the device being activated a second time, then I suggest you give me a straight answer.”

Gates licked his lips. “We don’t know for certain, Mr President.” From the corner of his eye he thought he saw General Stone’s face crease into a smirk, but when he glanced that way, the man turned his head.

“Mr President,” Stone said. “Give me the resources to at least put a plan into place. Let me prepare. Then, if the Secretary’s team doesn’t *come through,* we at least have a valid back up.” Everyone heard the inflection and several almost smiled.

“It’s too risky,” Gates said.

“It’s riskier not to try,” Stone affirmed. “The country’s independence is at stake.”

Gates flinched inside. He knew precisely what would happen if Stone found himself in command at Singen, but the sway of this room was leaning toward General Stone. With such support, the President would surely have to honor a simple request. But Stone was angling for glory, and almost everyone here would accept the General’s declaration that America possessed the bright minds capable of deactivating Odin’s device on spec. Maybe it did.

Trouble was, Gates thought. *Rather than working at NASA or studying at MIT, the mindset they needed now was more likely to be that of the peculiar loner slapped in jail for hacking supercomputers or the weird bedroom lout hitting the top of the leader boards of the new Tomb Raider game.*

Courage, strength, skill, a trace of crazy and the flair for fantasy. It was what they needed. He thought of it as the motto for SPEAR. If what the team had learned so far was true and the old gods were again part of all this, then the crazy and fantastic might be the only things that saved them all in the end.

CHAPTER THIRTY THREE

Karin Blake knew it was a race against time. Though the last week could best be described as an intense, stressful whirlwind, she knew that these next few hours would move swiftly from excessive to extreme.

She was alone in the new HQ. Komodo had set out hours ago on his quick jaunt to Pittsburgh, aiming to meet up with Romero, Smyth and two other Delta soldiers. Patterson's wife was still being held prisoner inside their compact home. Even though the professor's release had been effected a relatively short while ago, Karin had expected something to have happened up at his suburban house, but it seemed the head Russians – Razin and Zanko that they knew of – were far too busy to take note. Or perhaps the news hadn't filtered down yet. Karin ran a last check through Komodo's comms.

"Going smooth so far, T-vor?"

"As Mountain Dew, my little Kazmat."

Karin smiled at his use of their pet name. "I take it the soldier boys haven't arrived yet?"

"Still waiting. These comms are amazing, Karin. Sounds like you're sitting next to me."

"I wish." Karin was nevertheless quite excited about being alone in the HQ. It showed the level of trust Gates had in her. It showed that her future, through Jonathan and SPEAR, was bright and full. It showed she could have a life again.

"Heads up," Komodo said. "They're here."

The team leader went off comms for a little while to explain the situation to his new crew. Karin expected him to return in a few minutes and readied the loop that would patch them all through the same piece of equipment, linking them to each other and, via satellite link, to her. The new HQ was a little undersized, with no windows and employed the outdated parking-garage-only access method, but they had made it work. The cutting edge communications and surveillance systems took up most of the main room, the team's gear filled the second. There were no cells, no interrogation rooms, just a small basement that contained, in Karin's opinion, the HQs coolest feature.

An underground escape route that led straight into the Pennsylvania mall.

What girl couldn't love a thing like that? she wondered. Even better, it was an awesome, busy getaway location with dozens of exits, guards and places to hide. And to top all that, she could use the tunnel to grab lunch too!

But not today. Komodo and the team were relying on her to aid their assault. With the comms fixed up, she concentrated on the surveillance system, using the CIAs global mapping system to zoom right on top of the house. The magnification was tremendous and crystal clear. She remembered one of the weapons they had utilized on a previous mission – the one that could see through walls. Such a weapon would come in handy here, and in the future, but she just couldn't get the idea out of her head that Alicia would use it for something unsavory.

A double click told her Komodo was back online. "Game on?"

"It's in play. Herrera and Tyler are scouting and finding a place to hole up. We're gonna snatch the first one to show his ugly Russkie face, and use him to get inside."

"Sounds risky."

"Tried and trusted. Besides, it's all risky, babe. We're outside trying to get in."

Karin heard one of the men whisper about *canning the babe talk,* and guessed immediately it was Smyth. She had heard enough about the irascible marine to recognize his disposition even over the comms.

"Don't worry," Komodo said. "Poor ole Smyth's depressed. He texted Mai twelve hours ago and she hasn't replied."

Karin laughed. "Maybe he missed off the kiss kiss at the end, eh?"

There was a short silence, then Smyth's voice came over the airwaves. "Miss, I can only say you're lucky I'm Delta. If I were a marine I'd have told you to go fuck yourself after that."

Komodo burst into laughter. "He's got it bad. Hey, Romero, how d'you live with this all day?"

"We ain't married, sir. He can see whoever he wants."

"I think Drake might have something to say about that." Karin watched as two figures – Herrera and Tyler – cautiously approached the Patterson house. The two Delta soldiers competently worked their way to the foliage and waist-high decking that fronted the house, concealing themselves within. They did not rush. Karin counted twenty eight minutes of waiting and shuffling.

"We're all set here."

Komodo paced the inside of their white builder's van. The cover was sound. The house across the road was being renovated and demanded different amenities every day.

Romero said, "So how's Drake? This all part of some new exploit?"

"Babylon," Karin heard Komodo reply with amusement in his voice, then, "Don't ask."

"See, we've been wondering," Smyth said. "Since our team hasn't yet been renewed, if you might put in a good word."

Karin could almost hear Komodo's brain ticking. "A what? Why?"

Silence followed. Maybe they were communicating through eyebrow and hand gestures.

Then Komodo spoke with excitement in his voice. "You're kidding? Really? You want to join SPEAR? Well, Drake speaks very highly of you, Romero. I'm humbled that you asked me to speak for you."

"Any time, man."

Smyth's voice broke in. "Did Mai speak well of me?"

"She said she never could have survived without you."

There was another silence, and then Karin heard Romero's whisper. "Don't start crying, for fuck's sake."

"Fuck you."

She shook her head at the displays of military humor. With nothing else to do for now, she walked over to the little fridge freezer and took out a bottle of water. As she stood swigging the cold liquid, it suddenly occurred to her that she couldn't remember the last time she'd been alone like this. An odd thought for her. Karin was used to being physically alone in the darkness of her apartment, and mentally alone in the darkness of her mind. Her last alone moment must have been in her apartment, just before she told Ben she was going to Hawaii to help.

She had slotted into her new existence with ease, reasoning that she'd been born to lead this life. All her tragedies had prepared her for it. The moments she lived in now, these fine days, were the best she had ever known.

And Komodo held firm at the center of it all, her anchor. As that thought crossed her mind, the double-click of a live comm caught her attention.

"We're in play. Side door just opened."

Karin ran back to her seat, switching between the satellite display and Komodo's helmet-cam. He was focusing between the barrel of his gun and the van's inside handle as he waited for the go. Karin switched to Tyler's head-cam. Through gaps in the foliage, she saw a bulky figure moving toward the man. Tyler's light breathing punctuated the other man's steps.

"Target outside. Do we have a go?"

Karin immediately switched to the overview. Nothing else moved in the vicinity of the house. "All clear."

"Move."

Komodo's command started the team's offensive. The back of the white van burst open and three men jumped out, racing across the sidewalk and up the garden path. Tyler stepped out from concealment and dragged his opponent down to the ground, executing a perfect choke hold. Karin heard desperate struggle and frantic grunting noises, but it didn't last long. Herrera joined Tyler and, between them, the two Delta soldiers trussed the Russian up tighter than a Christmas turkey.

Karin watched through Tyler's head-cam as Komodo passed them on the path. The tiny camera swiveled to watch Komodo, Smyth and Romero press on through the half-open door. Then, Komodo's head-cam showed an empty hallway, paintings on the wall, the steep stretch of a staircase, a washing basket full to overflowing. The comms system picked up coarse laughter coming from down the hall.

Komodo signaled, and the three men headed that way. Komodo's gun barrel made controlled movements from side-to-side. Karin quickly checked the overview. Still clear, but a paperboy was making his way down the street.

A bull-like man emerged from the room at the end of the hall, surprise written almost comically across his face when he spotted the three armed soldiers approaching him. Immediately, the testosterone kicked in, outweighing the intelligence by at least five-to-one, and he reached around the back of his waist for a gun, shouting.

Komodo's weapon bucked. The bull hurtled back against the frame, changing the paint from white to vivid red. Komodo pushed on. A shot was fired blindly from inside the room, burying itself into the wall.

"Tyler, Herrera, check upstairs," Komodo whispered into his comms.

"One in the kitchen," Romero reported. "Unfriendly."

Smyth had checked the rest of the ground floor. "All clear."

Komodo turned quickly. "Finish it." He moved fast down the hall, tracking Tyler and Herrera up the stairs. "Smyth," he said. "Don't forget the garage."

"On it."

Karin watched as Romero's helmet-cam kicked back heavily. The man fired heavy rounds through the kitchen's plaster walls, leaving holes the size of side-plates. A brief scream signaled that the coast was clear.

Smyth ran inside, double-tapping the Russian to be sure. The inner connecting door that led to the garage was slightly open. Karin watched him approach it swiftly, but carefully. He nudged the door wider with the barrel of his weapon.

"Contact," he murmured under his breath. "The wife's here and not alone."

As if to verify, a high-pitched command rang out, *"Get back! You come no closer to me!"*

Karin winced. The last remaining Russian stood behind Audrey Patterson, one arm across her throat, the other holding a pistol to her head. The woman looked terrified and tears streamed down her face.

Smyth moved forward, probably hoping to force the assailant into the classic mistake and move the gun away from the hostage in order to point it at the bigger threat. But the Russian didn't comply.

"I shoot!"

The gunshot rang out, deafening through the comms. Karin saw Audrey Patterson shriek and go limp, but the bullet had only shot past her forehead.

"The next goes in!"

Komodo grunted as he joined the scene. Karin watched as four head-cams fanned out into a semi-circle. The fifth was aimed at the rough concrete floor, creeping slowly.

"Nowhere to go, fucker," Smyth said with typical testiness. "Put the pea shooter down."

"You let me go!"

"End of the line, Boris," Smyth growled. "Be a good Russkie. You don't want to end up smeared across the walls like your friends back there."

Komodo stepped forward. "Calm down," he said softly. "Both of you." Karin wasn't entirely sure if he meant the Russian and Mrs Patterson, or the Russian and Smyth.

"What do you want?" Komodo asked. "You let her go. We'll talk."

"Leave. You get out of garage, we drive away. I push her out when clear."

Smyth snorted. Karin felt every muscle in her body tense, every nerve ending stand on edge as the fifth head-cam, Tyler's, focused on the treads of a tire and stopped. He had to be only three feet away. Now, he would wait.

Komodo stepped to the side this time. The Russian followed him, gun wavering. "Why don't we all just calm down," Komodo said. "Point that gun away from Audrey's head and we'll talk."

"Alright!" the Russian screamed. "I aim it at you!"

It all happened very quickly and clinically. Tyler got the signal from Herrera, stood and fired twice. The Russian's head exploded, spraying the professor's wife and the side-wall. The woman collapsed to her knees, hysterical but alive.

Smyth and Romero rushed to help her.

Komodo addressed the comms. "Mission complete," he said. "Be back soon."

Karin checked the overview again. The paperboy had disappeared. The houses were all quiet. She would inform the authorities that they could move in. The peace and quiet of suburbia would live to see another day.

With time to spare, she fished out her cell phone and speed-dialed her parent's number, wondering how life was treating them over in Leeds. After that, she would call Ben.

CHAPTER THIRTY FOUR

"This could be the fight of our lives," Mai Kitano commented.

Drake crawled through the desert, ignoring the morning sun that beat down hard on his back, weapons ready. Their packs were comprehensively packed, even to the tools they might need for entering the dreaded pit. But, for now, Drake's eyes fixed firmly on the prize ahead.

The three large, camouflaged tents that belonged to the ragtag group of Razin's men pillaging the ancient pit of Babylon and, if they survived that, the Devil's Tower, the Tower of Babel, where Zanko and Razin hunted for ancient treasure.

"Nah, no worse than the battle around the coffee machine first thing every morning."

Alicia crawled at their sides, equally tooled up. "I've had harder times pulling my bike leathers on."

Mai eyed her. "But not so many taking them off, I bet."

Hayden, Dahl and Kinimaka approached from another angle, the two groups connected by a hardy communications system. Their objective – acquire all the swords at all costs. Ominous events were afoot in the world, and this was the team's only viable link to them.

The Russian perimeter was loose, made complacent by weeks of indolence. Judging by their careful surveillance, it seemed the Russians had a compliment of around a dozen men, including two bosses – a man and a woman, neither of whom were Zanko or Razin.

They will have stationed themselves at the Devil's Tower, Patterson had guessed. *Whilst their men acquire the remaining swords.* Patterson, Akerman and Yorgi had been left back at the all-terrain vehicles for this little jaunt. The civilians would only cause distraction.

Alicia blew a gust of sand out of her mouth. "Oh yeah, I'm lovin' this."

Drake surveyed the tented area through a pair of high-powered binoculars, identifying the positions of the guards. "Aye, it's bloody hot out here. Could be worse though. At least we haven't come across one of those mental camel spiders yet."

Alicia swiveled her entire body. "What?"

"Y'know. Six, seven inches. Move at ten miles an hour. Jaws like a croc. Those camel spiders."

"So I'm lying here up to my tits in sand, and *now* you mention them. Thanks." She cast around as if expecting one of the beasts to pop up out of the dunes.

"The scorpions are worse." Kinimaka's voice came over the comms. "I just crawled over one. Luckily, I squashed it, I think. They might survive a nuclear strike, but there ain't no surviving the mighty Mano."

"Let's just go." Alicia started to crawl again. "I'm starting to like the look of these Russians."

Drake kept pace, crawling with his elbows, nose an inch off the jagged, dusty terrain. The early morning sun was already beating down. A steady breeze billowed the overlarge tents ahead and stirred mini dust devils. The trio topped the last little rise and waited.

Hayden's voice came over the comms. "Go."

They rushed the perimeter. Drake's weapon spat. A guard fell instantly. Others followed suit around the rough circle. The team's rush ate up the ground between them and the enclosures. Within seconds, they were amongst the utility vehicles, packing crates and diesel drums. The tent flaps burst open and a swarm of badly dressed men flew out, weapons held high or still strapped to their backs. One still held on to a half-empty bottle of Southern Cross vodka.

Their shouts of pain stung the morning air.

Two more figures burst out of the tent. "Victoriyah!" one of them yelled. "Call Nikolai!"

The woman, black-haired, half-dressed like the men and sporting a confident, superior expression, threw her own vodka bottle in the direction of Hayden's team. "Of course, Maxim. I have little else to do."

Maxim discharged a stream of bullets into packing crates. Drake ducked as one nicked off the frame by his head. More bullets thudded into the crates as Maxim's men caught up with the situation. Mai leaned out and picked one off with a perfect head shot, sending him flying back into his boss's legs, crumpling him.

"Idiot!" Maxim yelled, scrambling to his feet and kicking at the corpse, face a livid red. "Victoriyah! Hurry up!"

"Suck it, Maxim."

Drake turned an almost amused look toward the women. "Sounds like those two are practically married."

Alicia peered out, and almost got her head blown off. Splinters of wood cascaded across her hair. "Bollocks."

More shots rang out. Hayden's team advanced, drawing the fire. Drake climbed on to the lip of a badly stacked crate and peered over. In the two seconds he had spare, he put a bullet through someone's throat and saw the through-and-through pass tantalizingly close to Victoriyah's skull.

"We're thinning them out and they know it," he said. "Let's move."

The trio burst from behind the crates, passing close to three haphazardly parked trucks, and out into the open. Only forty feet separated them now, and the pit of Babylon lay off to the left like a festering, exposed sore.

Drake focused on Maxim, but the Russian hit the dirt fast. Victoriyah threw herself alongside him, throwing the cell phone at his head.

"Dumb fucking thing doesn't work."

"No, Victoriyah. It's the dumb fucking thing trying to work it!"

Drake fired as Maxim rose, his shot whizzing by the Russian's head. By then, it was too late to do anything about the object clasped in the man's other hand – a grenade.

Maxim threw the pineapple shaped explosive. Drake hurled himself to the right and rolled. Mai and Alicia were an instant behind. Plumes of dust and sand rose around them. In three more seconds the grenade exploded, sending shrapnel shards spinning every which way.

The ground shook. Alicia let out a sharp cry. Mai struck Drake's bottom half, still rolling. Drake heard the terrible, death filled fizz of deadly objects passing by him at killing speed. The ground rumbled again.

At last he stopped, fully alert, bringing his gun up and looking to the tents. Dust clouds obscured his view. Beside him, Mai reached out for Alicia, pulling the Englishwoman into her.

"Are you hit?"

"No. But I think I saw one of those fucking spider things."

Drake peered through the clouds. Hayden's voice shouted in his earpiece, "Come in. Are you okay?"

"We're good. Just—"

And then their entire world shifted. The very ground they were lying on began to subside, to crack. Narrow fissures ran from the site of the grenade explosion all the way to the pit of Babylon.

Drake saw what was about to happen. "Uh, oh."

The earth collapsed beneath them.

CHAPTER THIRTY FIVE

Drake tumbled forward, clawing at anything that might arrest his fall, but the rocky earth fell away in a steep cascade, taking all three of them with it. Evidently, the cave-in wasn't confined to their area, but extended all the way to the tents, as Victoriyah's echoing voice berated Maxim for his insanity.

Time stopped as Drake fell. Their lives hung in the balance. This could be an endless fall down a bottomless pit or a sharp plunge down a steep slope. He tucked his body as it bounced off the sides, drew his head down as shale and stones poured all around it. At last, he hit the bottom, plainly a narrow space, since he immediately rolled a short way up the opposite side.

And that meant . . .

He dragged himself to his knees, head spinning, limbs howling with pain. He steadied himself by staring at the ground and bringing a pile of rocks into focus, then looked up.

A Russian's top half protruded from rubble further up the slope, partly buried, but still miraculously holding his gun and staring wild-eyed at his situation. Two more guards groaned and crawled through the debris that had collected at the bottom. Beyond them, Drake saw Maxim and Victoriyah sprawled across each other, struggling hard.

Rivers and streams of rock continued to run down both slopes.

Far above, Drake saw one of the tents leaning over the new crevice, balanced precariously and slowly slipping.

Crap! He pulled at Mai and cast about for a weapon. Their guns were nowhere to be seen. Alicia ran past him then, leaping nimbly from pile to pile, drawing her army issue knife as she closed the gap on the fallen Russians. Drake followed her. Alicia slammed the hilt of her weapon under the first man's chin, giving him no chance to react. The second struck out at her, glancing a blow off her shoulder. Alicia caught the arm and broke the wrist as Drake drove his own knife through the man's throat. Only Maxim and Victoriyah remained.

Then a bullet blasted into the rubble nearby, raising a mini explosion of shale. *Damn, how the hell were they going to cancel out that bastard?*

The Russian half-buried up the slope was laughing, making a point of taking careful aim. There was nothing they could do to stop him. "Hold still!" he cried. "I want to take your stupid heads off."

"Wing them," came Maxim's authoritative command. "We can bury them down here. A fitting end, I say."

"Get your fucking arse off me!" Victoriyah shouted.

Alicia, never a girl to stay put and take it, exploded into action, sprinting through the debris and shrieking like a banshee. Drake ran in her wake, feeling the itch as crosshairs lined up on his exposed back.

Mai screamed from behind them, "Drop—"

Then the cry of Torsten Dahl crashed down like thunder and the big Swede came feet first, slipping and sliding down the crumbling slope, torrents of rock streaming around him, smashing into the half-buried Russian and almost breaking him in two. Both men plummeted to the bottom, the Russian bent and shattered, the Swede brushing himself off and seeking out his next target.

Alicia hit Maxim hard, tackling him around the waist. Drake came up against Victoriyah, thrusting with his knife, but thrown off balance by the shifting mounds of debris. When he realized he was falling, he threw his body hard against the slope. Victoriyah laughed at him.

"What's this? You want to play?"

Drake crouched as she came at him, almost wincing at the sight of her shapely bare legs bloodied and scraped by the headlong tumble. He caught her lunge by dropping a shoulder, and heaved her aside. As he turned he noticed, beyond Mai, that the far edge of the fissure was slowly collapsing into the pit of Babylon.

And the drop-off point was running fast back toward Mai!

"Run!" he yelled. At that point, a thick rope slithered down from above, anchored by Kinimaka, Hayden and, Drake momentarily saw, Yorgi.

The little Russian thief must have disobeyed him. Thank God.

He launched his body on top of Victoriyah and took a blow to the ribs, but brought his weight to bear and lowered the knife. Her hands came up, stopping the tip of the blade an inch before the bridge of her nose.

Drake bore down harder. The Russian woman spat and thrashed about, screaming expletives. Alicia beat Maxim down hard, turning his face into pulp before ending his misery with a thrust to the brain pan. Mai outran the crevice's collapse, leaped for the rope and held a hand down to Alicia. "Hurry!"

Drake removed one hand from the blade, then brought it crashing down on top of the hilt, beating at it as a hammer beats a nail. The tip sliced through skin.

Victoriyah glared coldly into his eyes. "Fuck you all to hell," she said and let go of Drake's wrist.

The knife, unimpeded, drove down through her forehead. Drake left it in place and grabbed the flapping end of the rope, planting his feet against the slope and leaning back, right beneath Alicia. They all started to walk upward.

Dahl ran hard up the collapsing slope at a sharp angle, his course planned to intersect the rope just above Mai.

Kinimaka and the others took the full strain. The Hawaiian's voice could be heard clearly through the sudden stillness. "I've pulled many pigs out of many pits back home before, guys, but this takes the trophy."

"Hurry, Mano," Hayden urged. "This is far from over. We can't let Razin get away with those other swords."

Alicia peered over her shoulder and down at Drake. "Enjoying the view?"

Drake sent her a smirk. "I dunno, love. It's just not quite the same when you've seen it all before."

CHAPTER THIRTY SIX

Above ground, Drake saw that Akerman and Patterson had also been part of the rope-pulling team. Everyone except Kinimaka fell to the ground exhausted, as Drake, the last man, stepped over the top.

"Thanks, Mano." Drake slapped their enormous colleague on one meaty shoulder. He noticed straight away that Dahl was already stalking toward two trussed up guards.

"Answers," the Swede said. "Give them to me, men, and we might let you live. Stay quiet and you can take your chances in the pit."

Both men stared into space, their expressions a mix of despair and hangover. One of them wrenched at his bonds. "We tell you shit."

"Olle," Dahl said to Akerman as he passed. "You'd better look the other way."

As the Swede hammered his point home, Drake took a moment to approach Yorgi. "Thanks for being useful, mate."

"It is my new job." The thief laughed. "Saving your life."

Drake took a momentary look at the site of the Tower of Babel. "Can't see a thing. You think your old mates are there?"

"If they are close to finding your swords, they will not just leave. They will fight."

"Good."

Drake brushed himself off as he approached Dahl. The Swede was watching Hayden and Kinimaka approach a solitary crate positioned beside the furthest tent. "Our songbirds say they found three swords. Two are inside that crate. Razin and Zanko took the other."

Patterson heard the comment and rushed up. "Wait. Why did Razin take the other sword?"

Dahl raised questioning eyebrows at their captives. One of them spat blood. "He called it Great Sword, like Alexander the Great. I do not know his meaning."

Patterson practically wet himself. “No! They cannot have the Great Sword. It is the key. The key to understanding the whole inscription. The key to all the earth energy. The key to the vortex. It is—”

Dahl patted him on the head. “Calm down, boy. We’ll get it back.”

Mai and Alicia stationed themselves to watch the distant hillock. Time was against them now, and every second that passed increased the danger and the Russians' chances of stealing away with the prize. Drake drifted over toward the crate with Yorgi and Patterson.

Kinimaka smashed the side open with a discarded crowbar, then stood back as the contents spilled out. Packing foam littered the sand, amongst which several tightly wrapped packages tumbled.

Hayden reached down to her feet and picked up a long bundle. Kinimaka scanned the rest, but saw no shapes consistent with that of a sword. Hayden knelt down in the sand and quickly severed the wrapping twine.

The bundle fell apart. Two swords clattered against each other, their blades suddenly revealed and catching the light. Drake shielded his eyes as the sunlight flashed off a polished blade, still potent after all these years, ablaze with promise, fire and the sparkle of unfulfilled prophecies.

Hayden held one easily, turning it before her eyes, letting the fire of the sun flicker and flare down the deadly length of the blade. “Stunning,” she said.

Kinimaka stooped down for the other. “I’ll say.” The sword was short and stylish, with a wicked, curved double-edged blade and some kind of ancient pattern on the hilt. It looked to be made of cast steel.

Patterson ran up to them, frothing at the mouth. “My God, they're real. My God. Let me touch it!”

Kinimaka handed his over. Patterson turned it to reveal the ancient symbols, a set of characters that ran down the middle of the blade. Akerman walked up to him, staring. “That, my friend, isn’t the language of the gods. At least, not as I know it.”

“But the swords, when seen together and read in order, should tell us how to deal with the device.”

Akerman let out a long sigh. “The characters, though similar, are not the same.”

“You are questioning Alexander?”

“I’m not questioning anything,” Akerman breathed. “I’m stating a fact.”

“Alright,” Dahl shouted. “We'll worry about that later. Are you sure they’re the swords we’re looking for?”

Patterson nodded. “They bear the seal of Alexander. The portrait head and the spear thrower.”

Drake swallowed his awe. Right now, they had God-Zanko to deal with.

Mai stood a little apart from the rest, making a show of watching the indistinct tower, but actually only focusing half of her mind there. Behind her, the majority of her team members talked quickly and listened hard to Patterson’s descriptions of the tower, its history, and what they could expect there. Hayden outlined a plan, but without time-consuming surveillance, they were still only a step away from swinging in the wind.

Mai attempted to shut down the creeping contemplations of her own past, particularly the terrible memories that had moved stealthily to the front of her mind during the past few weeks. The knowledge that she was being sought by the clan smoldered through her mind like the inactive embers of a fire, just waiting to flare into life. It was an outrage that these people even believed they owned her. How could their arrogance attain such a level? The Clan Master, who had offered her destitute parents a great sum of money to take just one of their daughters off their hands, had seemed such a great man at the time, almost like a loving grandfather. Living in a poor and remote area of Japan at the time, many traders and shady dealers offered desperate, impoverished parents cash to take a child off their hands. For the parents, losing one child sometimes meant that at least the other would survive. A horrific choice, but an essential one.

Mai had been sold to a Clan Master in need of pupils. Her parents had cried; they had fallen to their knees, grasping the hand of their remaining daughter tightly so that she wouldn’t run after her sister;

realized the depth of what they had done and probably never recovered. But she never saw them again.

And for Mai, being literally torn from the arms of her parents was one of the easier trials of her younger years.

And now the men she had learned to both hate and fear were searching for her again. For a long time, she had believed that she had broken free. Now she knew. They would never stop, never give up their claim on her.

She was stuck in the middle of a lethal situation with two distinct outcomes – death and vengeance. For both sides.

At last, she became aware of the conversation behind her. Professor Patterson was quickly explaining the origins of the tower.

"They built this stone tower straight up to the sky. They reached for heaven. They used slaves, tens of thousands of slaves, and whipped them till they died, burned from the midday sun right through their flesh and bone. They were challenging God, you see." Patterson swept his arm around the general area of Babylon. "All this – a challenge to God. What we know today about the tower comes from a smattering of archeological evidence and ancient writings. According to one account, the builders of the tower said, 'God has no right to choose the upper realm for himself. We will build us a tower with an idol on top holding a great sword, so that it may appear as if intended to war with God'."

Yorgi whistled at that. "Hard words."

"Indeed. Some members of that generation even wanted to assail God in Heaven. More learned men with sly ambitions encouraged them by saying arrows they shot amongst the clouds returned to earth dripping with blood. So the people believed they could wage war against the inhabitants of Heaven and were persuaded to build the towers."

Drake's voice rose. *"Towers?"*

"There were two near Babylon alone. The Tower of Babel and the Tower of Babylon, though no one knows where the latter existed. There are the remains of towers in Central America, Mexico, Africa, Nepal and within the lands of the Indians of America, all surrounded by similar traditions. One holds that the Great Pyramid of Cholula was built in order to storm Heaven. Or . . ." he paused. "A quote from a scribed legend found in Lozi mythology, supposedly taken from an account by David Livingstone, states – *to follow the gods who fled back up to Heaven.* The tradition of towers being built to facilitate an entry to heaven exists all over the world."

"But *why?*" Hayden questioned. "To kill the gods?"

"No. To escape their wrath." Patterson smiled. "All these towers were built for one overwhelming purpose – to escape the next great deluge."

Hayden cleared her throat. "As in the Great Flood, and Noah's Ark?"

"The first great deluge. Those who survived or *read* about the event thought that challenging the gods might lead to further reprisals. So they made many men sweat and die so they could sit atop their mighty refuges and watch the great waters lap away down below."

"And what happened?"

"Well, right there is where we get the origin of the Tower of *Babel.* It is said that the gods – or God – seeing these monstrosities being constructed *confounded the language of the builders.* And that is why all the countries of today speak in different languages, my friends. Because once there was only one, and in order to confuse mankind and halt the erection of the towers, the gods created many. No man could understand the other and they all went to separate parts of the earth."

"Babel," Hayden repeated. "As in *babbling.* Each man thought the other was babbling. Is that the origin of the name?"

"Yes, it is."

"So the towers are inextricably linked to the gods," Hayden said.

"Yes. There are some old legends that tell of thunder and lightning bolts being sent to destroy the towers of Babel, shooting and *channeling* from one to the other."

Hayden picked up on his use of the word. "Channeling? As in earth energy?"

"Yes. They were all built atop an earth energy vortex. It is—"

"And there we have to end it," Mai spoke up suddenly. She pointed at the distant hill where tiny figures were frantically rushing around. "We need to hurry. We have a fight to get to."

Patterson's rhetoric, pitched low, still reached every ear as the team moved out at pace. "The battle for Babylon is about to begin."

CHAPTER THIRTY SEVEN

Jonathan Gates exited the new SPEAR headquarters via the parking garage and decided to walk the few blocks over to his own offices. Karin was running the show single-handedly from this end, as he had always known she could, but Komodo was due to return in a few hours. The rough-looking Delta officer with a heart of gold had already requested a private chat and Gates had a good idea as to what it might entail.

Romero and Smyth. Technically, the two soldiers were still without a unit, although, of course, they could slot in anywhere. Gates already thought they'd bring good extra cover to the team.

As he walked, Gates saw the figure approaching from his peripheral vision. His heart immediately gave a thud of alarm and he stopped mid-stride. The form moved closer, inescapable now, much too close to avoid.

Gates sighed. “Miss Moxley? Are you well?”

The wiry redhead showed no qualms about invading the personal space of the Secretary of Defense. “Yes sir, thank you.”

“Back on the job already?”

The newspaper reporter’s façade cracked a little. “Work is the place I go to heal, sir. Always has been.”

Gates studied her anew. It was the same for him. “I’m sorry about the deaths of your colleagues.”

“Me too, sir. They were good men. I tried to contact your office for an interview, but they stonewalled me.”

“They're under strict instructions to severely limit my media exposure. It’s the same for everyone.”

“Why? Is there something going on?”

Gates almost smiled. The bloodhound instinct of this reporter would never be quelled. He noticed the bright blue of her eyes and grew a little wary of her winning, open smile. “There’s always something going on in DC, Miss Moxley. Being a reporter for the Post, you should know that."

"Is that a quote?"

Gates laughed despite himself. "Do you ever let up?"

"No, sir. It's not in my nature. And, please, call me Sarah."

"And nor in mine," Gates checked his watch. "Look. I believe I owe you one, Sarah. Despite our many warnings, you stuck to your job and almost paid the price. Your colleagues did pay the heaviest price. If you were soldiers we'd be giving you medals for that. So, give me the afternoon. I'll clear your name at the office. Then call and arrange an interview. Alright?"

"Thank you, sir." There was no mistaking the happiness as the lights danced in her eyes. But the stare. The speculative look. It wasn't like the Secretary of Defense to get nervous around women, but her sudden interest made him almost feel young again.

She held out a hand. "See you soon, sir."

Gates coughed. "I hope so."

The touch of her skin would stay with him long after Sarah Moxley had departed. He started to walk again, but then his cell vibrated. When he checked the screen it was the call he'd been dreading.

"Yes?"

"Stone won, sir. He's been allocated the funds to configure his plan."

A bad day for the world, Gates thought. "Thank you." He ended the call abruptly. He firmly believed in stopping a charging rhino before its legs had even got going. And he would stop General Stone.

Hard.

He already had a plan.

CHAPTER THIRTY EIGHT

Drake and the rest of the team piled into the nearby vehicles and took only a few moments to find two sets of keys. The third was nowhere to be found, probably thrust deep in the pocket of someone still falling to their deaths down the bottomless pit of Babylon.

But two were enough. The team raced hard for the vague stack, reloading weapons and readjusting vests and straps as they got closer. The vehicles bounced along the rough terrain, sometimes travelling hard up slopes, other times barreling down the other side, but rarely staying straight.

"The bastards can see us coming a mile off," Alicia said, handing Drake a pair of binoculars.

"As soon as we're within range, split up," Drake said. "That'll give 'em two targets to worry about."

Hayden's voice crackled in his ear. "My thoughts exactly."

Drake ducked as bullets clattered around the vehicle's framework. The ride wasn't bulletproof, but it was still built of good quality, sturdy steel and the chassis gave them some protection. As they drove closer, they saw that the Russians had erected a makeshift slide, built out of wooden poles and boarding, rough but robust enough to cope with several heavy artifacts being slid down to the desert floor.

"Well," Drake admitted. "It's better than dragging them down by hand. Bet Zanko didn't think of that."

More bullets clanged off the bodywork. Hayden's vehicle peeled away to the left, circling the embankment. Sparks flashed as they too came under fire. Drake drove through the camp – nothing more than a large tent, several crates and a heavy-duty truck. The windshield exploded as he neared the bottom of the slope, but he was where he wanted to be.

Quickly, they all piled out, taking cover behind the vehicle. Drake had positioned it so that it was directly underneath the Russians' line of fire, ensuring they had to peer out and down the slope to find a target. The first man who did lost a head, courtesy of Dahl's pinpoint accuracy.

The team set off running around the hill. At various points, they left a person behind, ensuring numerous inroads up the short but steep slope.

Then they waited for Hayden. It only took a minute for her voice to fill the airwaves. "Check. We're all good here. Send in the bird."

Drake watched the skies. Camp Babylon wasn't far and had been on stand-by, awaiting the order to join the SPEAR operation with a fully tooled-up, army Sikorsky Blackhawk. Orders had been secured through Karin and Gates in DC. The chopper had instructions to strafe the top of the mound, and force the men up there to abandon their positions.

Then a voice, like thunder, roared down from up high, "Matt Drake! Are you down there? Is it you, my friend?"

Drake said nothing. Let the big hairy bastard wonder.

"Ahhh, don't be like that! So you lost. It is no big deal. Everyone loses to Zanko!"

Drake spied the bird in the distance before he heard its rotor wash. His lips curled. Zanko was about to lose big time.

The distant thud of the chopper became obvious. Hayden spoke up, "Let's get ready for this." The entire team popped up as Razin's men redirected their attentions to the oncoming helicopter. Of all the men up there, three had made the mistake of rising too high in their panic. Drake, Dahl and Mai made them pay.

Then the chopper swooped overhead, engines roaring, a wicked, almost prehistoric bird of prey, bristling with Hydra rockets and Hellfire missiles. Its main guns opened fire with a resounding roar, staccato bursts thumping around the top of the ancient hill. Drake saw two men flail immediately, puppets animated by hot lead, jerking and toppling head-over-heels down the slope. Pandemonium reigned above. Shouts, commands and cries for help, all suddenly drowned out again as the chopper let loose a second salvo.

"Go." Hayden gave the order a moment after the noise of the guns died away. Drake sprinted up the hill, saw a group of men milling around on the edge above and fired several shots. The chopper backed away, still hovering. Drake switched his run to a zigzag pattern as someone tried an opportune potshot down the hill. To either side of him, several meters apart, both Mai and Alicia ran hard. The team would assault the short rise from all angles.

Hayden whispered one more time in his ear as Drake crested the rise, "Remember, it's imperative we discover the location of the Great Sword."

Drake hit the dirt as a contingent of men fired. Bullets whizzed overhead. He rolled, trusting his team to assail them from another angle. Within seconds, the volley was over. Dahl and Kinimaka were amongst them. Drake took a moment to get his bearings. The widespread but low knoll stretched away from him in an almost rectangular pattern. If this was the lower reaches of the real Tower of Babel, then the foundations must be unimaginably huge beneath him. Any real archaeological mysteries within may have already been ransacked by Hussein's men, but then maybe not. The Iraqi ruler hadn't been known for his smarts.

Drake saw an excavated area near the right side, partly obscured by half a dozen men. Amongst them he saw Razin and then Zanko. The Russians looked like they were leaving. Then, the group parted and a loner stepped out, grenade launcher balanced across his shoulder. Before Drake could aim and fire, he had let loose a missile that flashed across the gap between it and the chopper, passing dangerously close to its undercarriage.

Hayden jumped on the comms. "Back off. We've got this now."

The chopper whirled away. The Russians mistook it for victory and cheered. The team pointed out their mistake by peppering them with bullets. Razin looked like he was hit and Zanko stepped over him.

Drake pressed forward. From out of nowhere, a Russian attacked his flank, tackling him at shoulder height. Drake stood his ground and shrugged the man off, quickly using the butt of his gun to render him unconscious.

They needed survivors.

Then Zanko threw Razin bodily across his shoulders. Drake heard the bellow he aimed at his men even from where he stood.

"Cover our escape! Die if you have to, but make sure we are clear first! Take them!" Zanko threw four shiny weapons amongst his remaining men. The swords of Babylon were his safety net.

Only four.

Drake dropped to one knee and squeezed off three quick rounds. Through his rifle sights he saw Zanko flinch once before leaping off the hill. Drake cursed. One bullet would barely faze the monster. And if the entire team was up here, then Zanko and Razin might indeed get away. The swords were imperative at this point.

Gunfire crisscrossed the hill. The Russians were unprotected but well-armed. Hayden and her team could not risk rushing in. No one wanted to die today. One by one, the defenders fell, at least one of them shot in the stomach so that he would survive, at least for a short while.

Drake lined the last of them up in is sights. "Drop your weapon! There's a way out of this, pal. At least listen to me."

"I never say where Zanko go. You think I am stupid?"

"No. No. It's not Zanko we want. It's the sword he took from the pit. That's all." Drake inched forward as he spoke. The last man was now covered on all sides.

"That is all?" The Russian's face was livid and spittle flew from his lips. "Are you fooking crazy? There are worse things," he panted. "Worse things than Zanko."

Drake was momentarily stunned. "Like what?"

"She asked for the Great Sword so he sent it. Days ago. It is no longer here."

Dahl stepped closer. "She?"

"No, never! *Never!*" As he screamed his last word, the Russian fired, not even bothering to aim his gun. Death by solider, it seemed, was preferable to revealing the name of the woman Zanko had sent the Great Sword to.

Hayden cast about the top of the dusty hill. "Let's see if any of these other clowns will talk to us."

With the battle over, Hayden recalled the chopper and used its occupants to help secure a perimeter. Razin and Zanko had vanished so completely, Drake wondered if they had a hidey hole in the area.

The pair of them were slippery enough, he knew, and unlikely to have revealed its location to their men. Nevertheless, the four swords were added to the two they'd already liberated and all set on the ground, inscription side up.

Akerman and Patterson cooed over them like grandparents over a newborn. Akerman again voiced the concern that the language differed from the one he'd been deciphering in the tomb. "But," he pointed out hopefully. "The properties are very similar. We should start as soon as we're able."

Drake stared down at the weapons, stunning yes, but hardly a weapon that might save the world. "You sure these things can stop Odin's doomsday device?"

Patterson looked stressed. "Alexander crafted them for that purpose. They are the swords of the seven veils. Priceless. Given place of honor at Alexander's deathbed. The real message is on the swords themselves – the inscriptions, but I can tell you now – it will center on the many earth energy vortexes scattered around the world."

Hayden stopped at his shoulder. "C'mon, Drake. It's hardly more surprising than when we first found out the gods were once real."

"Still." Drake stared up at the skies. "I sometimes get the feeling I'm just a main character in a story, y'know? Prancing around and not really getting anywhere."

"Shit." Alicia heard and laughed. "No one would be daft enough to make you the main character, Drakey. They'd choose me to help give the story a big pair of bollocks."

Drake shook his head, trying to purge his mind of the idea, and turned away. He desperately needed some downtime and maybe a touch of Mai-time. He saw her now, staring off into space yet again as if expecting someone to materialize out of the dust and the shimmering heat-haze that stretched across the horizon. It looked like she was chatting on her cell.

Hayden broke out the team's satphone and put in a call to Gates, through Karin, on the speakerphone. The Secretary sounded surprisingly upbeat at first.

"I'm sure you have nothing but good news for me, Hayden."

“Well.” Hayden paused. “We have six of the seven swords, sir, so at least that's something. We're working on the inscriptions now. No luck yet.”

“I thought you had that language expert. Akerman, isn’t it?”

“He says the inscriptions don’t quite match the ones in the tombs.”

Gates sighed. “Of course they don’t. We really do have nothing here. You should also work on a plan for a last case scenario.”

Hayden flicked a glance across to Drake. “We should?”

“Yes, if you can find out what needs to be done if it comes to fight or flight. Hayden.” He went quiet for a long moment. “I'm counting on you.”

“Thank you, sir.” Drake studied her, wondering why she didn't question the odd moment, but then she'd been dealing with Gates a lot longer than he. “Has Cayman resurfaced yet? Or his boss?”

“No. It feels a little like the calm before the storm here in Washington. All the main players out there are still jockeying into position. We don’t know their agenda. They won't reveal their intentions until they're good and ready.”

“Still,” Hayden brooded. “It infuriates us all, knowing they're up to something so terrible and we're powerless to stop them.”

“That's what makes you the best team for the job,” Gates said. Drake tuned out as the Secretary continued and crossed over to Dahl and Kinimaka, who were crouched over a twitching body.

“Get what we need?”

Dahl turned around, his eyes wide. “I'm not entirely sure. If we're to believe two out of two men, questioned separately, then the seventh sword has been sent to Zoya.” The Swede hesitated.

“Where the hell is Zoya?”

“Not a 'where', a 'who'. Zoya is Zanko's grandmother.”

Drake's face fell. “Fuck off, Dahl. This isn't the time—”

“I'm not joking.”

Kinimaka turned equally shocked eyes his way. “He's not joking.”

Drake chortled, drawing attention from the others. “Zanko's *grandmother*. And you believe them?”

Dahl's gaze was speculative. “I get the feeling that although this is Razin's operation, Zoya can start calling the shots at any time.

Grandmother or not, it seems Razin has a very powerful sleeping partner."

"Fine. Fine. I guess someone related to Zanko might not be quite what you expect. And in any case, we need that sword. You get an address?"

"Of course."

Drake saw Alicia approaching. The expression on her face made him bite his tongue in order to stop the insult that was about to fly out. "Don't say it."

Alicia tried to grin but didn't make it. "I only came back to help get you outta jail, Drake. Lomas needs me."

"We need you. The world needs you."

Now Alicia did laugh. "Don't be a dickhead. You'll be fine." Her gaze turned to Mai. "Both of you."

Drake took her in his arms, surprised at how soft her body felt in his embrace. You fought alongside someone so long, you watched them kill, bleed and struggle, you occasionally tended to forget they were just a girl.

Maybe that was part of why she was leaving.

"I hate saying goodbye to you," he whispered into her ear. "Twice in two weeks is two times too many."

Alicia grunted. "Bet you can't say that again when you're drunk."

"I don't get drunk anymore."

She pulled away. Drake held on. "Don't worry. It's okay. I know you didn't mean anything by it. We're family now, Alicia. You, Mai, me. Those idiots over there." He pointed out Dahl, Hayden and Kinimaka. "You ever need us. Just say the word."

Alicia's lips moved against his throat. "My family ripped apart when I was eight. My dad started beating up my mum, and me when I stood up for her. I was too weak to do anything about it, so when I got older the first thing I did was join the army. I got out of there. My dad forged my fire, but the army molded it into an art. All these years, Matt, I've just been fighting my dad."

Drake swallowed hard. He couldn't believe that here, in Iraq, atop the ancient Tower of Babel, Alicia Myles was finally opening up to someone. "Is your dad still alive?"

"He died of alcohol poisoning four months after my mum died of an overdose. Believe me, he was the lucky one."

"I'm so sorry."

"Thank you for my new family, Matt. I will try to visit."

"Make sure you do." Drake cleared his throat, averting his eyes until he felt he had some control. Alicia would join the crew on the chopper and head back to Camp Babylon, and from there back to Lomas and his biker crew. The rest of the SPEAR team would depart soon in the two vehicles that remained intact.

He sat down hard in the dust. Goddamn, he needed a rest.

The first thing Mai did in the aftermath of the battle was to check her phone. Sure enough, a message had been left. It was from Dai Hibiki, and the contents could not be good. She cast around first to make sure she was alone, walked closer to the edge of the mound, then ignored the message and hit the call-back button.

Hibiki picked up so fast he might have been sat on the receiver. "Mai? Where are you? Are you alright?"

"What is it?"

Her friend's voice quavered half a world away. "The name of the man searching for you. It's . . . it's—"

"Gyuki?"

Hibiki's silence affirmed her worst fear.

The man known only as Gyuki was her old clan's personal wetwork expert, a fact that alone substantiated his skills. Every member of her old clan were all experienced ninja assassins on a par with Mai's own skillset – but Gyuki was the man they turned to when the shit really hit the fan.

Hence, Hibiki's trepidation. "No fiercer opponent exists in this world."

"And what does he want?"

"According to my source," Hibiki swallowed drily. "Blood vengeance."

CHAPTER THIRTY NINE

Jonathan Gates leaned back, letting his recliner do all the work. His door was open, but the office was quiet. He had sent the staff home early today. He needed some quiet, uninterrupted time to reaffirm his decision.

If he went ahead with his plan, he would be breaking the law. More importantly, he would gain himself and his employee a very powerful enemy. Was it worth it? Did General Stone have the resources and the smarts to activate the doomsday device?

Of course, even that scenario depended on Hayden's team successfully translating the inscriptions on the swords. But if that did happen, Gates didn't then want to be in a position of defense or even conflict. The time to take steps was now, when his action would be a deterrent. He imagined the lengths to which Stone must have gone to secure the approval of not only the VP, the Joint Chiefs and their advisors, but the President himself. A man Gates greatly respected, although his decision-making hands had become tied somewhat since he took office. The old Coburn was the one Gates wanted to see again – the military strategist, the fighter, the vigorous contender. A risk taker – like himself.

One thing Gates knew, if General Stone ever possessed the means to activate the device, visions of greatness and glory would blind him to the obvious dangers. It was that simple. Stone was a hard line militarist, and gung-ho enough to believe a team of NASA techs would save the day if anything went wrong.

Decision made. He punched out her number.

She answered impatiently. "Who the hell is this?"

"Jonathan Gates."

"Shit! Sorry, Mr Gates, sir, I didn't know."

"It's fine. I don't have much time, Miss Fox, but I may have a highly sensitive job for you."

“Just lay it out on the table, sir, and, um, that wasn’t meant to be suggestive.”

“Never crossed my mind.” Gates went on to explain what he needed, all the while questioning its merits, its morals and what he imagined would be a low key, violent backlash.

Lauren Fox, to her credit, grasped the entire situation immediately and asked the most telling question of all. “If I do this, who will protect me?”

“Assuming he goes for it, Lauren, there’s a good chance we can keep your true identity out of it all together. If not, you'd be under my protection and SPEAR’s. There would be no reprisal.”

“You’re asking me to potentially give up my life.”

“And it’s only your first job. How long would it take?”

“Damn.” The line went silent for some time. Gates didn’t rush her. When she spoke again, Lauren’s voice was firm.

“I’m good enough to get this done in two days.”

CHAPTER FORTY

Russell Cayman arrived in Singen on Thursday morning, German time, around the same time as his boss, Zak Block, was finding it increasingly hard to get the idea of sitting on Odin's throne out of his head.

Cayman had returned from Hawaii, collected the remainder of the bones of Kali, and driven them just over four hundred miles west, almost in a straight line, bypassing Munich, and finally heightening his vigilance as he entered the industrial city. The mountain of Hohentwiel, with its ancient fortress ruins and extinct volcano, reared majestically to the west of the city, the ruined castle itself no stranger to violence – it had resisted five imperial sieges in its time.

Cayman parked the car carefully well before the foot of the mountain, hearing the two oversized holdalls shift in the back, their weight giving them their own inertia or, as Cayman liked to believe, Kali reminding him of her presence.

With difficulty, he wrenched his thoughts away from the goddess and surveyed the mountain. Again, he was a little early. Block's men were only hours away, but Cayman had never been one to mix with or wait for others. Besides, he was hungry.

Making sure the tiny part of Kali's finger bone still nestled in his pocket, Cayman exited the car and began to make his way up the mountain on foot. The archaeological exploration was being conducted all the way at the top and, out of respect for the locals, was minimized to that area. So the tourists and Cayman, and Block's men, would be able to get all the way to the perimeter without immediate detection.

No doubt the pesky Americans would have secreted a few hidden cameras amongst the trees, but by the time their contents were properly scrutinized, it would be way too late. So Cayman walked contentedly but warily, the sunlight dappling his face, the patchy shadows calling his name. He had time to kill.

Not to mention tourists.

Zak Block allowed the fantasy to take him over. He was already a god – a secret, shadowy god, but when he took that throne – when he took his rightful place upon the very seat of Odin – the destiny that was rightfully his would come to wondrous fruition. When three like minds came together, wishes boosted by the latent power and energies inherent inside tombs literally built and occupied by the gods, then Odin's power would truly be his.

It stood to reason that the three tombs would be connected in some way, perhaps through earth energy. Block had read about many such phenomena before. Places where the natural electromagnetic energy of the earth vitalizes an area and enables the existence of power. Energy could move vertically or horizontally. If the tombs had been built atop vortexes and along lines of vital, natural energy then it was clear that they were linked in the same way.

He was not unaware of the fact that Jakob Hult's translation of the ancient text had gone on to state where each 'like mind' should stand. Probably an ancient trigger for the device. But it was all speculation, and not something he cared too much about anyway.

For now, his efforts should be concentrated solely on the third man. Cayman and he were not enough. They needed a third individual. The Shadow Elite always had a kind of waiting list, a small group of people desperate to join what they thought were the world's decision-makers. Among the men on this list was one Dmitry Kovalenko, the Blood King, but he was unavailable due to secret incarceration in a godforsaken prison even Block couldn't locate. Truth be told, Kovalenko was too crazy and unpredictable anyway. He'd probably want to kidnap the US President or something. Block had heard of his blood vendettas and blood vengeance. Not quite the Shadow Elite's way.

Another name on the brief list was that of Nicolas Denney. The aging European had made respectable money through dot-com businesses in the early days of the Internet and had consolidated with sensible land and financial purchases over the last two decades. In addition, he was a thrill junkie. Block didn't know anything this man hadn't tried for kicks and, even at sixty, he had recently completed another round of Himalayan trekking. Add these qualities to the common trait of a rich man always wanting more, and Block had found the perfect fool.

Partner, he amended rapidly in his head. Best not to get ahead of himself. One of his secure lines rang, and he answered quickly, listening without comment to the vital information being eagerly spilled on the other end.

When the man had finished, Block simply said, "You will be rewarded." And hung up. *Interesting.* The US and their local allies were moving to secure all three tombs, perhaps somehow aware of an evolving threat. He wondered if Cayman had showed himself. That psycho and his damn prize. What made a man fall in love with the bones of an old god? Far better the tangible power they had once commanded.

Block thought back over the killers he had employed through the years. Cayman was probably the oddest, but there was one other he knew of – a woman, deeply embedded even now inside the British . . .

He paused with his line of thought. The critical call was coming in. He stared at the satellite phone, unable to believe the time had finally come.

From now on, it was the Shadow Elite versus the rest of the world. The battle of all battles.

"Yes?"

"Sir. All four cells are in position. One at Singen, one in Iceland, and two in Honolulu. We're ready."

Block's heart started to pound with excitement, fear and anticipation. This was everything he had been waiting for. "Go to war."

Cayman ignored the vibration of his cell phone as he peered through a canopy of overhanging branches into the heart of a clearing. Dangling from his left hand was the corpse of a rabbit he'd used a makeshift snare to trap within an hour of getting here. Blood dripped from the rabbit's neck, the same blood Cayman had coated his lips and chin with. He just hadn't been able to resist. Ah, the sweet, thick nectar of life. Spilled blood being the consummation of death.

But now, literally laid out before him, was quite a different prospect.

A young couple, hikers, enjoying the silence, the solitude and, perhaps, the unspoken thrill of being caught, to enjoy a different kind of consummation. Cayman watched intently. Once the couple had clearly lost all awareness of their surroundings, he crept silently forward until he stood directly behind the male, unseen, in their blind spot. He waited another minute and then simply bent over, jabbing the man several times in the ribs with his knife. Cayman leaned in and covered the man's screaming mouth, then flung the writhing body aside. The woman's shocked eyes stared into his own, glazed with ignorance, terror and denial until he fell upon her, ending her life with a single slice.

Her life force pumped into the ground, drawing Cayman's eyes and attention. In another moment there was movement behind him and a man wearing camouflage fatigues stepped out of the underbrush, closely followed by many others, state-of-the-art weapons at the ready.

"The boss says answer your damn phone, Cayman," the man hissed, holding out his own device. "Good job that phone he gave you holds a tracking chip." He glared pointedly. "For *your* sake. Here, take this. Wipe off your damn hands and talk to the boss."

Cayman sat back and pushed to his feet. The time for play had ended. It was time to go to work.

CHAPTER FORTY ONE

The first of Block's cells hit Iceland's tomb like an arctic storm. With little to do for months, and orders for heightened vigilance having only just being issued, the defending force was more than a little unprepared for the professional team of crack mercenaries that attacked and overwhelmed them.

Shooting mercilessly, the dozen-strong team killed or incapacitated every guard, but made sure they took several civilian hostages, most in the form of scientists and archaeologists. Their boss had said they need hold out only for a day and a half – this seemed the most proficient way.

Leaving a few men to keep an eye out for the cavalry, the leader of the cell proceeded to secure the remainder of the tomb of the gods that had been found first.

Though not in direct contact, the Singen cell struck at exactly the same time. Their job would be more difficult at first, infiltrating the harder-to-reach tomb, but, after that, keeping the local forces at bay for the allotted time shouldn't be a problem. They took Cayman with them – the man they would make absolutely, terribly sure would stand at the center of the tomb when ordered to by the boss – and lugged along his double holdall of bones. Their leader didn't question a thing. Their payday would be nothing short of the stuff his dreams were made of.

In Hawaii, the first cell achieved a strike so precise it could have been sliced by a scalpel. Their initial incursion took them all the way to Odin's daunting black throne, past defenses they had scrutinized for days, and caught an acceptable amount of scared civilian specialists in the process, some of them especially high up the local pecking chain. The leader was pleased, and only when the mission had ended did he experience an unusual stab of agitation.

Now, his team would wait for the arrival of their boss.

The second Hawaiian cell positioned themselves where they might prove most useful, dormant for now, but prepared to move at a moment's notice . . . if the boss demanded it.

CHAPTER FORTY TWO

Throughout that same day, the SPEAR team and their helpers sought to unravel the mystery surrounding the swords of Babylon. Akerman read the inscriptions again and again, compared them to all current translations of the language of the gods, which were being stored online in a secret server very few people so far had access to, and lamented about the close relation of the symbols Alexander had chosen to use.

Patterson helped him, bringing all his archaeological expertise and knowledge of Alexander to bear. Dahl stayed with them for a while, but eventually lost interest and went to call his family. Drake and the rest of the team assembled in the kitchen quarters of the billet they had been temporarily assigned in Camp Babylon.

Hayden poured coffees. "Time for a sit rep, I think guys. We have Zoya's address in Moscow. Zanko and Razin are on the run, their operations shut down. We have six of the seven swords, but not the leader of the pack. Hopefully—" she motioned next door. "The old boys will quit wasting time and crack the code."

"Problem is." Kinimaka accepted his mug with a smile. "Short of knowing that Cayman and co have another way to activate the doomsday device, we're not aware of his role in all this. I don't normally dramatize but that's—"

"A big problem," Hayden finished.

Drake stared at them "You two should be a double act. You've definitely been working together too long."

The couple looked affronted at exactly the same time. Mai laughed and pocketed her phone. Drake wanted to ask who she'd been texting, but knew this wasn't the time. Her buried past had risen to haunt her and, as soon as this Babylon thing was out of the way, it would be time to exorcise that malevolent ghost.

"A trip to Moscow sounds good to me." Dahl wandered in and stared out of the single, sand scoured window. Arid desert met his gaze, the earth already encroaching on the man-made camp, reclaiming its own. The sounds of men shouting and vehicles being driven over short distances hard and fast, the consistent clanging and booming of an army base, gave life to the environment but it was still an arid, life-sucking landscape out there.

Drake was about to reply when they heard raised voices from the next room. Patterson had mentioned something and Akerman had praised him. Dahl raised an eyebrow. "That means one of two things. Either Patterson just gave Olle an idea or showed him a picture of my wife."

They moved into the living quarters. Akerman was almost capering with glee. "Listen to this, ja? We mentioned that Alexander the Great embraced many religions in order to rule so many lands. He embraced many myths and local beliefs. He was a king, ja? A pharaoh. And do you remember what we initially said about the language of the gods?"

Drake tried to remember back a few months to when they had first encountered Olle. "We had just escaped tomb three at Singen when Dahl called you. Didn't you say that the language was a complete *syllabary?"*

"Spot on. A syllabary is a complete writing system that uses symbols to represent all the syllables of a language, ja? Remember?"

Hayden and Kinimaka both nodded. "Ja."

Drake grunted. "A mix of Greek, Chinese, Mayan and so on."

"Exactly! And that is also what Alexander's inscriptions are based on. It's why the symbols are slightly different. The writing system draws on scripts used in many of the lands he conquered. And purposely so. It's a kind of code, impossible to crack until the tombs were discovered and, consequently, the language of the gods. If we never found the tombs – the swords would never be translated and never actually be needed. Very clever."

Patterson positively glowed.

"Can you translate them?" Hayden asked.

Akerman gloated. "Put me in front of a computer and a light fingered female." He stared at Mai. "I'll have it down in no time."

The Japanese woman gave him a dangerous look. "I save these fingers for killing."

"Then at least I'd die happy." Akerman was incorrigible and scooted across the room to the little corner PC. He began to type, humming happily. Dahl grabbed a chair and sat next to him, sending a look of apology across to Mai.

"Speaking of dying happy," Drake murmured. "Have you heard from Smyth lately?"

Mai's expression remained hard for almost two seconds before she allowed a slight smile to curl the sides of her lips. "What do you think?"

"Not getting under your skin is he, *Maggie*?" Drake joked.

"Matt," Mai sighed. "Smyth would have more chance with Maggie Q, believe me."

It took hours, and Akerman would not reveal even a single word until he was finished, but, slowly, painstakingly, the inscriptions on the six swords began to make a sort of sense. Akerman insisted he reveal the swords in order – as best he could divine – and moved to stand before them like a lecturer in a classroom. The team gathered around and Hayden made sure to include Karin and Komodo by speakerphone.

"Okay," he said. "First sword. It says this—" He cleared his throat and began to narrate. *"The device that was made by the hands of the Gods can be unmade."*

"A direct reference to the doomsday weapon," Kinimaka said immediately, voicing the thoughts of everyone. "This is for thinking." He tapped his head and pointed at his feet. "These are for dancing."

Hayden shook her head. "Well, at least we know we can stop – or even destroy – the device. At least that's something."

"But not how," Yorgi spoke up, trying to get involved.

"Sword two." Akerman shushed them *"What was suspended at Ragnarok can be recreated."*

Minutes of silence followed, then, "Armageddon?" Hayden wondered. "Are they saying the swords could bring about Armageddon?"

"I don't think so," Karin's tinny voice warbled through the little speakerphone. "If you remember Odin purposely *prevented*

Armageddon at Ragnarok at that time because he knew all the gods would die, but he didn't stop it forever. He prevented it so, at a later date, he could return. And Ragnarok was all about the deaths of the gods."

Kinimaka let out a breath. "I don't get it."

"The inscription – the message – says we can actually bring about the true deaths of the gods, preventing them from ever returning, and ending this threat once and for all." She coughed. "Forever."

"It's a thought, but listen further," Akerman interrupted. "And so to the third sword. *What was written in time can be erased.* Speakerphone girl, I think this corroborates your theory."

"Yes it does," Karin said. "The prophecy of the gods' return was written in time."

"And the fourth bears further fruit." Akerman paused. *"That which is only sleeping can be destroyed forever."* He nodded to himself. "The gods."

"Two to go." Patterson rubbed his hands together excitedly.

"Well these two are real doozies," Akerman said with a touch of gloom. "I have *no* idea what they mean together. First – *take two swords each to the tombs and the Great Sword to the pit.* And the last one – *and channel the fires of your own destruction."* He stopped.

Drake glanced around, seeing blank faces and knitted brows. Karin remained quiet. At last Kinimaka said, "What the hell does *channel* mean?"

Drake shrugged. "I have no idea. But we're clearly missing one thing here. The seventh sword. Actually the Great Sword. Its inscription might tell us all we need to know."

"And . . ." Karin spoke up. "Count the swords. Two swords to each tomb makes six. My guess is the seventh has a different purpose."

"If they can destroy those tombs," Drake said. "And the device, I'm beginning to think it's not such a bad thing."

Hayden looked a little horrified. "You can't say that," she blurted. "You work for the US government."

Drake laughed. "Since when did that ever stop us blowing things up?"

"Think of it," Mai said. "The threat of the device *and* the gods – gone forever."

Professor Patterson moved to stand beside Akerman. "Consider this. Earth energy is heavily involved here somewhere. Pure elemental power. I believe that is what the doomsday device was all about in the first place?" He looked to his left.

Akerman nodded.

"The swords were made by someone who knew all about earth energy and how to negate an earth energy vortex. Alexander. He knew about the gods and the device but wasn't dumb enough to try and use it. He sought instead to counteract its effect. Wherever earth energy gathers in a vortex is called a sacred place, and, in many of them, you often find standing stones placed there by the ancients who had – shall we say – more time to contemplate these things. The three tombs are more than likely built atop the three most powerful in existence. But there are also *vile vortexes* around the world. Think – areas where ships and aircraft disappear, where radios and compasses don't work, where regular upheaval occurs in the earth's crust, where monsters are seen, where people exist perpetually in a state of unrest. There are many, many reasons why these swords could have been created."

"But the existence of earth energy has never been proven," Hayden insisted.

Patterson sighed as if he'd heard it all before. "You should read more. When I say 'mystical energy' you immediately qualify me as a wacko. If I was to tell you that I studied in *pseudoscience,* what would you say to that? Probably the same." He laughed. "There are literally hundreds of electro-magnetic aberrations around the world and no convincing explanation has ever been forthcoming."

"But there's still no proof."

"And there never will be. Do you think your stuffy academics want to be seen investigating events so far out of their comfort zone? The Daily Telegraph reported that the Austrians brought in local earth energy consultants to reduce the number of accidents on Austria's worst stretch of Autobahn. Roadside monoliths were erected to help restore the natural flow of earth energy. Since that day, over a stretch of two years, the number of accidents fell to zero.

But the biggest substantiation of earth energy came from none other than the great inventor himself and employee of Thomas Edison, Nikola Tesla. An electrical and mechanical engineer, physicist, and contributing designer to the modern AC electricity supply system, even he later became known as the 'mad scientist'. He found the earth to be, quote – 'literally alive with electrical vibrations'. Tesla believed that when lightning struck the ground it emitted mighty waves that went from one side of the earth to the other, a great tree of energy. 'The earth is a wonderful conductor,' he said. 'I could transmit unlimited amounts of power to any place on earth with virtually no loss'. He even said that it would be possible to split the planet apart by combining vibrations with the correct resonance of the earth itself. The earth's crust would vibrate so vigorously that it would rise and fall hundreds of feet, throwing rivers out of their beds, wrecking buildings and practically destroying civilization. And—" Patterson grinned. "He even tested his theory."

The entire team found their mouths agape. Kinimaka said, "Get outta here."

"He called it 'the art of telegeodynamics', described by him as a controlled earthquake. He stated that the invention could be used to the greatest effect in war."

"Of course," Mai breathed,

"Then there is HAARP," Patterson went on. "A huge $250 million project funded by the US Air Force and Navy, curiously located in the *same place* – Colorado Springs – that Nikola Tesla conducted his own earth energy experiments. They're studying the ionosphere."

Drake waved a hand. "Okay, you've convinced us, for now. But all this gets us no closer to finding out what Cayman and his backers are up to."

Then Karin's voice cut in. "This might. I have Secretary of Defense Gates on the line. And brace yourselves – I don't think it gets worse than this."

CHAPTER FORTY THREE

Karin patched Gates through on a conference call line. The Secretary of Defense's voice sounded strained, and Drake clearly heard the underlying exhaustion in the normally upbeat tones.

"The tombs in Iceland, Germany and Hawaii have come under fire," he reported. "Not only that, they are now in enemy hands. We still control the surrounds, but the tombs themselves are occupied by hostiles. God help us."

Hayden stepped closer to the phone. "Is it Cayman and his boss?"

"We don't know. They have hostages. We're having enough trouble convincing the local authorities that the hostages are the diversion, without wondering who ordered and executed the attacks."

"Leave that to us," Hayden said. Briefly, she reported their findings to date. Drake stated that it sounded like the 'three like minds in three tombs' translation was being followed to the letter. Gates sounded distracted, but seemed to take most of it in. When Hayden finished, Gates cleared his throat and took a moment to think before speaking.

"We're truly being handed our asses here," he said. "No one foresaw someone having the capability to organize a simultaneous strike against all three tombs and, not only that, but actually take them. You would think we'd have learned after the Kovalenko business." He paused. "But still, the serpents inside Capitol Hill distract those who would do good with their constant maneuverings and cunning trickeries. It gets harder every day to keep your eye on all the right balls, to keep them in motion. But now – now we will pay the price. It will take a miracle to get out of this one intact."

Gates ended with a brief call to arms. When he finished, the people in the little room, standing close the heart of ancient Babylon, in sand-scoured, sun-scorched Iraq, knew the heights to which they had to reach.

Higher than ever before.

"At least we now have a plan," Drake said. "We have three different tombs with three forces inside. These 'like-minded' men will be there too. We need to stop them activating that device by any means necessary."

Dahl moved to the table, staring down at the objects resting there. "And we'll take the swords with us."

CHAPTER FORTY FOUR

Jonathan Gates replaced the receiver in its cradle and put his head in his hands. It constantly amazed him how these egotistical sons of bitches found so many inventive ways to try to end the world. Or rule it. Or whatever twisted designs of supremacy these warped and pitiless individuals aspired to.

He sat back in his leather chair, staring intently at the Stars and Stripes that hung from a flag pole to the left of his desk. When he shifted, he could see its splendor repeated in the highly polished circular table where he held private meetings, not simply a symbol to him, but a warning to be heeded, a promise to be kept, a way of life to be maintained.

The photograph of his wife stared back intently from the right hand side of his desk. Not a day went by that he didn't miss her. Not a day went by that he didn't quell a rush of intense hatred for her murderer. He touched the frame lightly, a smile lifting the edges of his lips.

A moment later, one of the phones before him started to ring. As ever, even though a light was flashing, he had a moment's hesitation, making sure he picked up the right one. It was an internal line.

"Mr Secretary, I have a Sarah Moxley on the line. You recently approved her. She's hoping for a lunchtime meeting today, but asked that I stress this is not yet an interview. I have her on hold, sir."

Gates stared thoughtfully at the paintings above him. *Not an interview?* Was she trying to put him at ease or wind him up? It didn't matter, he could handle anything she threw at him. If only her timing had been better—

"Please tell her I have to reschedule."

"Yes, Mr Secretary."

Gates tapped the plastic phone, thinking. The attacks on the tombs carried with them a tiny sliver of silver lining. It appeared that now, General Stone wouldn't be able to execute his inane plan. The

President would be off the hook. As would Gates. But, he knew that with people like Stone, there was always going to be a next time. He made a decision and called Lauren Fox on a personal line.

"Things have changed," he said without preamble. "It doesn't have to happen."

"Jesus, are you kidding? I already made contact."

Gates frowned. "What sort of contact?"

"Not *that* sort. But—" the New Yorker paused, thinking hard. "The sort that, if cancelled, might seem suspect."

Damn. Gates reviewed his thinking one more time, but kept coming back to that old adage – *don't poke the beast.* There simply wasn't any gain in provoking a situation that didn't yet exist. Some men he knew did like to gather dirt, but it wasn't Gates' style.

"Sorry, Lauren. The fallout won't be as bad as if you went through with it, surely."

"It might be as bad. And you wouldn't get another chance."

She was right, but Gates just couldn't do it. "Abort the plan," he said. "I'll speak to you in a few days."

Now he stood up and paced his office, black polished shoes treading the plush blue carpet in the footsteps of the men who came before him. The pressure of office bore down so hard it felt like all the weight of the White House was upon him. His team, led by Hayden Jaye, were in the fight of their lives and separated. Even now, they fought an unknown enemy without a clear plan of action. The world was on the brink.

Again.

Damn these fucking tombs, he thought. *They should all be blown to hell.*

Quickly, he made himself calm down. Poured a glass of water. Stared without seeing out of the window. Then he called his secretary back.

"Come to think of it," he said. "I need the distraction. Call Miss Moxley back and arrange that lunchtime appointment."

"Yes, Mr Secretary."

*

The catering staff brought bottles of water, sandwiches and cakes minutes before Sarah Moxley was due to arrive. As soon as the Post reporter appeared, his secretary sent her through.

Gates rose and shook hands, remembering the touch of her skin from before. He invited her to sit at the round table. "Sorry for the formal setting," he said. "I don't have too long, Miss Moxley."

"Call me Sarah. Something still going on?"

"Always," he repeated his words of a few days ago. Gates picked at his food as she talked, moving half a sandwich around his plate like a general arranging battle formations, but he listened well. Moxley talked about her work, her life and the friends she had died beside, but she didn't ask a single question that put him on alert. Gates found himself interested, relaxing around her, and enjoyed the sight of her winning smile. But there were gulfs between them. He was fifteen years her senior. He was a widower. She was a reporter. He was sworn to this office in more ways than one.

But still . . .

When their time came to an end, Gates rose and smiled. "Good to see you again, Miss Moxley."

"I'm sure." She flicked her hair, redhead locks catching a ray of sunshine and holing every ounce of his attention. "Until next time?"

"The interview? Yes, we can arrange that."

"Who said anything about an interview?"

Gates stared as she left the room, cursing inwardly that he had to send her away so soon, cursing the old gods and the megalomaniacs and every other piece of self-important shit that made good men worry about the safety of others.

CHAPTER FORTY FIVE

Alicia Myles' feet barely touched the ground before she was whisked from the airport to the stylish Hotel Vier Jahreszeiten Kempinski in the heart of Munich, asked to wear a bikini by a very attentive Lomas, and taken down to the indoor heated pool, one of the very few inside any luxury hotel in the city.

Alicia was more than a little shocked, but she didn't ask questions, expecting that Lomas would explain when they got settled. But the sight of the biker gang, sprawled in their speedos around the rectangular, beige-tiled, blue-lit swimming pool stopped her short.

"What the fuck, Lomas?"

The big biker leader pointed to a far corner where, before a huge oval mirror, two women were receiving some kind of spa treatment. From the bright tattoos on their shoulders Alicia recognized the two as Whipper and Dirty Sarah.

"Did they *brainwash* you idiots whilst I was gone?" When Alicia left to help Drake, Lomas and the gang had been barely comfortable in the posh hotel the US had stumped up for, every single one of them wondering aloud if it was time to hit the road. Now, they showed all the signs of setting up a permanent camp.

"Look." Lomas pointed out Tiny, the enormous Harley rider, sprawled out over a rattan lounger, massive legs and arms touching the floor on all sides and snoring like a grizzly with hay fever.

Alicia took a deep breath. "Well?"

Lomas just shrugged his big shoulders. "The staff hate us. They're not sure whether to bow or run a mile. Let the boys have their sport for a day or two."

Alicia relaxed. "And then we're hitting the road?"

"Is there another way?"

"Nope!" Alicia ran and cannonballed into the still pool, splashing water up over the immaculate sides and across the nearest loungers. Fat Bob and Knuckler sat up complaining. Laid-Back Lex, the truest contradictory biker name the Englishwoman had ever heard, leapt to his feet and threw some abuse at her. Ribeye, the groups Vegetarian, shook his head in disgust. Alicia trod water and splashed them all some more.

Lomas, not an accomplished swimmer, thrashed around beside her. "Meant to say, your biker name was decided while you were off saving the world."

"It was? What is it? Believe me, Lomas, it better not be something prissy."

The biker didn't answer immediately, not a good sign. But then Alicia noticed him staring at her breasts. "Later." She swatted him. "Just tell me the goddamn name."

"Ah, well we voted on . . . Taz."

"What?"

"Taz. You know, the Tasmanian Devil from Australia. Carnivore. Strong bite. Hard fighters. Can turn crazy at the drop of a hat."

"I'm not sure I like it. You think I'm an Australian animal? And I thought biker names were supposed to be contrary to your character."

"Not all of them. It depends on your strength of character. Yours," Lomas grinned, "just shone right through."

"Taz?" Alicia thought about it. She didn't know a great deal about the Tasmanian Devil, but Lomas made it sound good. "I suppose . . ."

"Good, now come here." Lomas caught her in his muscular arms and held on tight. Alicia allowed herself to be hugged, just for a minute. A sense of peace settled over her, accompanied by the onset of dreadful, repressed memories. They only came when she relaxed. They were the reason she kept on moving, fighting, somehow always in motion. But the problem was rapidly becoming clearer – she couldn't stay in action for the rest of her life.

Dare she let the memories back in?

The way forward was confrontation. *Funny,* she thought, *how I love it in real life, but can't face down my past.*

"You okay?" Alicia heard Lomas' voice and focused. The biker had pulled away from her and was staring into her distant, stormy eyes.

"Old demons." She rubbed her temples hard. "Won't go away."

"Ah, I have those. Maybe someday we should swap horror stories."

Alicia fixed him with a contemplative stare. "Maybe."

Lomas doggy-paddled to the shallow end of the pool. Alicia watched him for a moment, grinning, then followed. The other bikers were all laid out in comfortable repose, some snoring, some flicking through magazines, others gazing out the windows as if they wanted to be out there, grinding up those gritty roads. Laid-Back Lex being the only exclusion, the young hothead sat glaring at everything as if trying to will it all to catch fire.

Through the half-open door, wafting from the kitchens, came the smell of newly cooked food. Alicia felt her mouth water. It had been some time since she'd sat down to a restaurant meal. *Maybe tonight,* she thought. *Just Lomas and me.* But the smell of freshly cooked food always caused that old vision to rear its ugly head, the one that had happened so many times it had become merely an event, each time indistinguishable to the one before, as her mother laid out her father's meal, still steaming, and her father reached out, not for his knife and fork, but for that already half empty glass of amber liquid.

"Just a sneaky one to shake off the day," he used to whisper, whilst trying to smile at her, not quite making it seem real.

Alicia blocked it out. The ringing of a cell phone intruded after a second and Alicia realized it was hers. Not only that, it was the tone she reserved for Drake. A little track by Pink called *Trouble.*

"Shit." She climbed out of the pool, dripping wet, and walked over to her bag. "What the fuck's happened now?"

"I believe you once said to call you for the next apocalypse?" It was Hayden using Drake's phone.

"You're fu—"

"I know, I know. You and Lomas – biker style. We've lost the tombs, Alicia."

The Englishwoman clammed up as Hayden went on to explain the most recent events. When she had finished, Alicia immediately spoke up.

"You want me back in Iraq?"

"We're thrashing out a plan. Between us we have to cover all three tombs. And Alicia, you're already in Germany."

It hadn't occurred to her until now, but Munich wasn't too far from Singen. She immediately grew suspicious. "Who signed off on this hotel a few days ago?"

Hayden was quiet for a second. "I did."

"Through Gates no doubt," Alicia grumbled. "That man has more manipulations up his sleeve than a banker."

"He would, he's a top-flight politician. And it's called *foresight.* Clever maneuvering of your forces. A good preparation. All much better words than manipulation, don't you think?"

"Whatever. Look, are you actually asking Lomas and the boys to help raid the Singen tomb? Cos they ain't military, you know?"

"We're spread pretty thin, and don't try to tell me they haven't had some experience. You would have some local military back up. But all you really have to do is get to Cayman and neutralize him. Oh, and get the swords in there."

"What swords?"

"We'll courier two swords to Singen airport. You need to collect them before you go in."

"Should I ask why?"

"It's a long frickin' story." Hayden sighed deeply. "And we don't even know how to use 'em. *If* we need to use 'em at all." She cursed. "We're way behind on this one, Alicia, and with no time."

"I'll ask them." Alicia disconnected and looked around. To a person, the biker gang stared hard at her. She sat down on the front edge of a lounger and laid it out. No one interrupted, but when she had finished, the first outburst came, predictably, from Laid-back Lex.

"Why would we wanna do that and leave this place?"

"This place is a reward for the last time we caused mayhem," Alicia reminded them. "Think of what might be next?"

"A grave," one of the older bikers mumbled. "Or a hospital."

Alicia nodded. "That's possible. This is a dangerous mission. The men who took the tombs are at least military trained."

"It would get us back on the road though," Whipper compromised. "Some nice open roads between here and Singen."

"You really wanna help out the government?" Tiny glared around. "Not like they ever bin good to us."

Trace and Fat Bob murmured an agreement. Dirty Sarah put down a nail file and wiped her hands on a wet-wipe. “Lomas? What’s your take?”

The gang leader cleared his throat. “If this were personal, I’d decide. If it were honor, I’d decide. But this ain’t for gang respect or credit. This ain’t like goin’ after Lisa and makin’ her pay for what she did . . .”

As he paused, Alicia reflected that she didn’t know much about Lomas and Lisa yet, only snippets of what her boyfriend had told her about his ex and how she had split to ride with a rival gang. Maybe she was his ‘old demon’.

“This has to be your own decision,” Lomas told them. “This ain’t gang business.”

Alicia nodded, respecting him for it. Truth be told, if Lomas had ordered them all to go, she would have protested. She listened to the rumblings and the moaning, the unruffled and the perturbed. But at the end of the day, they were a biker gang and, to a member, they wanted that open road.

Knuckler summed it up. “No harm in hitting the open road for a few days, eh mates? Then we’ll see if we fancy kickin’ some military arse an’ earning a year on Miami Beach. Ha, ha,” he cackled.

Alicia winced as overwhelming support rose for Knuckler, not quite sure how she was going to translate the ‘ifs’ and ‘maybes’ back to Hayden and Drake. When the guys started to rise, she turned her head. No way did she want to see half-a-dozen oiled-up bikers wearing trunks climbing off their sun beds.

CHAPTER FORTY SIX

Kinimaka watched sadly as the team made the decision to pair off. Memories of Vienna revisited him, of the night he had spent down at the bar with Alicia and Belmonte. Alicia had told him that her father used to be a drunk and beat her mother into unconsciousness at least twice a week. Belmonte had confessed that losing his protégé – Emma – had truly broken him. He would not work as a thief again for as long as he lived.

And the next day he had died saving Drake's life.

Now Kinimaka stared through cheerless eyes as the team decided to separate, each pair heading off to fight their own little apocalypse. Dahl and Akerman would travel to Iceland. Drake and Mai would go to Moscow, retrieve the Great Sword, then return here to Babylon, faithfully following Alexander's instructions. He would accompany Hayden to Hawaii. Their time was almost up.

"Stay in touch, and keep checking with Karin," Hayden told them. "She's the liaison for all our information. Gates will try to be on hand. And guys . . . let's all return to Washington in one piece, huh?"

"The minute anyone gets a shred of information," Dahl said. "And I'm talking mainly about you, Drake, with that last sword – let us know."

"Course I will," Drake said. "Once we kick Zanko's grandma's arse."

"We should watch out for Zanko and Razin," Yorgi said. "They are not done yet."

"I feel bad about sending Alicia and her new friends after Cayman himself," Hayden fretted. "But there was no other way. She'll make all the difference to that assault team."

"One thing's for certain," Mai said quietly. "Whether we want her to or not, she's most likely to blow up the entire tomb."

Everyone laughed. It was a poignant moment, not one reserved for Alicia, but one that encompassed them all. Amidst the brief silence more than simple respect, honor and concern passed between them. Something far deeper.

Kinimaka said nothing. Dahl made a point of inflating everyone's ego. Drake walked around purposefully, finalizing plans, but Kinimaka read the uncertainty in his eyes.

This time it was different. This time they didn't know what they were going up against or how to fight it.

We're going into Hell without a preacher, Kinimaka thought. *God help us lest we burn. And God help the rest of the world if we do.*

CHAPTER FORTY SEVEN

Zak Block loved the fact that Hawaii time ran twelve hours behind his own. It almost felt as if he were travelling back in time, enabling him to usher in the new reign of the Shadow Elite that much sooner. It was an illusion, he knew, but a comforting one.

The midday Hawaiian sun beat down hard on the airport tarmac. Being a first-class passenger, he was offered a lei and dutifully bent his head, smiling at the pretty grass-skirted girl as she spoke a greeting and wished him a pleasant stay on the island of Oahu.

"Oh, there's no doubt there's going to be a little fun for everyone," he said and headed over to his driver. The man lowered the card he was holding and showed him to a white sedan with blacked out windows.

So far, so good, he thought. The team had always known Block would be joining them inside the tomb and had spent many hours deliberating over the best way to get him inside. In the end it came down to a floating strategy with many alternatives. They could only predict the authorities' responses up to a certain point. After that, it was all conjecture and chance.

Block was driven around Diamond Head, with the sparkling blue of the Pacific to his right, and off the main road. Presently they transferred to an off-road vehicle, and the driver proceeded to bounce his way down a barely used dirt track. The man apologized, but Block barely heard. He was already tired of not being the world's decision maker, and filled his head only with visions of what he would do once he regained that power. He was a coiled snake waiting to strike and clamp his jaws on anyone who stood in his way.

They skirted three lava tubes, the first two of which were being monitored by the HPD. The third, somewhat further away, looked clear and it wouldn't matter if it was under CCTV surveillance. They wanted to get a man in – not get many men out.

Block accepted the pack offered by the driver and took a moment to check his email. Cayman was already inside the Singen tomb and Nicolas Denney was approaching its Icelandic equivalent. A message at this point would be bad news. But there were none. He sent a quick, unnecessary text, alerting the second Hawaiian cell that he'd arrived, warning them to prepare for battle.

The trek was arduous, but worth every laborious step. Block was helped down from the high ledge and, for the first time, observed the carved stone face of Wrath.

"Spectacular, isn't it?" The driver grinned.

Block ignored him, taking a moment for himself. After a while, he waved the man on, listening to his spiel about how the traps had been counteracted and how relatively easy it had been for a well-armed, well-motivated force to take the tomb. A little further on and they passed through Greed, the little, precious pots of riches now removed to prevent distraction and death. After that came Lust, and Block slowed despite himself, staggered and a little daunted by the extensive amount of carved and painted flesh on display.

"Those gods." The driver whistled, staying close to Block. "They sure knew how to throw a party, am I right?"

"Please," Block spoke just the once, expecting the man to understand. Luckily for him, he did and shut his mouth. In silence, they traversed the chamber and soon passed through Envy and Gluttony. It was after this level that the team commander waited for him.

"Sir, all is prepared." He came forward and gave a slight bow. "If you proceed to the ledge up there—" he pointed to a curved stone wall running around the top of the next rise. "You will see all that you came for."

Block braced himself and picked his way carefully to the wall. The sight that greeted his eyes beat everything he had yet seen and more, it was the most awe-inspiring, incredible thing he had ever seen in his life.

Odin's chair. The gargantuan, impossibly carved slab of obsidian hung from the cliff face before him, positioned over a bottomless abyss. An ancient silence filled the place, demanding deference, crawling and shimmering with an unseen, latent power. Only poised here, bowed by its glory, could he truly accept it.

"Now," he said. "Now I believe."

The team leader had walked up behind him. "I know exactly what you mean, sir. After witnessing something like this you start to believe anything's possible."

Block nodded, impressed with the man's insight. "I will show the governments of the world what is possible," he said. "Get everything ready, because after today there will be no government, no dictatorship, no insolent warlord, that will not bow down to me."

CHAPTER FORTY EIGHT

Not long after Zak Block cleared customs, Hayden and Kinimaka heard the wheels of their private jet squeal and rumble as they hit Hawaiian asphalt. Kinimaka mumbled a little prayer when they landed, not in lieu of their safe landing, but for returning safely again to his homeland. The aircraft had passed close to Diamond Head on its final approach, giving the two SPEAR agents a brief glimpse at the ongoing operation inside the depressed cone. Hayden contacted the local agents and captains in charge whilst in flight, ensuring they would be ready for action sooner rather than later, and smoothing over the inevitable rough corners.

Kinimaka stared out the window as the jet taxied in. "Mixed feelings." He touched the window. "Good to be back, bad to be here. Know what I mean?"

"Implicitly."

"You think Cayman and his buddies will switch on that device?"

"If they do, we will stop them."

"Sure. We ain't never faced a bad guy we can't put down." Kinimaka, seeing they were still alone, at least for the moment, placed an arm around her, conscious not to transfer its full weight to her. "And then, maybe we'll get a break."

Hayden turned and kissed him. "Sounds good to me. This damn job's becoming more intense than even I imagined. Good job we have Romero and Smyth on board now. We may even tie down a bit of vacation time."

"They say Hawaii's good this time of year."

"Really?" Hayden squeezed his knee. "I never would have guessed. You don't want to see Kono? We could spend a few days in LA."

"Hold that thought." Kinimaka clicked his tongue. "My sister and I should have at least one thousand miles of air between us when holding a discussion. Especially one where she tells me her plan to come see Mom again."

"She ran away," Hayden remembered. "It was a long time ago, Mano. She'll have changed."

"She broke Mom's heart and didn't care. I remember. We didn't know . . . anything."

At that moment, the co-pilot popped his head around the cabin door. "Hey folks, you're clear to disembark. Usual fast track checks in the terminal, then a car will be waiting to take you to the base."

Hayden surprised Kinimaka by kissing him once more. "Don't worry," she said, even more stunning up close. "It will work itself out."

She rose, grabbed her pack and strode down the aisle. Kinimaka hurried after her, a little bedazzled, then realized he'd forgotten his own pack and had to run back. They clattered down the juddering airplane steps and entered the terminal, greeted by a blast of cool air.

Kinimaka cast around, saw the relevant booth and headed straight for the stern looking man seated inside. Once they had presented their papers, the two were ushered straight through to the central concourse, the inner hub of Honolulu International. Kinimaka stopped to view the high-ceilinged, wide, airy space, basking in the sunlight that streamed in through the windows.

"Ahh," he said. "I'm relaxed already."

Shops stood to either side as the pair made their way toward the exit. A DFS Galleria and a Kona Brewing Company, the latter offering one of his favorite brews – the legendary Fire Rock Pale Ale – the sight so appealing he actually began to drift in that direction.

Hayden turned to him and spoke with a hint of warning. "Mano—"

Masked men burst through the doors in front of her. The car they had all piled out of idled at the curb in the public drop-off area, doors flung wide. Kinimaka counted five men before he yelled a warning and tackled Hayden around the waist, dragging her behind an artful display of Maui Divers jewelry exhibits. The leader of SPEAR tumbled ungainly across the floor and ended ass up as the bullets started to fly.

Glass shattered around them, showering down over their bodies. Hayden yelped as a sharp piece sliced the seat of her pants.

"Fucker got me in the ass!" She unholstered her Glock and disengaged the safety, dropping as low as her body would allow. The terminal erupted with noise, screaming and yelling, and the sound of an alarm. People scattered in all directions. Children were dragged into shops or lifted and shielded by parents' bodies before being tucked out of sight. Luggage slid and tumbled across the floor.

The masked men advanced slowly. More shots rang out and an airport security guard twisted and fell. The front window of DFS Galleria exploded into tiny shards. The sound of crying rose above the braying of the alarm.

Kinimaka took a fleeting look and fired off a shot. It went wide, but gave the invaders pause. Two dropped to their knees, covering. The other three peeled off around the side of the Duty Free. Hayden fired, her bullet hammering into a wall millimeters above her target's head.

"What is this?" Kinimaka hissed. "Is this for us?"

"I don't know," Hayden said. "But it's sure holding us up."

More airport security guards ran along the concourse. Hayden waved them to safety, showing her badge. She turned to Kinimaka. "They've taken a defensive formation," she observed. "A bit of mayhem, then digging in. I'm not liking the look of this, Mano."

"Agreed. I'm too big to hide behind this pillar much longer anyway."

Hayden switched her position, coming around the other side of the display cases. For half a second her enemy was in her sights. She fired and he fell, gun clattering across the polished floor. His companion didn't flinch, but trained his gun on her, then let loose a hail of lead on full auto.

"Shit!"

Hayden literally had nowhere to go. The deadly stream started at the exhibits, destroying them, and swung slowly in her direction. She hurdled a pile of glass, but came up against the side of a shop window. The flow of bullets drifted inexorably closer.

Kinimaka fell on his stomach, gun out in front and held in both hands, firing, but the shooter was hidden from him, his body blocked by a three-foot tree planter. Men fired back at him, their shots skipping off the floor three inches to the right of his body. He rolled back to safety, opening his mouth to shout—

—then saw Hayden shoot out the bottom of the glass window. Fragments cascaded like little bits of diamond, catching the sunlight, and Hayden dived right through them, rolling into the shop as the lead river blasted past.

Kinimaka let out a sigh of relief. He heard the shooter changing mags and rose a little to take advantage, but another shot pinned him down. This was a good team, working for each other, but they couldn't do this forever. The airport guards and cops were assembling down toward the Diamond Head concourse, quite a group. He looked toward Hayden and saw she was trying to convey a message.

Hand signals. No phones necessary. She was going through the back of the shop and aiming to take them by surprise. Kinimaka nodded and surveyed the shop to the other side. The Duty Free was open plan, different to all the other shops, and might not have a back exit. If he tried and failed he'd be stuck. Beyond that was a Starbucks.

Hmmm . . .

It was in the hands of God. Kinimaka exploded out of hiding, sprinting across the exposed area in seconds, and hurled himself forward as shots began to track him. He hit the ground hard, rolled, and came up again, barreling past a couple who thought it prudent to crouch down in the middle of the concourse, before running into the coffee shop. An easy chair gave him the bounce he needed to lift off and clear the counter in one. A barista, kneeling behind the display cabinet, squealed, making him jump and shout back. The space behind the counter was narrow, the stockroom further on crammed with boxes, syrups and metal shelves full to bursting. He flew past, listening hard, hoping Hayden was waiting. A cascade of white plastic lids toppled off the shelves in his wake. At last. He reached the end and spied a door.

Thank you Great Kahuna, he thought. Then he paused, collected his wits and pushed.

CHAPTER FORTY NINE

Kinimaka paused as the back of his enemy came into view. The man sported a buzz cut, a padded jacket and cargo pants. He clutched a rifle, aimed low, and carried several other weapons thrust into a utility belt around his waist. He was staring at a black wristwatch as Kinimaka pushed gently at the door.

He saw Hayden step out across the other side of the concourse opposite him, separated by hundreds of yards and four well-armed killers. She pointed her gun and yelled. Kinimaka gave it a second and then did likewise, hoping to cause confusion.

But these men were trained. The one nearest Hayden lifted his gun arm calmly, taking aim. The one closest to Kinimaka turned carefully, bringing his weapon around.

"Stop!" Kinimaka cried.

The gunman suddenly swiveled hard and fired, catching the Hawaiian off guard. Chunks of green and white signage erupted from a nearby wall. Kinimaka returned fire instantly, dropping the shooter where he crouched. His body shuddered and jolted back into his partner, knocking the man's weapon from his hand, but also making Hayden's shot go wide. The man went for a side holster. Hayden didn't miss the second time.

That leaves two. If he advanced here he would be totally exposed. Quickly Kinimaka ducked back inside the shop and sprinted through to the front. The barista squealed again, but at least had the good sense to cover her mouth. Kinimaka came around the front, just as one of the shooters advanced into the main concourse, rifle packed firmly into his shoulder. The Hawaiian could only duck and roll as the man opened fire.

He slid across the gleaming floor, stopping against a carpet. Rounds traced his movements, loud in the otherwise heavy silence. Something nicked the heel of his boot. He scrambled behind an abandoned airport electric vehicle, feeling ridiculously huge huddled behind it. Bullets smashed into it, spinning it one hundred and eighty degrees, actually opening up a firing line for Kinimaka as his opponent concentrated on blasting apart the vehicle.

Half a second, two shots, and the fourth assailant collapsed with two holes in the center of his skull. Kinimaka kissed his fingers and pressed them against the shattered side of the little buggy.

Thank you.

Now guards and cops hurtled down the concourse, shouting and screaming into radios. Kinimaka waved at them to slow down. There was still one more gunman. They didn't slow. The Hawaiian cursed, feeling the huge pressure of losing so much precious time on their journey to the Diamond Head tomb, and the crushing responsibility of trying to save these men's lives bearing down on him. He couldn't see the last man.

And where was Hayden?

Praying that his luck held, he dug out his cell and hit her number. The call was answered immediately.

"I'm inside the shop, near the front."

Kinimaka squinted. He could see her shape now as she peered through the open door. "Any idea where our last man went?"

"I have a good idea," Hayden sputtered. "Asshole's gone to ground, playing for time. This *is* for us, Mano. A delaying tactic."

"Some freaking tactic."

"Yeah. Look, tell those cops we have to get outta here. They'll have to handle the mole."

Kinimaka hesitated. "Are you sure?" He hated leaving anyone in harm's way.

"I have to be. World's safety's at stake. Whoever seized that tomb ain't just gonna wait until we get there."

Kinimaka waved one of the cops forward and explained the situation. The man conferred for a second, then pointed further down the concourse, near the wing that led to the Ewa concourse, past a huge red Avis sign. 'Exit'.

Kinimaka berated himself. He should have known that. "I'll join you," he told Hayden and pressed the red button. Pausing only to check his Glock for ammo, he ran hard toward Hayden, a juggernaut of solid flesh and muscle, all six senses firmly concentrated on his surroundings. One click, one shuffle, and he would hit the floor.

But nothing happened. Their quarry had to be well-hidden by now, probably expecting them to shut the airport down. But the SPEAR team had precedence here, and their mission was even more important than an offensive against Hawaii's largest airport.

Hayden looked to the skies as they burst out through the doors. "Goddamn, I hope we're not too late."

CHAPTER FIFTY

Drake and Mai took Yorgi and Patterson with them on the short hop to Moscow. This time, Karin paved the way through Jonathan Gates to guarantee that local reinforcements were committed to the op. Karin revealed that President Coburn had actually spoken with the Russian Prime Minister to help get things moving. A group of Russian Spetsnaz troops were on hand as Drake stepped from the warm interior of the plane out into a brisk Russian chill. Their commander had already been briefed of the operation's importance, and gave his full cooperation in perfect English, before standing aside and waiting expectantly with his men.

"This address," Drake held out a piece of paper. "Is where Zoya lives. It's just outside Moscow. Do we have transport?"

An hour later, they came to a stop along a country road, about a mile before the concealed gateway that led to Zoya's house. Aerial photographs received by the Russian commander's tablet computer showed a heavily forested area, inside which lay a rudimentary house, haphazard in shape as if it had had several impromptu extensions added through the years. The team was expecting heavy resistance.

As the driver brought their vehicle to a stop, the commander wordlessly handed over his tablet to Drake. On the screen was a recent picture of Zoya, Zanko's grandmother.

Even Mai did a double-take. Drake whistled. "Fuck, she's even bigger than Zanko."

"This is not a good woman," the commander, named Svechnykov, told them. "She has come under suspicion of the politsiya many times, and is also on Interpol's 'persons of interest' list. But nothing sticks to her."

"I know the type," Mai said, with a little shudder. "All too well."

Drake had been thinking hard about the assault. They had enough troops for a three-pronged attack. With no time to waste, they started deploying men. A stiff breeze whipped up and rustled the trees, tall sentinels observing and whispering their age-old secrets.

"The sword," Drake said as the men divided. "Is imperative. Everything else is secondary. Even Zoya."

By his side, Mai checked her gear as religiously as ever, but Drake noticed the faraway look on her face. The sooner they got this Babylon business out of the way the better, then Mai and he could concentrate on her problems. *Assuming,* he thought morosely. *They all survived this time.*

They stepped lightly, skirting the road and trees, coming upon Zoya's gate within minutes. Drake motioned toward the 'plastics' man. This was a full-scale assault. He smiled. There would be no pissing about with lock picks.

Ten seconds passed and a controlled explosion signified the start of the raid. Drake hugged the inside wall for a few meters before following the tree line just off the main driveway, heading for the front of the house. Zoya's hideaway sat deep inside the property, shielded from all but the most insistent of prying eyes. For about one minute there was almost total silence, just the swishing and creasing of men's fatigues and packs, the barest sound of boots skimming the undergrowth.

Then, all hell descended upon them. A barrage of bullets whickered through the trees a millisecond before the clattering tumult of gunfire rang out. Drake hit the dirt as a confetti of shredded leaves and branches fluttered around them. Mai rolled behind a wide, gnarly trunk. It soon became obvious that the shots were coming from above. *The defenders were in the trees.*

The Spetsnaz returned fire. Immediately, several bodies crashed through the green canopy, bouncing off the floor with the sound of shattering bones. A Russian soldier took a bullet to the shoulder and twisted around, cursing in pain. Drake sprayed the treetops, eliciting another scream. He saw bodies moving among the trees, so the defenders were also mobile. The tree growth was so dense it was enabling the men to jump easily from branch to branch.

"Fucking monkeys," the Spetsnaz commander murmured, and loosed a deadly salvo, his bullets creating a new hole through the foliage to the blue skies. "Least we can't hit one of our own."

With that, the soldiers rose and fired several volleys. Drake and Mai scrambled hastily past the skirmish, staying low. Two soldiers followed. Mai was about to break from behind another tree when the ground before her feet started to crack, crumbling vertically down. Her body swayed. Drake dived and grabbed her around the waist, wrenching her back. They landed hard, bruised and scraped, but alive.

One of the soldiers whistled, speaking in Russian. Drake pushed away from Mai and crawled over. The Japanese woman had almost tumbled into a crude trap, a handmade pit with a forest of sharpened stakes at its bottom. Instantly, Drake transmitted a warning to Svechnykov. The word went out – proceed cautiously.

As they advanced, a six-foot high palisade of sharpened timbers appeared through the trees ahead, the barrier effectively turning Zoya's home into a fort. Before Drake could take stock, a thud signified the landing of an enemy right behind him. He whirled to see Mai step up and whip a knife across the man's throat, then force him down to bleed out in the undergrowth.

The heavy sound of gunfire reverberated behind and all around them. Drake nodded as the two Russian soldiers pulled out grenades and motioned toward the fence. "Do it."

Making himself small, he felt Mai burrow in beside him. A loud explosion tore apart the air. Bits of tree and bark, fencing and soil thudded down all around. When Drake glanced up, he saw a ragged hole had been blasted through the palisade and, further on, he could see the front of the structure that Zoya called home. The windows were shuttered, the door barred. Nothing showed itself near the house.

The soldiers crept forward. More projectiles thudded into the trunks of trees and mounds of dirt around them, and Drake saw that the tree-defenders had moved closer. He cleared them out again, spraying indiscriminately until several began to tumble. Then he rose and moved fast.

"Go!"

As they neared the shattered palisade, a mid-size guard tower became visible, positioned off to their right. Drake swore. He had seen official military compounds worse defended. They saw movement – one man taking and returning fire to his left. The other team had advanced that far then. Using the distraction, Drake inched along, climbing carefully over the jagged bits of fencing and advancing further into Zoya's nightmare compound.

Drake tuned in all six senses and called on every ounce of his training to monitor all directions. Mai moved soundlessly a step behind, now fully engaged. He trusted her judgment to the max, even when she was at half speed. She uttered no words of warning—

—and Drake's heart almost stopped when the buried mine detonated a few feet before him. The explosion hurled an unlucky soldier high into the air, limbs suddenly as limp as a ragdoll's, discharging an energy wave riddled with fragments to every side. Drake was partially sheltered by a tree, but even the second soldier who stood out in the open only suffered partial wounds. Zoya's landmine was of old Russian manufacture, and built primarily to take out the poor man who triggered it rather than those around him.

Drake cursed and quickly surveyed the land to the left and right. A barely distinct channel ran in both directions, following the line of the palisade.

"Got it." Mai stepped to the right. Drake nodded, rose and let loose his weapon, aiming along the left-hand curve, detonating a string of land mines. Multiple explosions made the ground tremble. Plumes and mushroom clouds of dirt and foliage blasted higher than the trees. The Russian commander appeared through the dense foliage, running hard, his men only yards behind.

"Crazy bitch!" He spat, wiping his brow. "Who would have thought . . ."

Drake stepped away and kept moving. It was the only way to stay alive. Stay sharp. "You've clearly never met her grandson."

They moved as fast as they dared. Drake saw the second team lob a grenade at the guard tower in the aftermath of the landmine explosion, toppling it, and running through the debris, closing in on the house. He saw one man caught in a snare loop, the rope snapping around his ankle and lifting him upside down into the air, swaying helplessly until someone either found a way to release him or a sniper took him out. In another second, a horrible clash and scream from his left made him pause.

"Mantrap," the Spetsnaz commander breathed. "We saw two more back there." He barked an order for one of his men to attend the victim, then turned back to Drake. "We have entered a house of horrors, no?"

"Yes."

They rushed to the edge of the foliage that ended six feet from Zoya's front door. Drake's forehead creased. Was Zoya even here? He pointed out the shutters and door, indicating a multiple strike. The second team was about to hit the side of the house. Hopefully the third team was striking at the rear, but Drake didn't have time to check as the Spetsnaz soldiers assailed their target.

Then the front door opened with a crash, literally flying back and smashing against its hinges, before tearing half away and hanging lop-sided. From out of the doorway emerged a king-size nightmare – Zoya, the grandmother of Zanko, almost seven feet tall and wider than the door itself, cut-off vest showing arms that were thicker than some men's legs, a machine gun held easily in each paw-like hand.

"You fuckers!" she screamed. *"Mother—"*

The rest of her rant was lost as two Spetsnaz soldiers closed in on her. Drake cursed silently. They should have just shot and wounded this malicious brute, but chose instead to take her alive. It was their mistake. Drake never would have believed it if he hadn't seen it, but Zanko's crazy grandmother simply *batted* both special forces soldiers aside with her enormous arms. It must have been like being hit by a tree-trunk. Both men flew back, landing hard, rolling and then lay without moving. The woman boomed out a laugh reminiscent of some jungle animal's distress call and swiveled both machine guns around.

"Oh shit!"

Men scattered like leaves in a storm. The heavy thudding berserker sound of high-caliber machine gun fire sent Drake's heart into his mouth. Zoya's cackling screech was even louder. "This is me!" she bellowed. "This is what I was made for!"

Even the trees shuddered under fire. One younger specimen groaned and collapsed, blasted apart, toppling in the direction of the house and smashing against the roof. Drake saw two men risk a glance out of their hiding places, only to be torn to bits. He sat with his back against the thick base of an old oak, reloading as splinters chipped off the tree and flew past him. Mai knelt between his legs, facing him.

"Didn't see this one coming," she said.

"Yeah, but we should have."

Drake fired blindly around one side of the oak, Mai the other. Drake could see the Russian Spetsnaz commander pinned down behind a log, its entire length being chewed away by bullets. Drake sneaked a look around the tree and could barely believe his eyes. Zoya stood like a grotesque statue, unmoved, bleeding from at least three places, rock-solid and radical, the very expression of fanaticism taken to the extreme.

He looked back at Mai, barely believing his next words. "Grenade."

To her credit she only blinked twice. Then she unhooked a Russian-made grenade, pulled a suspicious face at it, and lobbed it around the big tree.

"Let's hope it works."

Drake followed its flight, feeling hopeful, but Zoya spotted it immediately and roared as if the very noise would create a barrier. She let her guns drop to her side and lumbered toward the grenade as it flew at her.

Then she drew back her foot . . .

Drake gaped. "Fuck's sake! She's going to volley—"

. . . and kicked out. Zoya's giant foot flew at the spinning grenade so powerfully her boot soared off, arcing up among the trees.

But she missed the grenade.

Drake ducked back in. Zoya's elephantine bellow drowned out even the grenade's initial blast, but ended abruptly as fragments shredded her body. A mammoth crash and sudden silence led to a dozen men popping their heads up.

Drake primed his gun. "Russian football." He shook his head. "Never was up to much."

CHAPTER FIFTY ONE

Drake, Mai and the Spetsnaz soldiers emerged warily, eyes fixed on the unmoving carcass blocking the way to the door. Everyone waited expectantly, but when no further defenders appeared, the commander looked to Drake.

"Do you think she guarded the house alone?"

Drake took a moment to reload and re-jig himself. "I wouldn't be surprised."

Mai crept toward the door. "Time to enter the monster's lair."

"Well, when you put it that way." Drake covered her back, eyes flitting everywhere. But it wasn't just enemy soldiers he was looking for, it was more of Zoya's booby traps. When they approached the mammoth body, Mai stopped, staring down in awe.

"She was three times my size."

"But she fell as hard as any extremist." Drake sniffed. "Just like Zanko will if I ever see him again."

They stepped over the body with the Spetsnaz soldiers coming up behind. Mai started up the steps and Drake almost put out a hand to stop her. A sudden vision had assailed him, of another person he loved being killed. He struggled to shrug the malaise off. It was something he'd labored under for too long, and he'd thought he had moved on. Maybe it was Mai's own current period of disquiet that was affecting him.

Because if Mai Kitano felt insecure, then something was majorly wrong, and the shit truly was about to hit the proverbial fan.

Staying his hand, he followed closely across Zoya's wooden porch and through the bullet-pocked door frame. Beyond that, they passed through a sparsely furnished living area complete with kitchen and king size bed. The dark, relatively small, space smelled of sweat and alcohol and, oddly, biscuits. Drake saw that the oven was lit, its motor whirring away, but knew better than to approach just yet.

One more open door stood before them and it was to this that Mai stepped next. But she stopped at the Zoya-sized gap and began to shake her head.

"You have to see this, Matt."

Drake stepped to her shoulder. The sight that greeted his eyes made him draw a sharp breath. There, piled high and almost reaching the roof, was a heap of treasure – everything from piles of banknotes to coins and trinkets; from machine guns and landmines, claymores and at least one RPG with scattered grenades; from works of art still in their original frames to swords, spears and wickedly gleaming mantraps.

Mai looked at Drake. "The monster's hoard."

"Oh aye. Damn right. What a crazy loon."

Mai pointed at the floor. It was the only room in the house that was carpeted. "Not a good sign."

The Spetsnaz commander ordered one of his men to investigate, but Drake was already on his knees, carefully prizing up a side of carpet. Sure enough a nest of wires ran underneath and he could see the pale gray side of what looked like a laptop bag.

"Pressure pads."

"Not a problem." The Spetsnaz commander pointed at the roof, and within ten minutes, his men had set up a lift-and-pulley system. Drake eyed the shifting treasure pile warily.

"At least we know what the bloody sword looks like. Call Patterson in from the van. He might be able to help. I'll go first."

Mai made a face at the Russian-made pulley system. "You sure will. Have fun with that. Oh, and Matt? The clock is ticking . . ."

CHAPTER FIFTY TWO

Dahl knew that time was running out fast. The journey by plane and vehicle, ending in rough terrain, had taken many hours. On the way, Akerman only made matters worse by reminding him of one of his earlier translations, 'The doomsday device is a weapon that will cause an overload of the elements. The earth will quake. The air will be split apart by mega storms of unbelievable ferocity. Chains of volcanoes will erupt. And the oceans shall rise.'

"It's happened before," Akerman said with cold certainty. "I'm sure you know about the startlingly factual proof that a continent once existed in the middle of the Pacific. This is where all the 'lost continent' theories find their roots. And proof does exist to corroborate a 'world-changing' event that occurred ten to fifteen thousand years ago."

"Meteor. Supervolcano. Pacific Rim eruption." Dahl counted the apocalyptical events off on his fingers. "Doesn't mean it was Odin's device, Olle."

"Doesn't mean it wasn't, either." The translator almost pouted.

Dahl slowed as Eyjafjallajokul reared in the distance. The car bounced along the winding road, alternately surrounded by mist and bright sunlight. Akerman pointed out the view to their left.

"Y'know, Torsten, that mountain over there is Mount Hekla, Iceland's most active volcano. It was known as the gate to Hell in olden times. Small world, eh? This place." He motioned around. "Has always had its ghosts."

Dahl nodded, not really listening. He was scanning the road ahead. During the flight he had contacted his Statsministern and secured the help of an SGG unit, at least two of them once part of his old team. On speaking to Karin, who was coordinating operations at the three tombs, he had learned that everyone was running late except Alicia – the gang of bikers were speeding along quite nicely to Singen.

Dahl pulled off the road, now quite close to the rendezvous point. He tapped the wheel. The SGG were late. They had agreed to meet here because Akerman, intimately familiar with the tomb and its access points, knew of an alternate entry point – one made by the coalition to facilitate dignitaries and less vigorous individuals. It might still be guarded, but it would make an easier breach than having to crawl single-file through a meandering tunnel.

Whilst they waited, the dark skies turned to black and the outline of the mountain stood out sharp against the clear sky. Dahl received a message to say his men were close and then, minutes later, they emerged out of the gloom.

"Did you *walk?"* Akerman asked pointedly.

Dahl held up a hand. "Quiet now, Olle. This is where the soldiers do their work. Are you ready to assault this volcano?"

His men nodded.

"Good. Because the world's future may depend on our success."

Dahl led the way, Akerman at the center of the group behind. If his calculations were right, and nothing else happened to slow the other teams en route to Hawaii, Singen and Babylon, they had about an hour to clear the tomb and find the third man. They had planned to make this a simultaneous strike on every tomb. Hayden had worked the timings out, but the time zone differences and estimated journey schedules were a bewildering web. Even so, everyone agreed, the chaos of a joint attack would confuse the enemy and hopefully throw their seemingly precise plans into disarray.

Now Dahl rested momentarily with his hand against an upstanding slab of cool rock. The ground underfoot was soft, shifting soil, the surrounding landscape shaded stark silver by the low-hanging moon. A gust of wind blasted past, its ice-cold jaws snapping. Dahl shivered. He had been spending too much time in warmer climes.

As one, the group moved stealthily into a man-made tunnel, supported in places by heavy-duty acrow props. The passageway had a temporary air about it, as if this insignificant warren would soon be reclaimed by the enduring mountain, but the men who searched and toiled here had at least tried to make it appear welcoming. A coalition flag hung across a wall marked at twenty foot intervals by

Pepsi vending machines, and chocolate bar and crisp packet dispensers. A leather bound visitor's book lay open on a desk half way along, a pile of flashlights, helmet-torches and other safety-equipment stood near the end. Dahl noticed two CCTV cameras, but neither of them blinked a red light.

At the entrance to the mountain, Dahl found the first body. A man in a white coat lay sprawled out and cold, the crusted red balloon shape on his lab coat revealing that he'd been shot in the back whilst attempting to flee.

What difference would it have made, Dahl thought. *If one scientist had escaped?*

A cold fury filled his veins. The work of mercenaries was seldom pretty, and was often marked by a cold, merciless dispassion, but such callousness as this demanded equal payback.

He paused. Akerman's description had this entry way emerging at the top of the bottomless pit, which had been hastily railed off, but if they followed the path to the right it led to the one thing the coalition forces had rigged that had made this fantastical excavation much simpler.

A lift.

A temporary elevator had been bolted to the side of the mountain, affording access to all three levels of the tomb, albeit the last level deposited them at its opposite end, giving them the choice of either a hair-raising climb or a short trip in a small capacity cable car that had also been recently erected.

Neither was recommended for the faint of heart.

Dahl spotted the lift right away. A sturdy red-painted array of metalwork with a simple box car attached to the side. As he emerged from the tunnel, he was taken back almost six months to when he had first accompanied Drake into this tomb, searching for the bones of Odin. The black abyss stood before him, seemingly overflowing with ancient power, vast and endless and hiding secrets in the deepest chasms that man could never hope to discover.

A little way above, he saw the first row of niches that signified the tombs of the gods, now brightly lit by a framework of lights. It all seemed a far cry from his previous visit.

"Clear." Bengtsson, one of Dahl's old teammates, surveyed the area. "Maybe they're dug in around the main entrance and Odin's tomb, sir."

"It makes sense." Dahl led the way carefully to the lift and studied the controls. Nothing fancy, but the sound of its mechanisms at work would alert everyone to their presence.

In another second it didn't matter. A figure appeared out of the dark beyond the lift, just the pale bloom of a face. Bengtsson fired first, the other man's shot going wide. Dahl cursed and leapt onto the lift, dragging Akerman with him. Their attacker crumpled as the rest of the SGG team joined Dahl, who thumbed the controller for level two.

As the lift ground into gear and started to rise, bullets shot out of the dark, peppering the lift's wire frame door and glancing off its surrounds.

Dahl crouched low, shielding Akerman. Bengtsson, Forstrom and Hagberg returned fire blindly, hoping to panic the enemy. The lift grumbled slowly, taking its time. Dahl looked up, thinking of the approaching levels, but saw no sign of defenders waiting up there.

"I get the feeling," he said. "That whichever force captured this tomb didn't expect to have to wait around long enough to defend it. And that is a bad feeling, my friends."

The lift juddered as it approached the first level. Dahl raised his weapon and fired through the diamond-shaped, wire holes as they ascended, taking no chances, but there wasn't a single guard positioned on the first level. They rose higher still, the view below switching from breathtaking to pitch black as the rock of the mountain got in the way. Then the second sloping level of niches came into sight. Dahl peered hard at the tombs, one of which he knew must belong to Thor, the other Loki. Time stood still for the Scandinavian. How he wished he had made the time to visit this place.

SPEAR isn't everything. And that was true, but he felt a deep loyalty to his friends now, and to Jonathan Gates, the man who had given him the chance to become a part of one of the most elite secret ops teams in the world. He owed them a debt.

At last the lift quaked to a halt at its highest level. The SGG team quickly threw open the door and stepped off, fanning out. Akerman followed Dahl and pointed out the cable car.

"Bollocks." Dahl tracked its twin support cables as they vanished on an incline up into the dark. They would finish at the very top, next to Odin's tomb. "We need a better plan."

It wasn't pretty, but it was the best they could do in the circumstances. The SGG team took off at pace, aiming to reach Odin's plateau the hard way. Dahl gave them a five minute head start and then climbed into the swinging cable car with Akerman at his side. He gave his friend a rueful smile.

"Sorry, Olle, but with so much at risk I need you with me."

"If I die I will haunt your bedroom, my friend."

"I feel like you already do." Dahl punched the green button, bringing the three man car quivering to life. It gave a jerk that sent Akerman to his knees, and set off. Dahl held out a hand. "No expense spared on the machinery, eh?"

The car swayed precariously as it travelled upward. Even Dahl made a point of not looking over the sides. Darkness soon swallowed them, and, for a time, he felt as if he were dreaming, all this effort merely the way out of a well-travelled nightmare. But when Olle touched his shoulder he patted the man's hand firmly.

"It's all good, mate. Won't be much further now."

Dahl peered into the blackness, fingers gripped tight around a thick supporting pole. Akerman stood next to him, the two men surrounded by a total absence of light, the only sound the slithering and grinding of wheel tracks over cable. Dahl almost jumped out of his skin as a heavy grinding sound fired his imagination.

"Now that sounds like something crawling up the mountain," Akerman breathed in his ear.

"It is," Dahl whispered back. "Us."

The cable car scraped slightly over rugged rock as it approached the precipice. The radiant glow of lights illuminated the dark above. Dahl prepped his weapon confidently without looking as the car swung over the final mound of rock, swinging into view out across the wide plateau of Odin.

His first impression was a memory of the crazy, pitched battle they had both won and lost here, of how he had leapt into darkness tethered with nothing but a length of rope to save Drake's life.

And back then, he hadn't even liked the thick-headed Yorkshire terrier.

His second impression was alarm. The welcoming committee was eight strong, fully tooled-up mercs with hard expressions and only one intention. To blast this intruder out of the sky.

Beyond them stood the tomb of Odin, empty now, but still as magnificent to him as when he had first seen it. An older man stood by the entrance and, even as he met Dahl's eyes, turned away agitatedly to check his watch.

A sharp bark from below indicated the call to action. Machine guns opened fire. Dahl grabbed Akerman and ducked below the vacant windows. The whole car swung wildly. Metallic pings punctuated the roar of automatic weapons.

Akerman swore. Dahl tightened his grip. "It's okay. The—"

A bullet tore through the floor of the car and exited the roof, leaving two jagged holes.

Akerman scrambled backward, but there was nowhere to go. Another bullet penetrated the floor. Men's laughter erupted from below. They were having a great time. The attitude of mercs.

Dahl sprang into action. To stay there was to die. Somehow, they had to keep moving. On the car's backward swing he leapt forward, reaching the front in one bound. He grabbed hold of the window frame and popped up fast, peppering the ground below with bullets. The mercs yelled and scattered, their sport interrupted. He slung his gun over his shoulder, took hold of the curved roof and hauled himself outside of the car. Using his legs as a piston, he thrust himself onto the roof of the car, holding tight to the edges on both sides to keep from falling. More bullets clattered around it, some pinging through and passing close to Dahl's body. Without pausing, he rolled and heaved, ending up on one knee, gun sighted immediately, and fired down at the mercs as the cable car swung wildly to and fro. Somehow he stayed on and planted both knees firmly apart. In another second, he heard shouts of surprise from below.

At last. Bengtsson and the others had arrived.

Dahl reached up and grabbed the car's guiding rope. Hand over hand he swung across the last few feet to the cable car's station, a minor rock outcropping with a vertical ladder leading down to Odin's plateau. As he swayed, a bullet fizzed past his shoulder. Dahl fought fire with fire, relinquishing his hold with one hand, unhooking his weapon and spraying lead at his target. The man scrambled clear, but caught a round in the vest and hit the ground face first. Dahl, hanging by one hand, threw his gun onto the rocky outcrop and swung over.

Suddenly, he had the perfect vantage point.

He fell to one knee and sighted in on the mercs. *This battle,* he thought, *is over.*

But then the civilian stopped checking his watch, screamed a warning to the mercs and raised his hands in the air.

Dahl's eyes flew wide as the rumbling began. The real battle, it seemed, was about to begin.

CHAPTER FIFTY THREE

Drake and his team had raced hard and fast back to the pit of Babylon. By the time they exited a military Humvee and stepped out into the cool desert night beside one of Razin's old tents, they had less than an hour before Hayden's agreed time came around.

But what the hell were they supposed to do?

The team had solved a part of the puzzle after rescuing the Great Sword from Zoya's treasure hoard. Patterson had used his experience and Akerman's cliff notes to decipher the last short inscription.

Take the Great Sword to the Pit.

"Is that it?" Mai had asked.

Even Patterson appeared disconsolate. "Crap. Yes, that's all it says."

"No instruction manual?"

Drake shook his head. "Not such a great sword after all."

"The inscription is enough," Patterson had speculated. "Could that be all we need to know?"

"It's gonna have to be," Drake had growled. "Tell us more about this bloody pit."

Patterson spread his arms. "I don't know any more. Not much is known about the pit of Babylon. It may also be an earth energy vortex. It was described as a deep, dark hole of sludge and dirt and just . . . nothingness. You understand? The remains of the original, most sinful city of all time were buried there and then dug up. What was left was an absence of *everything.* You surely know that some places which experience great trauma or tragedy *absorb* that disturbance and suffering. They become dark forever."

"You're saying the pit is haunted?" Drake cut through the bull and laid it on the line in true Yorkshire style.

"No. I'm saying that, like people, a terrible ordeal can damage a place, tainting it for all time. Need I quote factual references?"

"For God's sake no," Drake had finally moaned.

Now, as the world lay in ignorance of a possible doomsday event, Drake and Mai led Patterson and Yorgi past the gently billowing tents toward the edge of the pit of Babylon. Since Razin and his men had departed nothing had changed. Tools and crates littered the area. The winch stood idle, its man-size bucket swaying slightly. All four of them turned on their torches to survey the area.

Drake hefted the sword. "I don't see—"

The mammoth came out of nowhere; hairy, enormous, growling like an earthquake and bent on murder. Drake felt it hit his midriff, almost breaking him in half, his relaxed state actually saving his life as he folded easily instead of resisting.

Mai's piercing cry almost stopped his heart. *"Zanko!"*

"You killed her!" It was the bellow of a man turned insane.

Drake was carried for twenty feet and then hurled into the pit of Babylon, the sword clattering away into the darkness. As he fell helplessly, his eyes stared up – and saw Zanko jump right in after him

Hayden called the commander at Diamond Head as she and Kinimaka were driven at high speed toward the extinct volcano. Her words stunned him speechless.

"I want a full scale assault! Now!"

His lack of response infuriated her. "Did you hear me?"

"Y . . . yes. A full scale assault? Are you sure? I will have to confirm that through my captain."

"I *am* your fucking captain! Do it!" She signed off, knowing he would waste another precious five minutes seeking confirmation of the order she had given him.

Kinimaka squeezed her arm. "We'll make it."

Hayden shook her head. "We have less than an hour to stick to our simultaneous attack. If the others all strike and we're late, it could be disastrous."

"Call Karin. Put the time back."

"I did. Dahl's already inside his tomb. Drake's not answering. Alicia's pinned down." She met his eyes. "As a team we're disjointed, uninformed, and all over the place. We're losing this one."

Kinimaka pointed ahead. "We're nearly there. Hang loose." He gave her the ghost of a smile.

But Hayden shook her head. "Don't you *get* it? This is the big one. Not only for whichever whacko is in there playing king of the hill, Mano. It's also the last move of the gods. Their last chance. And it must become *their* Ragnarok, not ours."

Diamond Head's crater emerged up ahead, and they were driven up the long winding road to its entrance, through the short tunnel and out into a sunlit bowl. A military force gathered to their right, its point men thankfully already filing into the mountain. Hayden jumped out and raced up to the man in charge. Almost as an afterthought, Kinimaka grabbed the two swords of Babylon and followed.

"Thanks for clearing the way through so quickly. My partner and I," she indicated Kinimaka, "need to get down there. Fast."

"We just started the charge, little lady," the rugged faced officer told her stiffly. "You jus' jump on in wherever you feel comfortable."

Hayden checked her Glock and extra ammo as Kinimaka pushed his way to the front of the assault team. More than one soldier bounced off him, almost sent sprawling, but the Hawaiian's face brooked no argument. They stepped into the tunnel, instantly finding themselves under fire. A dozen soldiers crept ahead of them, moving in formation, bombarding a merc defense and pinning it down.

Hayden saw a sliver of an opportunity. "Go!" She slapped Kinimaka's broad shoulder, sending him off like a sprinter out of the traps. Shooting hard, they cleared the merc defense in seconds and raced down the passage beyond. A newly formed long slope brought them to the chamber where Cook's 'gates of Hell' resided.

Kinimaka gulped air. "Shit."

"Just go." Hayden dashed past him, knowing he would follow her into any kind of hell, and passed under the old archway, using her torch to light the smooth rocky path before them. A scuffle of feet behind betrayed the presence of at least one enemy soldier. Kinimaka slowed, but Hayden wrenched him along.

"No time. Just run!"

Bullets slammed into the rock walls. Hayden ducked her head and tore through the dark. Together they hurdled the eternal threat of Wrath, skipping over the inactive fire vents and threaded the needle through Greed, taking the trident paths at full sprint. Their pursuers at first struggled to keep up, probably surprised by their actions, but soon figured out their intentions of running all the way to Odin's chair.

Bullets impacted around them as they sped through Lust, shattering the outrageous statues, shredding the priceless, inventive paintings, but not slowing them down. They ran hard through the chaos, covered in dirt, rock and lead fragments, heads down, clattering across the temporary bridge that had been erected over Envy's sulfurous lake, capering on all fours over the belly of the statue of Gluttony, and even rolling part way down the passage that once held the enormous stone spheres.

Bruised, battered and determined, they came at last to the great cavern where the zip-line had once led over to the S-ledge that ended at Odin's chair. A new incongruous, blue metal bridge had been built across the great chasm. Hayden and Kinimaka leaped onto it and dashed across its length, sending it swaying, but avoiding grabbing the side rails which would only slow them down. Hayden fired over her shoulder as their pursuers – only two men – burst out of a tunnel. They dived to the ground, giving Hayden and her partner scant seconds to jump off the other end.

At last, they panted their way along the final hurdle. Odin's chair came into view.

And finally Hayden stopped, face stricken with horror. "Oh no, we're too late."

A man stood upright on Odin's throne, arms held straight above his head, face turned up to the roof that soared high above and the skies and heavens beyond.

Was the ground starting to shake?

Drake smashed against the side of the pit, its slope slowing his fall but not enough. His gun disappeared into the bottomless pit. Still he tumbled, and the nightmarish shape of Zanko fell after him, roaring with bloodlust. Then Drake slammed against a man-made platform, a few planks of scaffolding erected by the Russians, and groaned as his descent was abruptly stopped. Pain lanced through his spine, his ribs. But he had no time to assess any injuries.

Zanko crashed down beside him and totally destroyed the platform. Wood splintered and metal poles tumbled away. Drake fell again, clawing at the sides of the pit, but finding no grip in the squelchy mush that hung there. A hard-packed mud outcropping slowed him enough to get a grip, but his feet flailed over pitch blackness. He hauled hard, steadying his legs and rising up. Darkness surrounded him.

After all this, they had lost the fucking sword!

He looked up, seeing Mai at the top of the pit, struggling with someone—

—falling backwards, Mai put her hands behind her head and body-flipped herself straight back to her feet, surprising Razin as he aimed his pistol at her head. A side-kick relieved him of the weapon, but not before it discharged, the bullet almost taking Yorgi's head off.

"We came back here," Razin spat at her. "To avenge Zoya's murder. Where else could you go? This is where it all began."

Mai wasn't in any mood to chat. She struck hard at the older man, but he surprised her by skipping back and side-stepping into space.

What was she doing? The Mai Kitano of old, even the Mai of a few weeks ago, would never have let that happen.

She was compromised. She took a breath and tried to clear her mind.

"You came back to Babylon? Just to avenge *her.* Why would you do that?"

Razin swallowed. "Zoya was my wife."

Mai opened her mouth, but nothing came out. What was she supposed to say to that? It would be disrespectful to deride the man, despite his flaws. She wasn't Alicia Myles.

Then, Razin's hand emerged from behind his back. Yorgi screamed a warning, "Another gun!" Mai turned her body to minimize the target and dove at him. Her hands hit the dirt, bent and sprung her body into flight, legs aimed for Razin's head.

The blow snapped his neck instantly, snuffing out the spark of his life, but not before the gun discharged a single shot, passing millimeters before her torso.

Patterson screamed and slumped as the shot smashed through him, falling and tumbling over the edge of the pit of Babylon, following his dreams down.

Drake could only watch in horror as the body plummeted past. As the professor fell, the torch he held fell with him, its beam picking out a flickering kaleidoscope of jagged rock, trailing vines, black mud and—

—the sword!

Drake caught its glint about ten feet above him. The point had wedged into the side of the pit. Quickly, he sank his hands into the sides of the pit and grabbed hold, tested his weight and pulled.

The hand that grabbed his ankle was straight from the stuff of nightmare. It was the monster reaching out from under the bed, the beast crawling up from the pit. It was Zanko, covered in filth.

"Little man," he breathed. "We have a score to settle."

CHAPTER FIFTY FOUR

Drake knew his only advantage was in maintaining the higher position. Without thought, he relinquished his grip on the side of the pit and stomped down at Zanko's arm. The Russian had anticipated the move and twisted slightly. Drake's stamp grazed down the Russian's arm, serving only to unbalance him. He fell and twisted to his side. Zanko's other arm came out of nowhere, a hammer blow to Drake's chest. With the air forced out of him, he could only pant as Zanko hauled himself up.

But Drake recovered quickly. He threw a sod of earth at the Russian's face and let loose a salvo of punches at the immense torso, working around every pressure point he knew. When the monster came up hard, arms flailing, Drake stepped away and threw one of the hardest punches of his life at Zanko's face.

The Russian's nose burst, blood splattering across his cheeks, chin and eyes. Blinded, he made a lunge for the side of the pit to steady himself. Drake leaned back and brought his knee up, kicking out at the man's ribs. The blow would have sent a grizzly over the edge, but Zanko only grunted, half-turned, and raised his arms. With consummate care he took a sniff of an armpit.

"For you." He inhaled loudly, then roared at the top of his voice, face turning redder than the blood that coated it. "For Zoya!"

He charged at Drake, meaning to take them both off the outcrop and down into the pit. Drake saw no place to go. As he stared into the eyes of the onrushing madman he realized that this really was the end.

Alicia and the Bitchin' Motherfucking Hellslayers hit the Singen tomb with everything they had. Burdened with the suspicious package containing the two swords, but then happily finding an array of advanced armament awaiting them, they joined up with the local German forces and beset the third tomb with unstoppable force.

The passage that descended into the bowels of the earth had been greatly enlarged during the last few months and several tributaries added. To their credit, the German special forces' commander sent units down every pathway – as ploys and back up to the main force that pounded down the main artery. Alicia moved at the head of the pack, all fired up for battle, aware of the time limit that Karin had passed along to her, but unaware of how the rest of the SPEAR team were doing.

All she knew was that everyone she loved and cared for was now in harm's way, battling a mystery madmen to keep control of their planet.

Men fell before her, bullets winging them or smashing into their vests, with the occasional head shot, picked off by the cowardly mercs who crouched at the head of the corridor. Alicia and her crew fired relentlessly, pulverizing the rock walls around the tomb's arched entry, creating a mist of fragmented rock and spent bullets that helped cover their assault. Lomas, Ribeye and Laid-back Lex ran at her side, handling the advanced weaponry with ease. Ribeye, she knew, was ex-special forces, but as for the others, she had no idea where they had learned their skills.

Best not to ask, Lomas had told her.

Not a problem. Alicia had enough skeletons of her own not to question other people's. The only time she drew the line was after the terrifying recent realization that her new biker nickname – Taz – was also a video game character. A *sprite.* Every biker, on pain of castration or decapitation, had promised never to reveal it to any member of the SPEAR team – especially Mai Kitano. Now, worries cast aside, she leapt over the body of a fallen German soldier and rolled into the chamber, recognizing it from the last time she was here – the high, encircling walls of niches that held the most evil gods, the central ring of statues that had been built to accept the nine parts of Odin.

Now no longer needed since someone had found a failsafe, another way to activate the damn device.

And, horrifyingly, she could see strange pale glows emanating from the niches themselves. Were the god parts shining, the latent energy in this place powering them up?

She fired hard, blasting one of the statues to pieces and also the merc who hid behind it. The other entryways belched out German troops. The bikers filled the void behind her. Men fell to their knees and let loose lethal volleys, bullets crisscrossed the tomb of the gods in a hellfire hail of death. Screams punctuated the center of it all, rising on wings made of agonizing pain and murder, all gladly accepted by the tomb's crumbling, long dead occupants.

Then Alicia's mouth literally fell open.

At the heart of everything, like a dynamo at the core, stood Russell Cayman; naked, bloody, with his arms striking frantically at the air.

Real hell blasted her world to shreds.

Drake threw himself lengthways. Zanko hollered and clawed helplessly for him, but nothing could stop the juggernaut. His feet struck Drake's ribs, firing cannon balls of agony into his spine, and he flew headlong out into the center of the pit. Drake turned his head as the monster somehow managed to arrest his fall, hands like digger buckets clamping hold of the pit wall.

Drake stood quickly. Zanko hung helplessly in front of him, too far away to make it back to safety, too heavy to climb up to the top of the pit.

Drake didn't gloat. He needed that sword. He examined the walls above as best he could, pinpointed the sword, and took hold of a rock.

Zanko's voice drifted out of the dark. "Why did you kill her?"

Drake paused, startlingly aware that this man knew nothing of true values, of morals, nor did he possess much of a conscience, but also aware that it wasn't entirely the Russian's fault. "It comes back to the trafficking ring," he said softly. "You don't mess with the innocent, with their families, their kids. You don't kill another man's wife and expect to live."

When Zanko failed to answer, Drake took a step up, then another. The rock and earth muddle held well, despite being hidden behind a layer of pure muck. He was about to take another careful step when the question he had once asked Yorgi stole back into his brain. He wiped his hands and felt his desperate need get the better of him.

"Have you ever heard of an operative called Coyote?"

At first there was no answer. Then Zanko's resolute voice broke the silence. "Little man, you are worthy adversary. Perhaps one of only few I have encountered. You did well in the prison courtyard, so I will give you this. Coyote is a shadow, a whisper, a ghost invented to scare big bad guys like me. They say she comes with the wind and leaves with your head, silent, swift, unstoppable. She will kill you before you can blink and take your eyes before you see her. Coyote?" A harsh bark. "She is a demon of legend made flesh."

"Who says all that?"

"Zoya. They met. Once. It is said that if this Coyote respects you, she will only take your life."

Drake shifted. "Only?"

"But if she dislikes you or if you've done something very bad, she will go further . . ."

Drake licked his lips. The darkness hung heavy around him. "What do you mean – further?"

"She subjects you to the *Devil's cut.*"

"The Devil's cut?"

"So they say."

With that, there was the faintest rustle and then the sound of something huge chasing shifting shadows down into the everlasting dark. Drake took one look, sighed, and fixed his eyes upward.

To the sword.

Take the Great Sword into the Pit.

His hand closed over the hilt. Well, here he was.

What next?

He looked up. Mai was staring down at him.

"Look out. The sky's falling down!"

Drake remembered the old Dinorock tune. "This is no time for—"

Then he recoiled as a lightning storm collapsed on him.

CHAPTER FIFTY FIVE

Hayden ran like the wind, noticing the chasm ahead, gauging its width and leaping across without hesitation. A tall man, who looked to be in his early fifties, stood above her, laughing as he paced around the black granite throne of Odin, finally spotting her and bellowing out a command.

"Kill her. She is too late anyway. The Shadow Elite will soon once again control fate itself!"

A man stepped into view beneath the throne, aiming a pistol. Hayden flinched, totally exposed, but then a Glock cracked behind her head and the man's pistol flew out of his hand, struck dead-on by a bullet. Kinimaka had fired first, seemingly his last shot as the next one clicked on an empty chamber. Hayden ran at their attacker as a knife appeared in his other hand. She body-swerved as he lashed out and dug her stiffened fingers into his larynx.

He choked, but didn't go down. He thrashed at her again. She caught the wrist and broke it, but the man was tough and he was trained. He too stepped in and delivered a blow to her abdomen that doubled her over. She went down to one knee. She sensed an elbow being raised above her in preparation for the final blow that would break her neck.

"Hey! Look up!"

The scream made her look sideways in time to see the spinning blade of the sword arcing toward her. The man above hesitated, half-backing off, and that was his downfall. Hayden caught the sword's hilt and spun in a single calculated move, feeling the blade slice through the gristle of his neck.

Kinimaka made for the ladder that led to Odin's throne.

Hayden started to follow, but at that moment she felt the onset of something huge beginning to build all around her. The sudden crackle of unseen energy made the air smell of static electricity, like ozone created by thunderclouds. When she looked up she saw a bolt of lightning strike the rock near Odin's chair.

Crap, what had Akerman said about the doomsday device being a weapon that could harness the elements?

It was already too late.

Dahl saw the greater threat immediately and shouldered his weapon. The suited individual was at the center of all this and his capture would surely end it. He grabbed the ladder, hands and feet to each side and, within seconds, had slid down its full length. Reaching the bottom, he exploded into a fast run, seeing one of the mercs turn his way and rolling to upset the man's aim. The bullet whizzed by. Bengtsson put an end to the threat with a head shot. It had been the last of the merc resistance.

The man in the suit had seen Dahl's intent, but didn't bat an eyelid, just continued to glare up at the roof of the volcano toward the starlit skies beyond. In his right hand he held what looked to be a long, thick bone. Could it be one of the Gods'?

"We are joined," Dahl heard him say, and then gawped.

A squall began to gust inside the mountain, whipping through the man's jacket. The very air crackled. The bedrock began to tremble and shake. Lightning bolts struck before his eyes, fizzling and flickering, charging the air with electricity, swarming around the man's body and shooting off up into the air and, beyond that, into the skies.

The storm to end all storms was coming.

Alicia ran straight at Russell Cayman, but then a storm of elements erupted around him and a discharge of energy flung her back. *Was this earth energy?* The vortex was erupting, the failsafes and conditions of the gods met at last.

"Are you crazy?" she screamed at Cayman. "You've switched on the fucking doomsday device."

Cayman's face was bathed in sweat and glory, and starkly lit by lightning. He clasped a giant skull in one hand, undoubtedly the head of Kali. Alicia saw bright energy bolts shooting through the eye and mouth sockets.

Cayman's terrible visage turned upon her. "Now," he said. "Now I have come home."

The flickering tree of lightning climbed higher and higher, gusts of wind scoured the chamber. Alicia scrambled on her knees, for once helpless to do anything about it. The niches above trembled and quivered before her eyes, starting to shake in the throes of an impending earthquake.

At every tomb, a towering column of light shot up from the bowels of the earth. The three vortexes erupted together, unleashing their potent earth energy in one almighty blast. Energized by the tombs, charged and activated by the bones of the Gods, crackling bolts of incandescent energy blew the tops off every tomb and fired up into the clouds and skies. The core sizzled around the three men; Block, Cayman and Denney, enveloping them in a cocoon of white fire.

Hayden lost her grip on the ladder, fell backwards, and hit the rock plateau hard. Kinimaka made a tough choice, and jumped down to help her, cradling her head.

"Oh, Mano," she whispered. "You keep saving my life."

He bowed his head until their noses touched. "Without you there is no life worth living."

Dahl struggled toward the bright glow, raging through the lightning, cursing when his gun was wrenched out of his fingers as he neared the suited man. His thumb brushed the man's wrist a second before he was thrust backwards on his knees, pushed by the force of the gale, his slide only arrested by Bengtsson and the other two SGG soldiers.

Heads bent, they struggled to stand upright in the screaming vortex . . .

All three tombs started to collapse. First the cliff faces around them gave way, blocks of rock and stone shearing off and sliding down to crash and burst against the floor below. Then the niches themselves started to crumble, a cascade of smaller stones dropping like a devastating waterfall. Extensive cracks ran from niche to niche. Bigger blocks began to shift and rumble, the ominous shattering of enduring rock striking terror into the heart of everyone who heard.

Hayden's eyes bored into Kinimaka's. "We have to get the hell out of here."

"Not yet."

Kinimaka left her and started to climb the ladder, sword slung over his back. Hayden took a breath and followed, reaching the seat of Odin's throne a second after he did. Kinimaka strode ahead and literally barged through the power that coursed around Zak Block, shoving forward until he stood face to face with the Shadow Elite maniac.

"Stop it," he yelled. "Shut it off!"

The fanatics eyes flew wide as if just realizing he had forgotten to do that very thing. "It works," Kinimaka heard him say. "I have the power."

"Then prove it. Turn it off!"

The leader of the Shadow Elite dropped the finger bone he was holding, and at first appeared to try and concentrate and clear his mind. Then he closed his eyes and walked away. Finally, he slapped himself.

"I can't."

The earth energy, unleashed and unfettered at last, twisted like an electrically charged whirlwind high into the sky.

Unstoppable.

CHAPTER FIFTY SIX

All of a sudden, Kinimaka saw the branches of the towering, crackling tree of lightning stretching towards him. He was instantly reminded of Nikola Tesla's *tree of energy* description. He flung the Shadow Elite man aside, thinking he was the source, and backed away fast. But the blazing tendrils continued to test for his presence, as if sensing something. Then, one of the stalks shot towards him like a spitting arrow, striking his back. Kinimaka squealed, not ashamed to do so.

"What the fuck!"

Hayden fell in beside him. "Oh crap. Now we're in trouble."

"Why?"

"That lightning bolt just struck your sword."

Kinimaka stared in horror as the whole soaring column leaned toward him.

Dahl stood transfixed as the lightning tree bent over toward the swinging cable car. He screamed for Olle, and when the Swedish translator stood up, he was grasping both of Alexander's swords in his hands.

"Thought they might come in useful," he started and then saw the astonishing display of earth energy. "Ah," he mumbled. "Ah . . . Torsten . . ."

Alicia scooted across the rock-strewn floor as the energy tower, containing all the earth's elements, bowed down to the ground, a dazzling supplicant. Lomas brandished one of the swords. She picked up the other. Fear and wonder kept her rooted to the spot. Here was a primeval force that could tear the world apart. Here was real power, real might. The kind of display that might persuade a man to worship the gods.

Then the earth energy gathered its white fire and flashed straight at the swords held by Alicia, Lomas, Hayden, Kinimaka and Akerman, surrounding their blades in a writhing wreath of flickering flame before exploding and firing upward in a shining column straight through the top of the tombs, now channeled from their original purpose by the earth energy inherent in the swords and re-tasked toward something new.

Alicia watched in awe as the column of light reached its apex and then *veered away.*

Drake held the sword aloft and felt the energy exploding. Above him, beyond the rim of the pit where Mai and Yorgi's faces peered down anxiously, he saw fires illuminating the skies. The dark night was sunstruck. A wondrous array of crackling and sparkling lights swept the black curtain aside, a spectacular aurora borealis. Was it the end of the world? He didn't know, but had foresight enough to thrust the sword higher, its tip now clearing the top of the pit.

Instantly, the world ignited. Vivid bolts of lightning blazed brightly and blasted toward the earth with the sound of a thunderclap. Vital energy struck and channeled through the entire length of the sword, then flashed down from the hilt to be totally consumed by the bottomless pit of Babylon. A stunning symmetry of shining energy surrounded Drake and the sword, mini bolts of lightning crackled in his hair, between his fingers, across the tops of his boots, but he remained unharmed.

"It's a goddamn lightning rod," he said, amazed. The other six swords were the same, but infused with less power. They attracted the energy and sent it to their more powerful cousin.

The pit of Babylon devoured every spark of power like a hungry black hole. Nothing stirred down there. Nothing existed. Drake remembered Patterson saying that even the pit itself might be an earth energy vortex. But now he knew better.

It was a *negative* energy vortex, consuming everything and anything that was thrown at it.

Except for Matt Drake. With the help of his friends, he climbed and pulled himself up over the edge of the pit. The sword still flickered, expending the last of its force below, so Drake held it out over the black hole until the lights chasing along its blade finally diminished and the skies were reclaimed by the night.

Together they sat for a while, mourning the death of Professor Patterson and rejoicing that the world was now safe, but, most of all, worrying about the fates of their friends and team mates.

CHAPTER FIFTY SEVEN

Dahl bounded over to the suited man as the last crackles of energy subsided. He smashed a fist into the side of his head, sending his entire frame slithering to the ground.

"Questioning can wait."

He balanced on the spot, listening. At least the dissipation of the energy tree had temporarily slowed the crumbling of the old tombs.

Bengtsson stepped up. "What on earth happened here, sir?"

Dahl eyed Olle Akerman, still swinging in the cable car. "We won. And now we need to go."

Akerman stared forlornly through the empty windows. "Any chance you can get me down now?"

Dahl jumped for the ladder. "Just be a moment."

Alicia saw the last vestiges of earth energy fade away, then cringed as a high-pitched mewling started up. Her eyes sought and found Russell Cayman, bent double with his nose to the ground, the shattered skull of Kali clenched between his bleeding fingers.

The tombs still crumbled around them. She thought it really was time to get the fuck outta here, but could they risk leaving Cayman alive?

Not a chance. Alicia had no intentions of bringing the psycho back to the real world. She stepped among the statues, now at the center of the tomb, and raised her gun.

"You can't kill me," he hissed.

"Just putting down a rabid dog. And this is you getting lucky, Cayman, believe me."

Cayman looked up at her, eyes wretched and lost. "I don't want to be taken from my home again. I don't want to be left by the side of the road. Do it. Do it now."

Alicia hesitated for a second, wondering what his story was, but the sound of a Desert Eagle booming put an end to any second thoughts. Cayman's head exploded, his body falling backwards, fingers still not relinquishing their grip on the skull of Kali, even in death.

Alicia turned. Lomas shrugged at her, pretending to blow smoke from the end of his barrel. “We have to get away from here, Taz. Place is falling to pieces.”

The Englishwoman fell in as the bikers and German special ops troops jogged their way back up the shaking passageways. Behind them, the tomb started to steadily cave in. Alicia ignored it and, surrounded by her gang, repeated the words one last time to reinforce the gravity of her message.

“Never, ever, mention that name to anyone beyond this gang. You hear me? If you understand me right, your balls should be starting to shrink.”

A few 'ayes' went up, even from the women.

Alicia ran with her new family toward the light.

Kinimaka forced the Shadow Elite boss down the vertical ladder, throwing him the last four feet. All around them, rock faces were crumbling. Even the throne of Odin was starting to develop a myriad of tiny cracks.

Hayden met his eyes. Kinimaka nodded. *“Run!”*

Dragging their captive, the two SPEAR operatives chased their own footsteps back through the redundant trap system. Mini earthquakes threatened to upend them at any moment, but thankfully the major damage seemed to be confined to the tombs. It was the spectacular end of the gods, the final destruction of their resting places now adding to the insolent disrespect of their deaths. By the time Hayden and Kinimaka neared ground level, the rumblings had stopped, making the Hawaiian pause at the entrance to the gates of Hell.

“I guess that’s the last of the gods then.”

Hayden cast her eyes over the archway, the so-called portal, and wondered about the two devices that complimented it. Whatever had happened to them?

“I guess so. And in truth, Mano, despite what we may have learned, it’s not a bad thing.”

"Damn right."

"I just hope it's the same at every tomb. I wonder how the others fared." Hayden stared at her cell until the green bars flickered into life.

Kinimaka strode out into the open air first, throwing the Shadow Elite boss to the floor at the feet of the gathered military forces. "Last guy we walked out of here," he said, "is still wallowing in some top secret prison. No one knows where. I expect nothing less but the same for you, asshole."

Then the day became a blur for Kinimaka. Hayden called Karin and confirmed events at the other two tomb sites and Babylon. Jonathan Gates came on the line and thanked them publicly, along with half the military and cops in Honolulu. A Japanese family somehow managed to wander into the facility and started to take pictures. His sister, Kono, called and said that she needed to see him. She was sure she was being watched. She knew he was in Hawaii, and maybe he could stop on the way back to DC. And finally, ultimately, Hayden pulled him to the side and led him over to the low rim of the crater.

Beyond, the glittering Pacific lapped at Waikiki's golden shore.

"We should call a hotel," Hayden said after a while. "Get cleaned up."

Kinimaka grunted. "Are you kidding, makamae? My home's a short drive away."

Hayden pulled a face. "You want me to go meet your mom?"

"Doesn't every man want to take home his beautiful girlfriend?"

Hayden still hesitated uncertainly. "Ah, the Hard Rock's in the other direction you know."

"I know. We can go there tomorrow."

CHAPTER FIFTY EIGHT

Jonathan Gates accepted the hugs from Karin and Lauren Fox, and even Komodo. This was a team he could depend on, enhance, and trust to always have his back. When Smyth and Romero came forward, he heartily shook their hands. It had been a good outcome to a terrifying situation, and one to be celebrated, but he had the dreadful feeling that it would not always be so.

What was coming next?

Monsters swam near the surface, and there was always another one waiting to rear its twisted head. New threats were the staple diet of the men and women who safeguarded the free world. For them it would never end.

Gates soon excused himself and left Karin and her colleagues to their celebrations. He took a moment to talk to Lauren Fox outside the main comms room.

"Thank you," he said. "I know you were prepared to see through all I asked."

Lauren had flown down to DC at his request. Now she explained her most recent experience in New York.

"My apartment was being watched, sir. At least, from the ground floor. Who knows if anyone broke in and bugged the damn place?"

"I find it hard to believe that General Stone figured you out, let alone found you so quickly. Are you sure it was his men?"

Lauren blinked, and fingered the threads of the old cardigan she wore. "Who else could it be?"

Gates voiced his thoughts. "You're on record as being part of the SPEAR team. C*onfidential* records," he stressed. "But records nonetheless."

Lauren frowned. "I don't like the sound of that. I've been around, sir. I *know* how confidential those things actually are."

"Then stay here." Gates didn't respond to her cynicism. His own impression was that the government's security systems were quite thorough. "Just for now. On my dime. I'll make some enquiries."

Even as the New Yorker started to smile, Gates turned on his heel and walked away. It was time to get back to his office. There still remained a matter that required urgent attention. As he walked, he passed by the heavily barred, steel door that led to the facility's underground escape route. Whoever designed it to surface in the Pennsylvania Mall was a genius. More escape routes than the New York Zoo.

He laughed aloud, then looked around self-consciously. It wouldn't do for a senator to be seen laughing to himself. No point in giving the opposition ammunition. He allowed himself one more grin by entertaining the idea of suggesting the same escape route strategy to President Coburn, before slipping his game face back on and stepping out into the open air.

He saw the Secret Service agents straight away. That was good, normal. Beyond them was a second car, government issue, also watching. Why would they send two?

Don't be an idiot, he thought. *We just escaped a calamity. Of course they would assign more men to your safety.*

Well, the calamity was over. And now he had that other urgent matter to attend to.

Pulling out his cell phone, he called Sarah Moxley. It seemed a good day for a celebration after all.

Matt Drake drove Mai and Yorgi through the sand dunes to Camp Babylon. The crisis across the world had been averted, and he was hoping it was time to take a break. He felt like he'd been fighting hard for months on end, ever since the gods first reared their divinely hideous heads.

Now it was time to soak in a little sunshine, a little Mai-time, and a little Dinorock time. All the good things in life.

He chose not to think about Mai's crisis, not yet.

As they bounced over the rugged roads and sandbanks Mai took five minutes to call her sister, Chika, and then Dai Hibiki. She asked about Gyuki and about the old clan. She asked about recent sightings and recent assassinations across the globe. She listened quietly for a long time, eyes unreadable in that true Japanese manner. When she ended her call, Drake spoke up.

"You know, Zanko told me that Zoya knew Coyote."

Mai didn't take her eyes off the road. "Hmm, well, I saw Zoya too, Matt. I wouldn't put much faith in Zanko and Zoya if I were you."

"But still," Drake breathed. "We should revisit her place sometime. Maybe we'll find some clues."

"Maybe."

The US army camp came into view. Drake showed his ID and, after confirmation, drove through the inner gates and took a little time out in the camp barracks. After a shower and a meal he sought a quiet corner to make a call.

"Hey mate, how's it going?"

Ben Blake grunted down the line. "Not bad. Finally got myself a new bird, anyway."

Drake laughed. "Thank God. Thought you were licking the other side of the stamp for a while there."

"Piss off."

"What's her name?"

"Stacey."

"Stacey?" Drake laughed. "As in 'Stacey's Mom'? Has *she* got it going on?"

"Like I haven't heard that one already. Even my dad said it. What the hell do you want anyway?"

"I wanted to tell you," Drake said somberly. "The Odin thing's finally over, mate. The tombs are gone. The device is gone. It's all finished. Thought you should know."

Ben was silent for a long time. Then, "Thank God."

"Well, thank *Drake*, at least."

"Next time you're in York . . ."

Drake smiled in the dark. "Yeah, next time."

Mai Kitano watched Drake's shadow from her own world of darkness. She could tell when he smiled, when he frowned, when he grew sad, all through observing his body language.

It was what she had been trained to do. By *them.*

By the clan. The people who owned her. The bastards who purchased her from desperate parents, without giving the barest hint of what they would ultimately use her for.

And what had they done? she thought. Turned her into a killing machine, a mindless, mechanical robot with gears so twisted they could never return her to her former self – innocent, free, full of promise. The young Mai had a whole life of potential before her. They had taken that with the selfish, detached greed of monsters.

And now, it seemed, they wanted everything she had left.

The assassin of assassins, Gyuki, had just called her cell. Using a minimum of words and with only the most basic of emotions, he had literally ordered her to meet him in the center of Tokyo on Friday at 1300 hours.

"Meet with me or die. You belong to us. And if you choose not to come . . . you will know our true vengeance."

Mai felt real, debilitating fear for the first time in almost two decades. If she hadn't been leaning against the window frame she would have slipped to the floor. Gyuki's key words cut deeper than any blade she had ever known.

You belong to us.

CHAPTER FIFTY NINE

The old man walked in line, keeping step, chains jangling between the manacles clamped around his ankles. The orange jumpsuit didn't flatter him. It was baggy and torn, and like nothing he'd ever worn before. The eyes of the prison guards latched onto him, running deep with pure hatred. He noted how each man's fingers went deathly white around the chunky stock of his gun as he passed them, and how confident they seemed when hiding in their own little cages.

Standing safe, for now.

Down in the mess hall, he sat apart. They were all seated separately, with only fifteen allowed to eat at the same time. Nevertheless, he was a man of limitless means and unimaginable power, and when he wanted a message passed on . . . someone died horribly if it didn't happen. Not in here. *Out there.* He had maintained contact with the outside world.

Today, his bought guard turned a blind eye when he momentarily paused between two tables. The guards, to the government's credit, had all proven fruitless sources of corruption for many weeks. But then something had happened. The old man was only too aware that something always happened. Something unforeseen. And that's when his men had pounced.

And the promise of a personal little island near Zanzibar never hurt when winning the heart of a peasant.

The Blood King dropped his plastic fork and bowed his head, speaking to both lieutenants at once.

"Are we ready?"

Mordant, his chief, inclined his own head. The man's appearance never failed to unsettle the Blood King, despite all he had seen in his life. Mordant was an albino. His huge, egg-shaped, perfectly white head was completely hairless. Now, a pink tongue flicked over pale lips.

"On your word."

The other lieutenant, Gabriel, a wiry African, concurred. The Blood King actually counted himself lucky that he had come across these two whilst taking a few months convalescence in this so-called 'secret' penitentiary. They were blood brothers – known as The Twins – despite their obvious differences. But more than that – they were far beyond the worst of the worst, sadistic nightmares that the real world couldn't cope with or contain, beyond skillful, highly intelligent, pure psychotic gold.

Either man made Kovalenko's old lieutenant, Boudreau, look like a newborn kitten by comparison.

Indeed, they were so violent and ferocious, the Blood King always remembered to show them respect, a fact in itself that complimented them. It was something he had never afforded any man before.

"Thank you," he said and, standing upright, made his way to his table. The food on his plate was piping hot, the coffee smelled good. But he wasn't really in the mood. He was already looking forward to a much more satisfying meal.

And much more than that. His question hadn't merely been aimed at the state of their preparedness in this prison. It had also been querying the readiness of their forces *out there*, on the outside. The very same enquiry he had been making for weeks. The proposal he had originally outlined for The Twins had brought simultaneous grins, the monsters inside them shining forth. Later, it had been passed on to his concealed forces on the outside and had taken months to put in place, involving the deaths of many innocents, the greasing of countless palms, the purchase of much hardware and White House secrets, and of course the constant surveillance of a chosen few.

His plan was monumental. In one stroke, he would devastate the Americans, leave the country crippled and bleeding, and show the world how he, the Blood King, extracted his terrible blood vengeance.

THE END

For more information on the future of the Matt Drake series, read on:

Next time, everything changes as the Blood King gets his revenge in Matt Drake 7 – 'Blood Vengeance', due for release January 2014.

. . . Matt Drake's team is torn apart around him. Washington DC is under siege. The President has been taken . . .

The Blood King is back.

Prepare for Hell . . .

And since I often get asked about when the Coyote will make her appearance, I'd like to say, now that I positively know, that it will be resolved in Matt Drake 8.

As some might already know, I have taken one or two small liberties with the US army camps of Iraq in this book, and the general layout of Honolulu airport. I hope it didn't spoil your enjoyment.

Word of mouth is essential for any author to succeed. If you enjoyed the book, please consider leaving a review at Amazon, even if it's only a line or two; it makes all the difference and would be very much appreciated.